FRIENDS WITH DEATH

James Wright

PROLOGUE

Across a grassy hillock, in the pouring rain one shambling mass of flesh followed another. Both were emitting a general groan. One was Barry Williams, an ex-estate agent from Birmingham, the other was a horde of the living dead.

It would be fair to ask how a man the size of Barry found himself in this situation. Moreover, you could ask how he lasted this long in the first place. In your typical zombie apocalypse scenario, you didn't see many obese males over forty going the distance. The truth was Barry relied on the help of others. They were gone now, and he was left in a literal race for his life.

Barry let out another wheeze as he tried to outrun what appeared to be the end of his journey. Now sure, the undead deal with the soggy English countryside like a spider crawling through custard, so he still had a chance. Navigating this terrain wasn't his strong suit either though. Despite this he was gaining distance, even with the incline of the hillock putting a further strain on his already overloaded joints.

Sadly, the effort exerted in escaping his fate sealed it. His wheezing reached a crescendo. His veins expanded, contracting his clogged arteries to the point of bursting.

His heart was straining like a geriatric librarian on a ladder with a large stack of books. They reach across an aisle to shelve a particularly large book on Herodotus. Their arthritis is playing up, their legs start to wobble. The rest is history.

Barry grasped his heaving chest and doubled over in pain. A look of abject terror was plastered over his face. The mass squelching he could hear slowly approaching promised his last few moments to be agonising. Being eaten alive or dying in a wet field of a heart attack, it was a toss-up really.

Death watched the man keel over and was reminded of an over-stuffed sausage flopping onto an awaiting pan. It was callous and removed thoughts like this he was trying to work on. While he had operated closely with them for millennia, he never really understood humans.

Everything seemed so imminent for them. They only had a short amount of time to exist and had to make the most of it. Death, not subject to such worries, often found most situations either glum or at best mildly amusing. It was only a job after all.

Things had changed.

Before, he would always appear as a human died. He was summoned to whisk them away to the next stage of existence by an unknown force. He was a cog in the never-ending cycle of gained understanding and mild disappointment. Now his part in the process had ended and Death did not know why.

When humans like Barry dropped dead in the present, their 'being' would not emerge. This essence would stay inside its shell, shortly after re-animating sans-being. It would then start lurching around consuming any living soul in the vicinity.

This was type of thing that could give Death a bad name.

Not that there was anyone to hold him accountable. His origins and overall existence were a mystery even to himself. All he knew was that he had been created to serve a purpose, and now that purpose had been taken away from him.

The shepherd of souls was flockless, and whoever created him did not seem to give one.

Death could not recall exactly how long it had been going on. It could have been a few weeks, months, or decades. When you are a being with no clear beginning or end, telling the time becomes very difficult. Whatever the case he was getting tired of this state.

A long time ago Death decided to mask himself from the physical world. He became incorporeal and aloof. He would still appear to the souls of those recently departed. Work was work after all.

However, he shrouded himself from the living, appearing only after their mortal coil had been shuffled. There were the typical exceptions; animals, small children, the pure of heart, it is to be expected. No matter how much they worried about him or tried to understand how the whole thing worked, no one else could see or sense his presence.

On Death's part, this was less to do with some mysterious sense of ineffable elusiveness and more about practicality.

When someone saw a tall, dark figure in a hooded robe, they were likely to be on the defensive. It is one thing to tell a person who already died that their time was up. There is only so much begging and bargaining one can do when you tell them there is no going back.

It is quite another issue when a person about to die sees the embodiment of their demise. Their desperation takes over and they try all manner of things to get out of it. None of it worked, but it was quite annoying.

Like the difference between being a train conductor when someone who was late for their train sees it has left, and when they spot it is still sitting at the station. Even though the doors have already closed, and the result is the same, the chances of things getting out of hand are greatly increased.

It was not just for his sake. All these people upon seeing him would use up their remaining time with pointless bartering. They would miss out on enjoying their last moments with loved ones. Furthermore, it was rather traumatic for the surrounding people, quite justifiably possibly jumping to the conclusion that Death was there for them instead.

Then there were annoying slip-ups. Whether serendipity or divine intervention, sometimes things worked out differently in the grand scheme. The saying goes 'when your time is up, your time is up' but that was not always true it turned out.

Death would appear, all 'come hither my weary traveller'. Then lo and behold the person somehow made a miraculous recovery. This was great for them, but he would be left holding his scythe and looking like a colossal tit.

This is exactly why there are so many depictions of Death stemming from the early days of man. Some auspicious fellows would survive and then go on to tell others of his coming. They would make all types of judgements on his appearance, and it all got a bit overexposed for his tastes.

There were also those accounts of bystanders of course. Some often even believed he caused the passing. It was terrible for his reputation.

Thus, Death chose to take himself out of this part of the equation. To not get involved with the various human problems that arose from being present in situations concerning ones perceived end of existence. He would observe, but he never got involved until after the events.

While less hassle and arguably more professional, it made him more removed from humanity than his vocation dictated. He had grown to feel almost separate from the mechanisms of life, even though he was an essential part. It was a little like wearing a pair of headphones on the on the tube, comforting yet somewhat distorted.

What could already be a potential problem now was a real trouble. There was a difference between opting to hide away and not having a choice in the matter. Now he lacked the purpose for digression, what with most people already dead. In this new world to be constantly hidden seemed downright anti-social.

When he collected souls there was always the promise of a little chat once all the physical stuff was out the way. Most of it consisted of "What happened?", "Who are you?" or "Where am I going now?" Still, it was something at least. Without these interactions Death was starting to get very lonely indeed.

He was seriously considering abandoning in-corporeality for a more substantial presence in the world.

Perhaps doing so would allow him to help people, most of which were having a bad time. He could have prevented the death of dear old Barry for instance. Or at least have acted as a bit of a cheerleader for him trying to make his escape. Besides, the general dread invoked seeing a robed figure with a scythe was probably negated due to the hordes of undead.

Death had not become corporeal for more than an age. There was a good chance something would go wrong. However, he could not wait any longer. He imagined shutting his eyes, the only real step in this token process of transfiguration. He could feel his physical form coming into being, the fact he was feeling at all signalling that it was working.

He suddenly realised materialising in this place, amongst these things, might not have been the best idea. He thought about rotten sets of teeth gouging into his newly formed flesh. Grasping hands could be tearing out his pristine insides before they even got a chance to get warm.

Being torn into a million pieces and having to sort out all that mess would not be pleasant. He thought about the passing through putrid intestines and entrails. Let alone having at least part of his consciousness eventually flopping out of the hole in their backside that used to have some control over itself.

None of this happened.

Instead of waking up in an abattoir it was more akin to Oxford Street on a busy Saturday. Decaying bodies jostled his newly formed flesh. The smell was a bit off putting, apart from this the mass of near humanity did not seem to be threatening at all.

Still, there was no need to put up with that kind of odour. Death willed his nasal ducts to close. After all, for him breathing was a luxury, not anything essential.

He pictured the scene and realised he was not imagining but seeing. For the first time in a long time, Death saw with real eyes and felt with real senses. He looked down and noticed his hands; his skin was a similar grey pallor to that of the shambling husks all around him. A few shades darker maybe.

He was for all intents and purposes in human form, albeit one who could easily be mistaken for a statue. This appearance must have been something he willed on a subconscious level. It most likely came from one of the more flattering of his artistic representations.

He looked down at one of the corpses, it indeed had no intention of consuming him. If anything, it was giving him a look of slight admiration. It felt like he was a vaguely disconnected father figure. This was almost endearing in a way.

He realised after a moment that this undead convert was the deceased Barry Williams. Apparently, the mass of teeth was not able to consume him before he had turned. This likely due to the cardiac arrest he suffered before they even reached him. He only had half a face now but apart from that he was intact.

Now reborn, Barry looked to want some justification for his new state of being. It was an experience familiar to him, but unfortunately Death had no solace or answers to give. As far as he was aware, in this new world there was no hereafter, and he no longer had the power to guide those who were lost.

All he could do was pat Barry on the head in a generally friendly manner and start to push his way through the crowd of animated corpses. He wanted to see if he could find anyone to have actual conversations with. It had been years and he would need all the practice he could get.

Unbeknownst to Death, he started to follow along, slowly but with an ungainly conviction. The rest of the horde travelled along in this general direction too, some still chewing on Barry's ample cheek flesh. Five seconds in the physical world and he already had an entourage.

CHAPTER ONE

Most people in the zombie apocalypse have problems. A lot of this stems from loved ones. Either losing them or finding them, or else said loved ones dying, coming back, and then forcing an unwanted reunion of sorts.

Steve Carpenter was fortunate in a way since he did not have to worry about any of this.

In the week before people started rising from the grave, he lost all those risky attachments. He hadn't seen his fiancé in a month due to her teaching abroad. The patchy replies and succinct messages made the voices in his head whisper that she was cheating on him in some torrid holiday romance.

He received a call from an unknown number on Monday. He braced himself for some expected bad news. Instead of one type of heartbreak, he received another by being told that his mum had died. It was fair to say he was unprepared.

He was close to his mum, but they were never the type to message frequently. They had an understanding. This was that they both weren't very social people, so in general no news was good news. Not this time, however. He hadn't even known that anything was wrong.

During his grief, he went to see his remaining family on the Wednesday. He was never comfortable or felt like he fit in with them. They themselves, he believed, only tolerated him in the token sense of 'family is family'. This already present strain led to a stupid argument over trifles, causing him to storm out and vow to never see any of them again.

Even under these circumstances Steve welcomed this for the most part. He had only ever kept in touch with them out of a vague obligation. He simply couldn't see the need for them.

Through all these mixed feelings, he did finally hear from his MIA fiancé on the Friday. As he tried to tell her about his traumatic week, she shrugged it off. Instead, talking about the wonderful time she was having and how she had decided to stay there permanently. She assured him that there was no one else. It was just that she needed to leave him to be truly happy.

There is nothing quite like being told by someone you devoted your life to that they would be better off without you in theirs. To make it worse, he had forsaken many of his friends for his partner years ago and he was not really a social butterfly to begin with. So essentially, he had no significant others left by the weekend.

It was safe to say at this point he was developing serious abandonment issues. After wallowing in self-pity for a couple of days, he vowed to pull himself together and face the world a new man. When the next Monday came however, he woke to the news that there was no world to go back to.

Everyone was dying, only now they were coming back.

Steve, at least, was a pragmatist and saw that in hindsight the past week had prepared him a lot better than most.

Flippantly he considered how the dead returning could be potentially quite comforting for people with separation anxiety. It was the end of the world. At least the end of the world as he knew it and he felt fine.

Life and its complications never really appealed to Steve. Instead of aspiring to some lofty career goals, he attempted to live a simple life. He stayed two minutes away from where he worked at a construction supplies company. Despite his name he was not exactly a carpenter by trade, merely someone who facilitated building works through the distributions of materials. However, he had picked up a lot in his time and knew enough about it to get by.

People would tell him he was scared to truly get his hands

dirty. He acknowledged this was possibly true, but never really understood why it mattered. In his mind he was happy with his role in life, at least back when life was fundamentally functional anyway.

There was a general disconnect between him and most other people, who were constantly seeking satisfaction through big moves and changes in their situation. The problem with this as he saw it was once these occurred, they would always then be looking for the next thing. He could not see the actual point where they would be happy with what they had.

Despite his lack of ambition, he was educated. Although many would say he was wasting his degree in Design. He liked to dream up concepts for constructions, but the idea of doing it in more of a professional capacity didn't really appeal to him.

He had an innate talent for seeing how things fit together and felt a satisfaction seeing them perfectly fall into place. This could all be done on the page though. The actual construction was prone to human error, especially when forced to work with others.

Again, he would draw criticism from those around him for this view. His estranged family insisted that working for a mere supply company was keeping him from using his true talents. They would have possibly changed their minds now however, if they were somehow still alive.

Even in his somewhat dishevelled state, Steve had taken the opportunity of society falling apart to help himself to what the massive yard had to offer. It became the perfect means to fortify his street from the marauding undead that quickly began to pop up. He would see them on the TV before it went down, shambling about like nobody's business.

At the best of times, he didn't like the idea of strangers wandering about on his quiet little street. The thought of these lurching louts coming about to look for a snack was more than he could bear. Sealing up his surroundings was a motivation he could get behind.

When he had set to work in those first few days, he felt

bad for stealing. He got over that by telling himself that he was helping the company by safeguarding the grounds. He was even putting the stock to good use by protecting several employees living on the street with his efforts.

He had a head start when it came to fortification as his street was full of terraced housing. There were only a couple of gaps at one end that he would have to seal off. The road ran up a steep incline and at the bottom was a big pair of metal gates leading to the supply lot. The whole place was surrounded by a large, reinforced metal fence designed to keep out trespassers. So, the immediate area on that end was well protected.

This left only the top of the street to board off and seal shut. He also planned to use the only two adjacent alleyways running parallel to the construction yard's fence as the only means in or out. The small dimensions of the alleyways made sure any invading force could only enter in small numbers.

He tried to round up as many people as he could from the street to help. Some couldn't get their heads around it. Others only cared about finding friends and family. Additionally, some claimed that they did not want to be cooped up with a mad man. These comments seemed a little unnecessary to Steve.

Unfortunately, he had a reputation among his co-workers for being a bit eccentric. He didn't think his behaviour was that weird. It was just talking to himself on occasion, and the usual bouts of quietness and then streams of blathering that seemed to flow and never stop. Yet somehow this was enough to make people wary of him.

Despite the general unease he inspired, about a dozen or so stayed behind. Some of the deserters said they would return once they found their people. Steve was sceptical, but he tried to hold out hope that he was wrong. The gate at the end of the street was constructed by those who remained.

After a couple of weeks with no word there was a general consensus that no one was coming back. Some chose to gather up all the supplies left by the deserters and distribute them amongst those left. This was justified as a reward for all their hard work.

Steve had insisted that everything found be split into several locations rather than horded by individuals. He called it forward thinking in case outsiders found their way onto the street. Others thought it was paranoia, but they agreed, if for nothing more than to stop him going on about it. All except the local news agent, who had not let anyone near his shop since this whole situation began.

The TV stations started to slowly disappear over that first week. Then the internet went down a couple of weeks later, so no Netflix anymore. At this point it became impossible for news from the outside world to reach them. On top of this, a hum of low moaning started being heard from the surrounding area.

Steve kept insisting that staying behind the wall was the safest course of action. They would be rescued once all this was sorted out. Or else there was nowhere safe left to go anyway. Some saw this as sound logic, others disagreed.

The supplies were enough to hold them over for a while. Despite this some of the remaining inhabitants still wanted to check the neighbouring streets for more. Steve was not exactly a fan of this. But he didn't want to cause a fuss, he was already having trouble keeping on the good side of everyone.

While it had been his idea to fortify everything and bring everyone together, he was not really a natural leader. He liked to keep to himself and had a hard time clearly explaining his thinking to others. In the end he just could not inspire enough confidence in those around him to really hold authority.

When supply runs started, he'd stayed behind; preferring to guard the gate and make sure everything was secure. He told himself these were vital checks for the safety of their makeshift community. It was also a good excuse for him not to have to venture outside, even if it made those who did think that he was a coward.

At first, these runs helped ease some tension. After a few days though, those who risked going out hadn't returned. Steve agreed with the others that something must have happened to them. This validated him in his choice to remain in the shelter, but he tried not to go on about it too much.

A voice inside his head wondered if they found something better and left the rest of them behind. He comforted himself with the thought that they probably met a grizzly end, rather than abandoning the street. Steve could be a petty man.

Now there were only six people left.

There was Dave, who worked with Steve in the yard. He was older and seemed to always be looking for short cuts. They held a moderate friendship despite Dave's feckless nature.

Jenny was a former teacher who always kept to herself. He thought she looked like a nice person, although they only had the briefest of exchanges before all this. She was rather curt, but it wasn't something he had a problem with.

Then there was Michael, who ran the local newsagents at the top of the street. He was an 'old school guy' if Steve were to put it politely. He was only really concerned with keeping his little empire together despite all that was going on.

The final two were Michael's daughters, Joyce, and Lucy. Lucy was a university student back home for the summer. And Joyce had been looking forward to her final year of sixth form before the dead started eating people. Steve didn't really feel comfortable enquiring about anything beyond school status for women of this age.

Michael and Dave were both men in their late fifties and held no real interest in making any long journey to find other survivors. Dave didn't really have anyone, much like Steve now. And Michael wasn't about to let his daughters go out into the unknown. Instead, they chose to stay in the enclosure he built, and he appreciated that.

As for Jenny, he didn't know why she stayed. Maybe like him she had nowhere to go. She had lived across the road from him for a couple of years and he never really noticed any active social life being projected from her house. Not that he was a crazy stalker or anything; he just liked to keep an eye out.

He was always observant of people and how they acted.

Unfortunately, this often led to him getting the short end of the stick in social situations, rather than being an advantage. For instance, he noticed how many women got hassle from guys on the street. So, he made extra efforts to never even really look at women when they walked by. All this led to was him staring strangely ahead, looking odd and then them being bothered by someone else anyway.

The same was true when he occasionally did venture out to pubs or social gatherings. Before meeting his fiancé, even if there was a lady who looked to be interested, he was always too shy and reserved until he was passed up for someone else. He would analyse the situation until there was nothing left to act upon.

Steve could not count the times he told himself to break through these social barriers. To simply say things and see what happens. He tried drinking copious amounts. Somehow alcohol made him even more passive. Less shy maybe, but equally as removed.

This sheer amount of analysis in social situations affected him in most any scenario. This was why he could never handle small talk. It would either be about something he had already observed and was therefore obvious, or else too miscellaneous to notice in the first place.

He never understood how people could regurgitate their thoughts directly. He wondered if it was because they did not care about what they were saying. Still, most people appeared to find a comfort in this, rather than being insulted.

To him, the whole thing was an excuse to appear at ease with one another, rather than actual means of communication. These thoughts were a dangerous road to go down though. He hoped people were genuine in their interest for one another, not merely trying to fill a void with affectations of niceties.

None of this really had anything to do with Jenny. Steve's mind couldn't help itself. Any thoughts about interacting with people brought up a lot of his insecurities. It was no wonder he held most at a distance.

Now the inhabitants of the street were whittled down to

him and these few others, he felt like he should make more of an effort. He really wanted them to have a sense of community. Mostly in case they also decided to leave. Some might argue a street should have a pre-existing feeling of common interest. If it had then Steve didn't know about it.

Dave took the opportunity of people deserting to swap his wreck of a house with a much nicer one, which happened to be right next to Steve's. Well, it was as nice as you can make a terraced house in a low-income end of Coventry anyway. There was paint on the walls and everything.

Currently he, Dave and Jenny were all living in the three houses at the end of the street. He was glad they were near the alley exits in case something happened. Michael's family were positioned at the top of the road in the flat above his shop.

He wondered how they felt overlooking the gates. Even though they weren't bombarded by hungry shambles lurking outside, shuffling foot traffic was a constant feature. Maybe Michael was more comfortable with the sight of lurching sacks of rotting flesh than he was.

Steve had taken to calling them 'shambles' since he felt it made their presence easier to manage. The term 'Zombies' was loaded with associations and imagery, which could be a little overwhelming. Plus, quite frankly they were all a bit of a mess. The term had somehow stuck with the others too.

While he was grateful someone was keeping watch over the wall, it still seemed a bit weird to him. If he had a family, he would want to keep them as far away from those sights and sounds as possible. Then again, to his estimation there wasn't anywhere you could go to truly get away from it.

This was the catch twenty-two of an apocalypse. If you don't have a safe place, you are constantly exposed to danger. Yet, if you are protected then you become unprepared for the horrors sporadically visited upon you by the world outside. He was constantly worried what they would do if their boundaries were tested and failed.

It was all too risky.

Both states can get you killed. The only difference is the time it takes. Steve secretly hoped to bring in a bunch of people hardened by the outside world, ideally those who left before. The problem is there was nothing to stop them from simply taking over if they had the inclination.

The best case was a 28 Days Later scenario, where after a certain time the infected ceased to function. Surely a body can only stay reanimated and rotting for so long. At some point most shambles would become skeletal, and you couldn't walk around on bones and guts alone.

Even if they reached this point however, he had no idea what state the world was in. Everything outside the walls was a mystery. What Steve would give for some carrier pigeons or a rogue skywriter. A text from his mobile network letting him know about work being conducted in his area would do.

For all he knew the virus could not only reanimate the dead, but also restored them fully in body and mind after a time. Heck, it could turn them into vampires. Or else mutant freaks bent on world domination!

What if it wasn't a virus at all? It could be some elaborate alien invasion? What was to stop an invading hoard of little green men from bursting through the gates at any moment?!

Steve had a few issues with paranoia.

He was comforted by the fact that he had not seen any flying saucers, so hopefully aliens were off the table. No news was good news. In fact, he hadn't really heard anything apart from the occasional moan or cry in the night. Maybe everyone outside the wall was fine and simply having a massive orgy.

That would be just his luck. When the world was finally ready to lie down and open its legs, he would be trapped in a prison of his own making. All the orgy people probably looked at his barriers and thought it was a conservative protest against pleasure.

He didn't even like to vote.

With all these thoughts swirling around he knew that at some point he would be driven to go out. But were the risks worth the reward? What good was venturing into the outside world if all you found out was "yes indeed everybody is dead, and look, I'm next!"

Sometimes sitting with nagging worries was better than getting your leg bitten off. Others would have said "shit or get off the pot." But Steve liked long toilet sessions.

He was staring out his upstairs window. He could see all the sprawling fauna growing out of control in his back garden after months of no maintenance. At least the wildlife was doing well. It was also possible this mess would be a good defensive line against the undead if it ever came to that.

He saw some movement. His defences were being tested! Must the universe seek to prove him wrong so immediately?!

His hope was a stray cat or fox could be roaming about. He remembered a few years ago when the surrounding roads had been closed off for massive maintenance to underground pipes. He thought it was strange at the time, but he had gotten used to it, even liked it due to the lack of through traffic. Others who did not live right next to their workplace were not exactly happy. Ah well.

It was the dead of winter, and the night was so quiet you could hear if someone coughed three streets away. Steve took to going for walks around the area, just happy not to run into anyone. The main thing he enjoyed on these nightly jaunts was witnessing the unnatural interplay between the local cats and foxes.

The scavengers had become bold without the presence of people, possibly due to other prey going into hibernation. They had taken to pursuing the faux feline predators around the streets and back alleys. You didn't know how fast a cat could leap about until you saw it being chased by a fox.

The whole experience was fascinating. Although he would not have liked it as much if he saw it play out to its natural conclusion. Luckily that never happened. His presence probably put them off, continuing a theme.

He had a sudden fear that it could be Jenny. Maybe she was

sneaking off to escape from him and his awful company. He tried not to think like this, he was his own worst enemy.

There was significant movement now, bigger than a cat.

Maybe Dave was trying to help with a spot of extreme gardening.

Everything was an extreme sport now: going to the shops, driving to a friend's house, walking the dog. It all could end in your painful and immediate death. Steve supposed technically this was always true. The probability was only a lot higher now.

Whatever it was didn't look like Dave. He could see it was person-shaped now though. It was moving awkwardly, but not slowly like you would expect from a shambles.

It wasn't Dave. Dave did not wear a hooded black cloak. What's more, Dave didn't have grey skin. And Dave didn't carry around a massive scythe with him.

To be fair though, a scythe would be the perfect tool for extreme gardening.

Seeing the figure more clearly now, Steve confirmed that it was also not Jenny. The frame was too big. Either that or she had piggybacked someone while putting on the massive robe as a disguise. How far was this woman willing to go to get away from him?!

What if the undead started to gain intelligence? Knowing what they were and taking up arms?! It was Land of the Dead all over again. The next thing you know they would be coming together to unseat the establishment if they had not already done so in their own way.

There was something comforting about the idea of those who put all their stock in high living at the expense of everyone else finding out it meant very little in the end. When the dead rose, it might not be so easy to visit your country club anymore. You might find your meticulously crafted castle crumbling.

Then again this might be wishful thinking. The wealthiest of the world were most likely safe and sound in a bunker. They were probably still living better than ninety-nine percent of the rest of the world. However, in a more subterranean style than they were accustomed to.

It's understandable to want to be the one percent if you have all the privilege and everyone else toils away. When the 'unwashed masses' turn into slobbering ghouls clamouring for your flesh, you might feel a bit outnumbered. No one is left to do your washing or cook your meals. You might truly have to become one of the living for once.

A fear shot through him that he could now be considered part of the one percent. He didn't even get to have a private jet! In a world where everyone was dead, being a living human made you privileged.

His mind filled with images of zombie protestors, calling for him to be cancelled. Maybe that was what all the moaning was about. Was this figure in the garden leading the charge?!

Vague political machinations aside, Steve wondered how the thing even made it into his garden. There was limited back access. Someone might be able to hop a fence, but it would be difficult for a walking corpse to pull it off.

There were several possibilities floating around in Steve's head. The main one being that they were getting smarter and organising. The underlying worry persisted that this was only the first of many.

Admittedly, with all the ground floor doors and windows on the street boarded there was little chance of stray shambles getting through. He had been extra cautious when it came to sealing up the downstairs of all the houses on the street. He had gotten the thickest wood from the yard and nailed the planks airtight against any opening he deemed unnecessary.

It was hard for any light to escape through the boards, let alone anything to get in, or else a person to escape. Not that he was concerned about that. Some people had complained at the time. Still, others volunteered to do it for themselves. He didn't really like this either, what if one of them hadn't done a good enough job!

The only way to get through without painstaking hours to pry all the nails out would be to take an axe to them. At least for the ones he was responsible for anyway. Come to think of it, there was an axe resting against the backdoor in case of such a situation.

His brain weighed up a bunch of options.

He could do nothing and let the thing shuffle about down there getting up to potentially all sorts of mischief. He could go tell the others and have them help him. Or he could deal with it himself. All three options had problems.

The undead, at least in the movies, were a lot like weeds. One or two of them look harmless and inoffensive so you leave them. Shortly after you find yourself with a whole garden full of the blooming things. While Steve had enjoyed playing Plants vs. Zombies while his iPad worked, he didn't want to see a real-life version outside his window.

He also didn't want to involve the others, because if one of them got injured he might have to save or kill them. What's more, with all that had happened with people leaving he didn't want to look as if he could not handle things on his own. He could see Jenny rolling her eyes at him or Michael's mocking throaty laugh. It didn't make him feel good.

Plus, what if it wandered off in the meantime if he went to get someone? That wouldn't mean the danger was gone! It was the same as seeing a big spider in the corner of the room. If you took your eyes off it and it disappeared, you could never use that room again!

Nope, he was going to have to deal with it himself. The priority now was to figure out the safest way to go about it. His critical thinking skills were no use if he ended up dead.

He could lure it to the window and drop something heavy on it. His PS4 was useless at this point, but it didn't feel right to fling it out the window, too much progress lost. The memories of the good times he spent with it were still staunchly attached to the lump of plastic. All the stuff in his man-child room was soaked in association come to think of it.

He didn't want to throw down anything that would make a lot of noise while breaking either. This might attract more of the undead and would defeat the purpose entirely. Besides it's not like there were several conveniently large throwables lying around. He would have no reloads if more came.

Sharp objects were an option. He had no experience with them to guarantee any kind of success though. While he was fairly good at playing darts, the skill level required with one to kill a zombie seemed beyond his reach.

The problem of size came up, in regard to projectiles. He was not the type of person who possessed specifically designed weapons like throwing stars. He was not that far down a rabbit hole when all this had begun.

He considered dangling out the window with the axe and trying to clip it on the bonce. This strategy probably would not end well. As a child, Steve had a habit of dangling out of his bedroom window. He was a lot bigger now and wasn't sure it would work the same way, let alone with an axe in tow.

Thinking about delivering an arcing swing reminded him about the scythe the thing was carrying. He wondered where it would have picked up the implement in the first place. It wasn't exactly an everyday household object, locked in the grip of a recently turned former person.

If it was late October, then there might have been some explanation. Being as this all started in late spring, it couldn't be the remainder of a shoddy Halloween costume. Perhaps it was a shambles cosplaying as the Grim Reaper. If so, it had done a poor job. It wasn't even bony for a start.

He decided to concentrate on disarming it for now and worry about decapitating it later. A shuffling corpse tapping at your window was one thing; one using a sharp implement to do so was another. Even if it had not developed any form of real intelligence, a lucky swing might cause trouble.

He considered that the boarded windows could probably stand up to a few passing glances. Still, who knew how long the thing might be out there if he didn't take care of it. There was always the chance it was indeed sentient and therefore needed to be disarmed directly.

He finally formed a plan in his head and having settled on it, leapt into action. He called out to the second-rate reaper from the window. It looked up at him and without hesitation he dashed from sight and thundered down the stairs to grab his axe.

His plan was to dangle the blade down as the thing came closer to then hook the scythe before dragging it up. Even if the shambles somehow had the intelligence to know how to use the weapon, it couldn't reach him from there. What's more he doubted it had the physical dexterity to swing the heavy blade properly if it came to that.

There was a nagging doubt in his mind that a weapon like that didn't need to be all that fast or accurate to end his life. There wasn't really any turning back though, the process had started. He gulped through heavy breaths as he collected the axe and headed back upstairs.

When he got back the figure was closer, weapon raised in a threatening manner. The British summer time of alternating rain and sunshine had made the garden monstrous. This slowed its progress as it continued to move towards the window.

Steve started to psych himself up, trying to picture the act of taking the scythe out of its undead hand. He wondered if he should go slowly, like some kind of deadly claw machine. Or try with one great swing to disarm the thing before dragging it up. He thought he might be able to, but what if it dropped to the ground instead.

There was every chance that if the walking corpse picked up the scythe once, it could do it again. His breathing increased and he started muttering to himself. He clutched the axe and tried to put these questions out of his mind, pumping his arms getting ready to swing.

He hadn't dealt with any of the dead directly before, nor a dead body in general for that matter. He thought he knew what one looked like, he had seen enough TV. He didn't think their skin would be so stony, closer to marble than mould.

He also expected the movements to be stiffer. Surely the

decay of the joints and muscles would have more of an effect? Instead, there was a fluidity to the figure, an eerie ease. It came across as more like something from Twilight than any of the Living Dead movies.

This is why he didn't trust the media.

Sometimes you think things work a certain way because everyone says that's how it goes. Then you find out it's for the most part false, or at least poorly explained. For example, he still didn't understand why in health class the teacher had been insistent on telling the classroom full of boys that women had three holes. He had spent ages pondering where the third hole was.

Once as a teenager he got up the courage to ask a girl who he was on the verge of being intimate with. Admittedly it wasn't the best time to do this. But it had been bothering him for a long time and now was the opportunity. In a dry, sardonic manner, the girl had explained to Steve that the third hole was in fact the anus.

He was shocked. She mistook his surprise for enthusiasm and got the wrong idea. They did not end up being intimate. A little part of his outward curiosity to ask how the world worked died that night.

After that revelation Steve had begun to truly question everything in his own mind.

Why would a teacher, when talking about female sexual organs, throw the anus into the mix? In his experience women did not consider this a part of the bargain. At least not on the first date anyway.

Then again others seemed to believe it was like some sort of magical 'cheat hole'. For moral or religious reasons, it didn't count towards some invisible points scoring. It was a strange system that Steve had never really gotten his head around.

These thoughts flashed into his head as he readied the axe, the robed figure drawing closer and closer. The thing was nearly at the ground floor window now and he had to pop his head out to see it properly. Fearing a possible attack, he kept bobbing in and out of the frame.

The proposed plan of snatching a scythe with the swing of his axe wasn't the best. At this point he had very little else to go on. He was running out of time. Strategy gave way to situation.

"Hel…"

The sound the thing made triggered Steve's response. He found himself launching the axe down with a force he did not know he had. Feelings of nervousness and memories of failed sexual experiences drove the blade on through the air.

Intelligent or not, the thing didn't have time to react.

The momentum of the swing was so great that it knocked the weapon out of its hand completely on the first try. While this wasn't really the desired result it was something and Steve started to feel positive about his flailing attempt. That was until the wild metal edge of the axe ricocheted off an adjacent wall.

It sent a jolt through his arm, in turn making him lose grip on the handle. He was too slow to react, the axe slipped out of his hand. It tumbled down, blade first. He instinctively jumped back. Then all Steve heard was a wet 'squelch' from below.

CHAPTER TWO

The journey through Coventry was a slow one for Death. For one thing, he was getting used to the mechanics of walking on actual legs. It had been so long since he last manifested, he had completely forgot how they worked.

When ethereal he took more to moving with a mysterious glide. Nothing sells a person more on their time being up than seeing a spectral figure floating towards them with unworldly grace. The effortless movement promised something beyond the physical.

The tremendous scythe he carried did not hurt either.

Now though he had to think about moving two ungainly appendages, let alone where to put them each time. It was no wonder humans were always coming to sticky ends operating them. They tripped into woodchippers and fell off tall buildings. Sometimes they simply stepped awkwardly off the pavement, causing them to break their neck.

In some ways the struggling made him feel happy. He was starting to understand things about the human condition. The fact that he was feeling at all was a sign of that. It would make him much more relatable. In another way it was a huge pain in the backside, something that was also causing him problems.

Navigation was especially difficult due to all the uneven grassland he started out on. Death was deposited in the great English countryside a few weeks ago to escort a hiker who had broken her ankle while trying to get a stone out of her shoe. Of course, it was not the ankle that killed them. It was the crawling for miles before dying of exhaustion and exposure.

To be fair, Death was in a better position than they were. On the other hand crawling may be a better way to learn. The small humans looked like they had a fun time with it after all.

At the time he wished the hiker well and tried to show off how they would not have to walk anymore now they did not have a body. The hiker, whose name escaped Death, did not appear to be impressed. At the time he had shrugged it off and waited to be whisked to the next departed soul. Now that he realised this was his last interaction with a person it made him a little apprehensive.

On top of this was the worry that he could not remember the details of the person. It was usually a given for him. It was hardwired into his mind. This helped for his job since he was dropped into unfamiliar situations on a regular basis.

Maybe a subconscious part of him registered this failure in communication and that was why he floated about aimlessly for some time after. He was resigned to wait for a sign rather than act. Eventually he got bored of the woodland scenery and drifted more towards what he presumed would be a populated area.

The journey to civilisation felt like an age, even being in incorporeal form. Death usually did not have to actively travel. When he got there, he felt like he missed a party or something. Everything was a mess. The dead were all around. It was like Santa choosing to take a break and everyone carried on with Christmas without him.

He had never felt like such a useless figurehead. It was all rather depressing. This was why he wanted a new purpose.

The thought drove him on. He stumbled across fields and uneven pavement for what may have been days before he saw something other than empty houses. It made him wonder how the walking corpses behind him managed it.

Admittedly, the group following him dwindled a bit from the horde he first encountered. However, there were still a fair few hobbling along after him. These shuffling shells possessed little semblance of humanity. They were lumbering automatons following simple stimulus to the sense organs, which somehow clearly remained in operation.

You would be surprised where such mindless persistence could get you. Like a group of drunkards arguing for free food. Although in this case there was no overstressed night manager handing out chicken nuggets to quell the tipsy horde. Normally he might not know about such colloquial phenomena, but the number of fatalities around this scenario was enough for him to take note.

Their company had a sort of charm in how unchallenging it was, almost like training for when he met genuine people. He was concerned, however, as to how to explain the dozens of ravenous undead brought to the door of any surviving human he was able to find.

Despite this he put the problem to the back of his mind. His first concern was to discover where some of these survivors were hiding out. Then he would worry about his groupies and how the humans chose to greet them.

Death had thought that the further he went into the city, the more likely he would be to see humans. They did thrive in the most hostile locations after all. However, as the long roads became more cobbled and the buildings closed around him, he saw no significant signs of life.

His surroundings reflected his morose inner thoughts. It appeared the city of Coventry was fully home to the dead. A place once full of music and creation silenced. The mixture of centuries old architecture and modern commercialism now a sound stage for the groaning of animated cadavers.

There were some boarded up shop windows that looked promising. Sadly, when he rapped on these makeshift barriers he was only greeted by further undead. They looked pleased to see him at least.

After a few of these meetings he realised polite knocking probably would not be appreciated by potential people inside. Plus, pounding on a door might get him mistaken for one of his ghoulish grey companions. That was the last thing he wanted.

He would have to work on his introductions.

There was little else he could do apart from wander the city searching, pondering what he would do if he met someone. He cursed the forces responsible for his former employment. What was the point in dedicating your existence to something if one day those in charge arbitrarily decided you are surplus to requirement?

Being locked in the soul collecting business forever might not be a great deal. But he thought he had job security at least. It turned out even this was an illusion.

He began to drag his feet with every empty shelter. This made the foreign act of walking even more perilous. Several times he tripped over his own robes and tangled his legs in the shaft of his scythe. If there were any people around it would have been quite embarrassing.

At least the dead did not judge him. They looked towards him with rapt awe, even though at times he was more ungainly than they were. They were not so encumbered by reminders of their former identities. Often, they had very little in the way of clothing or accessories to obstruct them.

Death tried to imagine himself without the scythe and the robe. The options were potentially endless. It was intimidating. He decided he was not ready to let go of his usual iconography right at this moment.

The dead clustering around him was starting to give him a headache, an unpleasant new experience. He realised this was only happening because he was letting it. He shook it off and tried to maintain a positive attitude.

This journey was about self-improvement, not wallowing in potential problems. He needed to not get discouraged so easily. Now if he could only find someone to give him a nice warm welcome.

His wandering started to take him back to the outskirts of town, still hopeful of finding people. The persistence of humans went far beyond huddling against each other only for heat and safety. They were always able to adapt and eventually thrive. For all the ends he witnessed, there were millions of beginnings that brought forth new life and opportunity to the world.

While no people were present, he saw signs of the former world. There were tables set outside restaurants waiting for a summer rush that would never come and flyers for club nights that would never take place. The efforts people made in the former world to find social satisfaction made Death feel better about his own current desires.

His attempts to find life arguably paled in comparison to the desperate need for humans to find companionship, sexual or otherwise. He often heard the departed regret being alone, or else regrets of clinging to someone for so long to avoid this. Finding contentment in life through others appeared essential, yet potentially impossible.

As disembodied representative of the effects of time and circumstance, he was content with his role as rhetorical agony aunt. He listened but did not necessarily feel the need to give out advice. It was a bit late for that. Also, his perceptions were so removed that what these souls said was generally amusing rather than poignant at the time.

Take the many who felt the need to completely obliterate their motor functions and common sense to then find someone in a similar state. It did not sound like a recipe for success. They went into a hot and crowded room to rub against each other to feel some sense of social acceptance.

The whole ritual was ludicrous to Death. Plus, the logistics alone were a nightmare. What he wanted was a conversation. Copulation was far too complicated a concept to consider.

Still there must be a certain appeal to the whole process, otherwise why would so many people partake? After all, what did he know about creating life? It was fair to say his expertise was solely based on the period after.

There is only a limited amount you can garner about the human condition from regrets and hindsight. He was not the maker of the cake. If anything, he was the one who threw the cake out after it grew stale, and everyone was done with it.

In this moment Death noticed a movement different from the uncoordinated jerks of the undead. It was the quick trotting of a medium sized canine. More specifically a Border Collie. The black and white patches weaved through the shuffling corpses as they groped around in confusion.

They did not know what to make of the dog.

Clearly this was a living thing, moving and making noise. Yet the dead had a hard time deciding if they wanted to eat it. Maybe the shape put them off, or the way it sped about on all fours. Or perhaps the soul was a factor. Death never attended to an animal, so he did not know how the concept related to them.

Maybe they just did not like the taste of fur.

Death saw the Collie had something strapped to its back. It was a pack of some sort, filled with various bits and pieces. He could not make out exactly what it was carrying, but clearly this was not some stray animal.

When he focused his mind on the movement he started to discern more about the canine and its past. Any living thing exists for a select period of time. Despite only appearing at the end, he had been able to perceive the whole. Although before, this had only been of passing interest, and like everything else right now this power seemed to be a little bit shaky.

He had not understood it on a personal level, but in terms of facts about events he was infallible. It helped a lot with the small talk side of his vocation. Now he had to concentrate for even a brief glimpse into the past of one specific animal. Still, it was something.

He saw flashes of a street, a door, an owner. Then flashes of miscellaneous items; pain killers, needle nose pliers, a bottle of gin and some things Death did not recognise or understand. While he had a good knowledge of the living world there were always going to be aspects that he could not pick up on. He had never delved into the mind of an animal before. Even without faulty powers he would be in uncharted waters.

It was as if the Border Collie played through a visual list and directions in their head, remembering a mission. This was entirely possible; Death knew many animals could be trained to do any number of tasks. He also knew how this training could go wrong. In this case however, the clarity in which they were going over these thoughts was comprehensive enough to be akin to a human being.

This dog had no distraction. No attraction to shiny objects or miscellaneous movements out of the corner of its eye. It was to the point where he could see little else than the list it was repeating over and over. Intrigued, he tried to force the images away and go deeper into its past. All he got was a blinding flash and the sensation of pain before the animal was too far away, scampering off into the distance.

He considered following her. He gathered she was a bitch in the time inside her head. He would have to run though, and he doubted his level of coordination right now could handle that. Death was inevitable; he did not need to rush.

Despite this hesitance, he was getting better controlling his body. He barely tripped over his robes at all in the last few minutes. Given time he could most likely push his fabricated body further. For now, he was shaky and out of practice.

What he needed was to find somewhere he could put his feet up and get accustomed to his new state. Technically he could do this anywhere, but he would rather have a chat while doing so. Preferably with someone who could hold up a decent level of conversation.

He looked to his left and saw the whimpering shade of Barry. His steely gaze softened as the lumpy face continued to regard Death with a confused admiration. There was something endearing about him, even though he could not converse on a human level. He conveyed a kind of tragic beauty, almost like he understood what had become of him.

"Come on Barry." Death said. "We have people to find."

After a couple of hours, the myriad of boarded up and broken into shops gave way again to desolate row upon row of houses. Most looked the exact same, apart from an occasional smashed or burnt-out window. They all had drab brickwork, a rickety wooden gate, and reasonably thick wooden doors.

Anyone with the aspirations for an ornate door with a glass design in the centre would have fared poorly against the undead. Reinforced or not it was unlikely such a door would stand up to regular pounding. Neither would it be any good at drowning out the horrible sounds of a baying pack of ghouls hungry for flesh.

Death hesitated to think of the shape a band of survivors in those kinds of conditions. His search of the inner city had been fruitless, so there was little else to hope for. He puzzled at those who chose to take shelter in this suburban environment rather than moving into the city. There they would surely be better positioned for rescue and supplies.

He had trouble understanding human wants and desires that influenced their choices above the needs for safety and sustenance. It was a blind spot that made him sceptical of his own logic when trying to figure out their actions. For instance, that observed need for gyrating to obscenely loud music in dark rooms.

He assumed a correlation with mating dances and vivid colour displays in animals could be an explanation. However, he thought humans generally acquired a mate through sight and conversation. These two things were clearly greatly impeded by the proposed situation. There must be a nuance Death could not perceive.

Yet the results were evidently there. Copulation stemmed from these social activities as much as fatalities. Then again, he was not sure if either outcome could be claimed as desirable in the grand scheme of things.

That would be one of the challenges when he finally did come across people. Any anecdote he could tell to ingratiate himself included at least one person having died at the time. He held a hope that with all the constant death and bodies around it might not seem as morbid as it once would have. Or at the very least he hoped it would not kill the mood.

Death realised in his musings he had lost Barry, as well as the rest of the hoard. This made him a little sad as they passed for decent company in the absence of anyone living. He glanced around but could see no trace of them. Who knew they could shuffle off so fast?

Admittedly he mainly used Barry as a sounding board for his own ideas. There was something about the vacant face that made him easy to talk to. Not totally akin to a real human being though, a lack of mutual respect found him commenting on his actions; "Look at him sniffing at that drain like there could be people down there!"

It was amusing and filled the time. Death was beginning to appreciate what having a pet was like. There was a comfort there. But part of this came from a removal of the pressure felt by engaging with a being who could challenge you on your own level and behaviour.

The power dynamic was off.

He even scalded him like a pet, chastising him for things he had no real control over. "Put your entrails back in, they are dripping all over the pavement!" If Barry was any real type of companion, he would find his way back to him.

Maybe he should get a leash.

The division between his perception of the living and the living dead was strange. For all he knew they might still possess their minds. His incapacity to usher them to the next plain of existence did not mean they were entirely absent.

They may still possess thoughts and feelings, only having lost the ability to express them. A dog had things it liked and ways of showing this despite a lack of complex communication tools, even if most of these were entirely food related. These walking corpses might be the same.

Death was struck by the idea that perhaps they followed him around due to a latent memory of what his figure signified. Maybe they were expecting him to feed them. This made him feel a sense of misplaced responsibility. He could not go around rooting out humans to give his undead friends. But if the whole conversation thing did not work out it was always an option.

He tried to clear these thoughts from his mind. They were

dangerous. As removed from the human experience as he was, he would not start off this new chapter by extinguishing the little life that remained on this planet.

All this milling around was starting to bother Death. You would surmise that being around for over two millennia taught him patience. Conversely, in this time there was little rest and waiting. Instead, it was all purpose. Turn up for a departed soul, usher them on, then onto the next one.

Maybe he needed a hobby.

Before he could ponder the potential of needlepoint or wood carving, he spotted smoke coming from between one of the few gaps in the rows of terraced houses. While at most only a few stray puffs, there was no smoke without fire. The thought instantly revitalised him, after all this spark gave birth to human civilization.

He recognised there was every chance all he would find was a blaze created by an abandoned fire hazard. Or else, some undead stumbled past a cooker and managed to oven itself to destruction. Both would at least be something to look at, and if not, he could find the survivors he wanted.

Furthermore, they might need help, how fortuitous!

Death was determined to find a way past the houses that blocked his path. There was an alleyway, but it was completely barred for some reason. He walked around the brick maze and finally found the entrance to the street, but it was obstructed by a big set of gates.

The barrier looked professionally done despite its rushed and ragged appearance. It was almost as if someone aimed to completely secure this one street. And they were now trying to carry on as normal despite the hordes of living dead all around.

This was the perfect scenario for him!

He thought about giving the gate a few good bangs with his scythe, but then thought better of it. It was a prime place for someone to throw heavy objects down at him. While Death had always technically been immortal, he was a bit wary of the extent of his powers at this point.

If he was physically damaged maybe he could regenerate over time, or even instantly. He was not sure though. For all he knew he could lose parts of himself and end up being whittled away to non-corporeality again.

He may have the same physical rules as the undead. One swift blow to the brain and he was done. That would be the last thing he wanted. Just because he did not employ the manners to give a proper greeting, some idiot could end up exploding his skull from a great height.

He decided it would be better to go back to where he saw the smoke and try a more direct approach. It was better safe than sorry. If worst came to worst, he could hack a couple of doors down and get through that way. He realised this thinking might be counter-intuitive, but he was tired and fed up.

Until now there was no sign of human life anyway. Like waiting for a bus that should have been there fifteen minutes ago. All the hope felt started to give way to sulky pessimism at every sign being dashed. This sudden switch in moods felt off to him.

He grasped getting used to having a physical form again, emotional shifts were something new. He was not a fan. Death did not need the mess that came along with cascading feelings.

It had been a source of confusion how humans changed from moment to moment. Existing as a force of nature he saw the complex and course changing events of life as all flowing to one source. The end of the journey would always be the same so why get so caught up in the minute inertia of the minute to minute.

Of course, this was easier to say when you were removed from the world. He knew how transient such dispositions were. However, now being fully immersed in this reality, realistically he should expect to get caught up in the tide.

He would need to learn to dive in headfirst.

In the spirit of this, he steadied himself by embracing his more negative thoughts and resolved to find a way in no matter what. In this effort he went back on himself and arrived at a house that should lead to the source of the smoke on the other side.

There was a passage with a rickety wooden door that led to the garden. He gave it a kick to let out some frustration, this shattered the weak wood at the bottom clean off. As splinters sprayed into the air, he rethought his strategy. He did not want to start things off with an act of wanton destruction.

Death scooted away from the partially broken partition. Now with a much larger gap at the bottom than it had before. Instead, he would try a more traditional approach. He knocked on the front door and waited.

When nothing happened beyond summoning a couple of undead to the immediate area, he decided this was also a bad idea. He would have to face the fear of potential inadequacy and attempt to displace his physical form and phase through the door. It was unlikely the dwelling was occupied due to the lack of an answer.

Either that or they were being very rude.

He leaned against the door, trying to find the detached feeling he needed to lose his corporeal form. There was a slight hesitation due to the possibility that this transition could be permanent. He shook these thoughts away. He needed to take risks in this new world, leave the path of the removed observer behind.

Death refused to live in fear.

The sheer number of humans who devoted their time to a dread of death was terrifying. He was determined to never be afraid of anything that was a possible end. Above everyone, the grim reaper knew in most cases existence continued in some way or form. He was not willing to let apprehension keep him from progressing.

He felt his physical form fall away. For a moment there was only space and air. He created a picture of the door in his mind and willed himself forward. Slowly the door became a sea of woodchip, which became the modest living room of a lower-income house.

The room smelt dank and musty, not the nicest of places to settle. He realised since he smelt then he must at least be partially physical again, even if he was just a nose at this point. It also occurred to him that for most of the time before he was walking around without one.

It was most likely a good idea for him to keep it, despite the smell. The sensory orifice would probably help him blend in more. It might even come in handy at some point. He looked down using his eyes and saw his hands, as well as his grey toes sticking out from underneath his long robes.

This was curious. He had not actually made the full effort to reappear just yet. Yet here he was, in the flesh.

He tried to fade again. He did, but only for a second. Then he was solid again.

Ah. This was not as reliable as it could be. Well at least he phased through the door and did not get lost in space and time forever. A plus all things considered.

Death would have to remember that he was mostly stuck in his current condition now. This could be troublesome if the search for companionship did not pan out. There was a definite feeling of his options becoming more limited.

There were worse places to be stuck he supposed. On the other hand, he was unsure of his relative lifespan in this form. It might take him ten years to find any survivors, if there were people left at that point. That could be a problem.

He became distracted by the body of a woman lying in a chair in the left corner of the room. From the looks of it she was still intact, only worn by age and neglect. He concentrated and got a couple of flashes of meals alone and cats. There was little else of comment.

Along with a general musty whiff there was an artificial aftertaste of gas in the air. These were the dangers of having no companionship for a prolonged period. Even the most solitary person goes a bit funny and ends up departing.

They were in extenuating circumstances. Yet it served as an example to him of the pitfalls of an existence with no human contact. The longer you go without good interactions, the more removed you feel. Before you know it, you can do nothing but try to escape.

He did not want to become a phantom again. Everything was too unknown right now. All he could do was make guesses and take chances until he reached more solid ground.

Looking away from the body he prepared to leap into uncertainty again by heading towards the backdoor. Death was all set to try phasing through when he caught himself. He tried the handle. The door opened as if it was nothing. Doorhandles, he would have to remember to check for them before tempting fate by forcing his way.

He walked into a neglected garden in full summer bloom. Brushing overgrown shrubbery aside he could see the adjacent house. There was an open window. This must have been where the smoke came from.

He crossed the wild lawn to a part of the back wall a bit shallower than the rest. He proceeded to hop it in an incredibly undignified fashion for a man-statue in a flowing black robe. He nearly dropped his scythe as he scrambled over. This would not be the best thing due to noise and physiological concerns.

His entire being and wardrobe were fabrications of his mind, which also extended to the implement. Again, he had no real knowledge of his limitations when it came to this in the new state of things. The tool might still exist independent of his touch. Or dissipate and feed back into his general essence. Or it could fade away into nothingness and he would lose that part of himself forever.

Death reflected how questioning his current state, as well as how he continued to function, could be exactly how human beings felt all the time. How did they stand it? Maybe he should have been more visible in the world when he had the chance. He was not sure how this would have gone for him, but at least it would have saved a lot of uncertainty and worry on the part of everyone else.

Then again, everything he knew about the whole process

of dying had decided to pack up and go home. If he was already in the world at the time it happened, he would be some form of morbid celebrity he supposed. If looked to for answers for the world's ills he would have seemed like an enormous fool.

At this point if he gathered the remains of humanity and tried to tell them the mysteries of life, he would find himself at a loss. Admittedly this was not the informative reassurance one might imagine receiving when given an audience with Death. If he was a modern-day talking head this would be the name of his one-man show, however.

Once over the wall, complete with a messy dismount, he saw that this garden was even sloppier. It was hard to navigate, like a discount hedge maze. Maybe it was a defensive measure, but a pretty half-hearted one if so.

Wading through dense grass, he was sorely tempted to put his scythe to its traditional use. Still, he was not a gardener or the cleaver of weeds; he was the former reaper of souls. Also swinging a blade before coming to say hello could be seen as a bad introduction.

He resided to ambling through the overgrowth and slowly guided himself towards the back of the house to see if anyone was in. Even in the elaborate foliage he could make out boards were nailed across the ground floor windows. While this would obscure his view, it was arguably a good sign.

It indicated survivors, or at least someone trying to take a stand here. Then again, the place could have been abandoned long ago given the state of the garden. Either way, it was clearly not a military stronghold.

There was a movement above him. He was focused more on the surrounding shrubbery. Being faced with this botanical barricade he thought the best course of action would be to call up to the window in the hope that someone heard him.

This would be a nice clear indication that he was distinct from the corpses outside. There definitely had been movement so there was a good chance a person up there would have seen him. With any luck he would receive a warm welcome. Possibly they had already headed to the backdoor to let him in, or even called to some other survivors to come greet him.

Death realised his cowl was pulled over his head from his struggle over the garden wall. Fearing this might give him too much of a foreboding appearance, he took it down to bare his sculpted face. If you were going to take on a human form then why not craft a handsome one, even if the skin was more the colour of stone than marble.

Being in full preparation to actually meet living people he continued to consider what to do with his scythe. Brandishing it was not the best way to meet someone. Yet, his holding of it would signify his intelligence and distinguish him further from the zombie hoard in the vicinity.

He made a compromise and began holding it high over his head to show it was more for wading and balance than cutting and slicing. It was a carefree farming tool, not an implement of impending danger. That should help with first impressions.

He saw the face of someone in the upstairs and readied himself to put on his best smile. They appeared to be waving something out of the window and before he could finish saying 'hello' he was cut off by the swing of what was a rather sharp axe. Maybe it was just a warning, understandable really.

The blade continued its trajectory, however. It slammed into his casually held scythe, knocking it out of his unprepared hand. The panic at the idea of dropping his iconic tool turned to relief as he watched it clatter to the ground and then remain corporeal.

That was one less thing to worry about. He looked down at the piece of himself lying there safely breathed a little easier. He could still hear the clanking of metal despite the blade now being completely settled. He thought maybe it was a reminisce ringing in his ears, but it was coming from above him.

It was not an echo.

CHAPTER THREE

Death was aghast. He let out an astounded "...O", to finish his greeting. Steve was also taken aback by the sight and sound of the thing outside attempt to get the axe blade out of its head. There was clearly something wrong with it.

What kind of zombie doesn't die from an axe burrowing directly into their forehead? What if this was another stage of their evolution?! If so, it was a bloody scary one.

Before the whole 'axe to the head' mishap, it had tried to call up to him. Steve was sure of it. Not in some basic hungry desire, but with an apparent intelligence. The more he watched it, the more he was convinced.

It grasped the handle with both hands. This was too much coordination. It braced its back against one side of the garden wall and its feet against the house, problem solving too. Finally, using inhuman strength it managed to wrench the blade out of its head in one go.

They were all in a lot of trouble.

Death's brain was swimming. However, the damage to his physical state had not overridden his thinking being. Perhaps he should be annoyed. But Death mainly just hoped the sight of him removing the blade from his cranium would not be too off putting. Whoever dropped it must be having a fit.

There was no real harm done.

The axe came out with a sickening gurgle and a spray of something that resembled blood. Death was not sure if it was a manifestation of his mind or natural by-product of his physical form. A necessary lubricant if you will.

Now came the real potentially problematic part. He had no idea if his body would heal itself. And if it did he was not sure how the process would work.

Unlike phasing, healing was not part of his regular work. Even before he removed himself from the world he was never really injured. A few poor souls had taken a desperate swing at him. He was more ethereal back then. There had never been a connection.

Death dropped the axe and hoped for the best.

Steve saw the thing send the axe clattering to the ground, it was not effective. Rick Grimes would have been out of luck. If that wasn't terrifying enough, the robed figure turned to look at him directly as the gaping hole in his forehead started to close Wolverine style. All the while it wore this ghastly grin on its face. Its eyes burned into his soul, promising vengeance.

Steve gulped. He was going to die.

Death let out a sigh of relief as he felt the wound closing. He was fine despite receiving massive head trauma. Now there was no longer a blade embedded in his head he could fully see the human at the window. He should be able to get a read on who they were and why the best course in greeting him was to drop an axe on his head.

He wanted the first human he met not to be some kind of bloodthirsty psychopath. Then again, that could be what it took to survive in this world. Kill anyone on sight and ask questions to a corpse.

To be fair, if this fellow was an axe throwing maniac, it did not necessarily mean he was fundamentally a bad person. Or at least he could be someone able to hold a decent conversation. Death had no qualms over any number of sharp projectiles now he knew his healing capabilities.

Steve was paralyzed. He got lucky with that axe hit, and it didn't even do anything. This is where being proactive gets you. He was still at the window when the monster began to reach down for its weapon.

The robed destroyer scooped up the scythe with a grace so far away from one of the living dead it was almost a comfort. There could be no way something with motor skills this refined was a mindless killing machine. Then again, seeing a tiger stalk you through the long grass is probably a thing of beauty until it ripped your face off.

Death hefted the missing part of himself, the weight felt good in his hands. It was all relative. It was made of his own mental design. Still, he had an attachment to his tool. Although wielding it was questionable in this new world.

It appeared he was right in thinking brandishing it might come across as hostile. On the other hand, dropping an axe on someone's head for giving a polite "hello" was an overreaction also. There had been enough toing and throwing, he decided he would simply proceed with his social agenda.

He yelled "Cooie!" at the man in the window. He added a little wave in case this clearly paranoid person thought that was a kind of war cry or something. Death was unsure if this was a correct greeting, but it was the first thing that came to him.

It was possible his brain was still a little damaged.

Steve tilted his head sideways. He couldn't help but give a wry eyebrow raise. Had this thing really just said 'cooie'? What the fuck was that?!

Did this thing think they were in an 80s sitcom set in the 60s or something? Who said that type of weirdness outside of the North anymore? Maybe it was from Manchester, the dead could be different there.

The North was a mysterious place with strange ways and customs. They put gravy on chips after all. This being the case their walking corpses might be spryer and more skilled when it came to the usage of farming implements.

Steve realised it was waiting patiently for a response. His general terror fought against his pervasive English politeness. In the awkwardness of a now imposed growing silence he couldn't help but give a little wave and say, "Hello there!" back.

The devil gave an unnervingly broad smile.

"Could I possibly trouble you to let me in so I could have a word with you please?"

It definitely wasn't northern.

Once again in the face of being asked something in such a reasonable way, manners compelled Steve to cave in. This was frightening. Did it have mind control powers? How could he say no when he already made such a faux pas with his axe? This person had not even demanded an apology after his mistake.

"Well, I...I can't see why not. Hang on, I'll be right down." Steve was compelled to comply.

Death was surprised by the cordial response considering how their meeting had started. It just went to show you could always get further with etiquette than offensive weapons. This was the power of politeness.

Steve descended the stairs, puzzled over what was going on. A minute ago, he had swung an axe at this person. Now he was hurrying down to greet them so as to not seem rude. What did he expect to happen when he opened the door?

Would they say: "Terribly sorry, but would it be too much of a bother if I possibly have a little nibble on your brains?" Put like that the request almost sounded reasonable. Would he be compelled to oblige once again? It would be impolite not to!

This was the real danger. Not the dead evolving to use weapons or open doors like Raptors. No, the threat came from their development of proper etiquette!

Steve recalled the times he was forced to do something or put up with some sort of insufferable person out of fear of being rude. The power of potentially perceived social shame was immense. The examples were incalculable.

He once listened to a client go on about pebble dashing their house for two hours because it was technically part of his job. Another time he had to look at dozens of photos of an elderly co-worker's dog after it died because he was the only one in the staffroom at the time. He also held doors open for people to the point where he would be late for another social appointment and then end up feeling impolite anyway.

One real good thing about the world crumbling was not being a slave to unspoken societal norms. Now this thing was employing this toxic form of communication once again. It was a dirty trick.

He reached the backdoor and paused.

Here there was an excuse. It was boarded shut. The one counter to the pressures of politeness was having a legitimate justification that would make the other person appear impolite if they insisted. "Would you mind if I stayed for tea?" could be met by "Sorry the kettle's on the fritz." It worked every time. If you were to ask some of his relatives, Steve's kettle had been on the fritz for years.

"Sorry." He called out. "I'd love to let you in, but my door appears to be boarded up from the inside!"

Steve held his breath in anticipation. What would its next move be? Surely the thing had to abide by its own rules.

"Oh, fair enough." The reply came from the other side of the door. "I certainly would not want to inconvenience you in any way. Give me a moment."

Steve patted himself on the back for his quick thinking. All those years of dodging social situations finally paid off. He had won!

His attitude to life meant he had been almost completely alone in this apocalypse and mostly even before this, except for a scattering of girlfriends. He never did have many friends and the remains of his family, if there were any, hated him. At least he was not about to get his skull cracked open and the contents sucked out with a straw. He doubted a thing like that would use its hands, far too sticky.

As Steve celebrated conquering the wicked dynamics of social conditioning, he heard a racket from outside. There was a kind of whooshing noise, and all the air went out of the kitchen. When it came back it was decidedly mustier. Before he could turn around to see what was going on, he heard a pleasant and chilling voice from behind him.

"Sorry about that." Far too close for comfort. "My scythe

appeared to get stuck as I tried to phase through your door."

He whirled round to see a grey figure towering over him. Steve tried to speak. Instead, he passed out, polite sentiments echoing in his ear.

***

When he came back to the world he was propped up on the sofa. He did not know how much time had passed. He checked his vital organs and his head, everything seemed to be intact.

There was a tinkling of crockery from the kitchen.

It was safe to say that it was more than a few lifetimes since Death endeavoured to make tea. He was having a harder time than usual as the kettle was one of those electric powered things. He never really learned how electricity worked and held no idea how to heat the plastic thing up, let alone the water inside.

Little did he know the power was not working anyway at this point. So even if he knew how it would be impossible. He tried asking the human, but he had not been responsive. Death hoped he was not deceased, that would be a bit awkward. He would find out soon enough either way.

Luckily the stove was operational, so he lit it and grabbed a pan. He knew about general kitchen appliances, their usage summoned him often. It was just the way electrical versions caused this that was not so obvious to him. The water still ran, so he set about finding a couple of mugs and something to put in them.

Obviously, there were teabags, helpfully out by the kettle. He hoped the human did not take milk. Having witnessed many cultures, while he did not understand the ins and outs, he knew it was rude not to join someone when making tea. So, he was making it for two, even though he could not be classed as a traditional tea drinker.

Steve watched as the giant figure carried in what looked like two mugs of tea. The thing, seeing he was awake, handed one to him and kept the other for themselves. Once again, the ingrained sense of politeness took over and he accepted it with thanks.

Honestly if this thing meant him harm, then he most likely would not have woken up to begin with. That was unless this was all part of an elaborate ritual before killing him mercilessly. The entity collapsed into the sofa next to him and then as if it had forgotten itself, extended a hand.

"Hello...again. My name is Death. It is nice to meet you." It said, with an inappropriately pleasant smile.

Steve's uncomfortableness rose to unprecedented levels. Appearing in his kitchen was presumptive. Rummaging around his draws to make tea was invasive. Sitting down, right next to him was downright disturbing. To expect a physical greeting though, that was too far!

He stared at the outstretched appendage.

"Sorry, I should have introduced myself sooner." Death's demeanour cracked a little while his hand remained un-shook. "Although it was hard to get my bearings, you know, after what happened with the axe."

Steve resisted the urge to apologise and continued to focus on the hand. He did not want to give in to this blatant attempt to guilt him into accepting this form of greeting. At the same time, he did feel bad about the whole axe thing. Even in these times it was no way for a first introduction to go.

After a long moment of inner conflict, he took the hand and shook it. He was hoping that going along with this thing claiming to be Death would keep him alive. Also, the discomfort of having to hold out on pressing social needs was getting to him, damn it.

"Steve." He nodded, not sure what came next.

"So, is it just you here Steve?" Death said, straight faced.

"Uhhhhhh...well." He did not know how to reply. It was a loaded question. He could lie about there being lots of people, or say he was alone. Either way the actual answer that there were only a few of them felt inadequate.

"I noticed all the street fortifications so I presumed there would be quite a few people here...If there were people at all."

Death attempted to remain composed and not sound too excited. Surely it would be disrespectful to when first meeting someone convey that you are interested in talking to others. He needed to stick to what was in front of him and not get carried away.

"Oh...oh yeah. There are a bunch of us here."

It wasn't exactly a lie. It depends on your definition of 'a bunch'. At least this suspiciously cheery monolith wasn't hoping for him to be alone.

Death could not contain himself.

"Oh good! You do not know how long I have been looking for a group like yours!"

Steve hesitated in a conversation full of hesitations.

"Uh...That's good...I'm glad." He searched for something to say, having fully entered this perplexing process. "I imagine you meet a lot of people, especially now."

Death let out a cold laugh that killed the conversation. It was on its last legs to begin with. They sat in silence. Steve was trying to figure out what was funny.

"I was not joking about being Death you know."

This was not exactly the best remark to get things going again. Death sipped his tea. Steve's remained untouched.

"Sure...So, what's that like?" He asked, actively trying to take away the awkwardness.

"I am glad you asked." Death said, putting down his cup. "I have always enjoyed my job, but I have to admit that the past couple of months have been pretty challenging. The new lack of souls departing from bodies is a real problem."

"Yes, I can imagine that makes things rather difficul...wait, what?!"

Steve sat upright. Now less cautious and more engaged.

Death shrugged.

"You know, since this whole thing started happening." He gestured outwards. "People have been dying but their souls..."

He shrugged again and let out a sigh.

"So, wait." Steve put his cup down. "You're saying that as Death, you have no idea what is going on? You have no control over what's happening?"

"That is correct." Death said, keeping an air of matter-of-factness. Despite this, inside he was a little hurt at this line of questioning. Especially from someone he just met.

Steve tried to process this information.

Maybe there were no souls now, he felt the same though. Of course, the answer could be that he never did have a soul to begin with. That seemed a bit melodramatic really, if there was a substance classified as a soul, he probably possessed one.

Perhaps this essence was now going somewhere else this supposed Death couldn't see. He clearly wasn't all knowing or anything. Just because he was out of a job didn't mean the job was gone. He could have been replaced and was simply having a hard time accepting it.

Or the soul could now stay in the body, acting as a sort of battery. Come to think of it this could be how life worked in general, only now the process of death worked to scramble the connections. Like a door hanging off its hinges. Still connected to the frame, but it doesn't function properly anymore.

The human Steve had been staring off into the distance for some time. Death coughed; aware it might be his fault for not being the best company. His filter for social interactions was shaky at best and he would be hard pressed to recognise if he said something truly inappropriate.

Also, by outwardly suggesting his company was unwanted it might become a reality and make things even more awkward. Human beings had a tendency to cling onto things suggested, even if they never occurred to them beforehand. That is why over-elaboration could be described as self-sabotage to some degree.

Steve was pulled from his existential musings by a polite cough from the grim reaper, it was all very bizarre.

"So, how come you aren't all bony?" He couldn't think of anything else to say.

"Well, I can choose to embody any kind of form I want when manifesting physically." Death looked down at his stony, flesh-covered hands.

"Yeah, but why choose to look like that?!" Steve blurted out, being beyond the point of politeness after having such a philosophical bombshell dropped on him. Another counter.

"I like it." Death replied, an edge of defence in his voice.

In these situations, Steve found the best course of action was to keep on going. People often tried to have a dig at you if you backed down. He didn't really want to get picked apart by something that had seen the best and worst of humanity for possibly thousands of years.

"Yeah, but I mean, if you aren't going for the traditional 'big skeleton' look then why not do something that helped you blend in more?" He shrugged. "A tan wouldn't go amiss."

"Hmm, well I like to fit into the theme of the time at least somewhat." Death replied.

He paused for a moment, trying to come up with reasons to justify for the most part, unconscious choices. To be fair in willing himself into being, all the little details were pulled from somewhere. They already existed in his mind, but he had not painstakingly gone over them.

Death was not used to all this. In his interactions with passed souls he always managed to maintain the upper hand. They cared too much about what happened to them to really pay too much attention to him past the initial shock.

He might get the occasional "Who the hell are you?!" To which replying, "I am Death!" in a slightly spooky and ominous voice usually did the trick. There was no further interrogation over his nature or how he operated. This human was asking him to justify his choice of aesthetics and he was hard pressed to give an adequate answer.

"I suppose if I think about it, I also based the design on a painting I saw once." His mind whirled as he matched intention to vague memory. "It was by Leighton. I was impressed by the billowing robes and firm brow...The posing not so much."

He gave a 'humph', nodding to himself in satisfaction of an explanation well given.

"I suppose the bulging pectorals and rippling abs didn't go amiss either?" Steve said incredulously.

Death flexed involuntarily.

"Yes well, you know those artist types. They do like to get the anatomy right."

"I bet they do." Steve marvelled at his own sass.

Here he was, talking to the equivalent of a force of nature and he was handing out burns like they were mini sausage rolls at a work do. What else could you expect? The embodiment of mortality comes into your kitchen and tells you that he doesn't really know why the world ended. Humanity is basically down for the count and that's it.

It could make a person a bit snarky.

Death sensed discomfort on the part of Steve. Something was making him ill at ease. Outside of his appearance, which this one seemed fixated upon, he could not figure out what was causing it. He tried to engage any sense of empathy he held. It was hard. After a moment he thought of something.

"Tell me, did anyone in your family die recently?"

"What?!"

"Oh, terribly sorry. What I said was DID ANYONE IN YOUR FAMILY DIE RECENTLY?!!" Death repeated at an astoundingly inappropriate volume.

Steve stared at Death, who continued to regard him with complete innocence. Like the question was the equivalent of asking how the weather was outside. His mind boggled at how this ancient entity could think that was an appropriate question to ask. Surely even the most oblivious person wouldn't mention the weather if you were clearly holding a broken umbrella and drenched to the bone.

Then again, he supposed that if there ever was a time to ask such a poignant question in passing it was now. In a zombie apocalypse it becomes standard chit-chat to discuss how one's family members were killed off horribly. For Steve it happened a little differently, but there was still a fresh loss in his past.

There was just a complete lack of tact here, like he didn't know how to interact with humans properly. Regardless of the politeness he employed beforehand, face to face, Death didn't seem to truly know the rules. Steve could relate.

He realised he might have found someone who he could talk to without having to worry about unknowingly breaking social protocol. To be fair, he always found himself being overly polite when he first encountered someone too. He was trying to gauge who they were and how they felt before attempting to become more familiar.

His trouble with people was a lifelong problem. He found the best way to deal with it was to smile, be silent and reply in politeness. Only real mental cases would have a problem with this when they first met him. Otherwise, anyone would simply think he was a very quiet and boring person, and not bother getting to know him better.

This was the mask he wore in the world before. It was not something that made him happy, it was necessary for his social survival. When he tried to be himself from the get-go people looked at him strangely, as if something was wrong with him. Truthfully, he never really understood the difference between the things he said and what others did.

Now there was a chance to communicate with someone from the start in the way he really wanted to. Death thought it was acceptable to ask about dead family members five minutes into their first conversation. Surely anything Steve said would not be too bad. He realised his robed friend was still waiting for an answer to his question.

"Well…" He held out his hands and shrugged, searching for the right response. "Actually, my mother did die, just before all this started happening. Do you know what happened to her? Did you see her?"

Steve realised this was his best chance to get some real answers. He found it hard to hide his eagerness. He hoped with Death he could abandon the affected sense of reverence that usually came along with talking about such things.

The human appeared excited. This was progress. Still, he was faced with a dilemma.

To carry on the promising upturn of this interaction he would have to break a certain privacy barrier. This would let him find out more about this Steve than he could in hours of talking. However, it was not a normally socially accepted means of getting to know someone, which did not seem sporting or fulfilling. He decided to come clean to his new friend.

"Sorry Steve. I am not omnipotent, even in the matter of passings. To know who your mother was I would have to delve into your mind and memories. This might reveal to me much more than you may be willing to share."

The serious tone and straightforward reply struck Steve.

"Well, that's very decent of you." He said, he was noticing a theme.

This is how complicated social protocols were. Not only could politeness be used to manipulate it could also be a way to identify someone as being earnest. In Steve's mind, honesty was the best policy. This was so long as it came from the right place and the person on the other end was able to accept it of course. The only people who needed to be lied to were those who couldn't handle blatant facts.

"At this point I would rather know. So, if it's all the same to you..." He pressed on but left the end non-committal so as to not appear too forceful. Some habits die hard.

Death considered this.

If he was given permission by the person to look into their mind, then maybe it was alright. It would also be a good chance to test out his control. At this point he could use all the chances he could get. Moreover, there was a certain appeal in cheating a little, even with something he was trying to be disciplined in. It was an acceptable indulgence.

He remembered times he had seen humans do the same. They would drive through traffic lights as they changed. Sample food from someone else's plate of despite insisting they could not possibly order it themselves. Or walk on grass and hop over fences despite signs being placed that specifically forbade this. Although, his points of reference were a little off seeing as how most of these instances had led to the person's demise.

For some reason his mind stuck on the specific less deadly practice of opening several doors on an advent calendar at the same time. The debasing of a device designed for moderation, ruining the ritualistic aspect for a moment of joy. However, in these cases it would not matter so much since they would be deceased long before the rest of the doors could be opened.

From a logical standpoint this action was purely negative since it served to corrupt the standards the person wanted to uphold. Before he could only ascribe this to the illogicalness of human beings in general. Now in his current position Death was starting to understand. The allure of letting yourself slip a little bit, especially when someone else is urging you on.

"Well, if you insist..."

He stared at Steve and started to concentrate.

A picture began to be painted of his current situation.

The somewhat forced isolation.

His lost love and potential feelings for someone else.

The conflicting feelings of disappointment and content.

The glaring lack of people in this fortification.

His most recent bedroom practices.

Death had gone too far with the present.

He tried to go deeper into the past. Images whizzed by too fast to make out. Fighting for control, he saw a young boy. They were walking on their own on what seemed to be a usual route from the local child repository. Streams of small people at various stages of adolescence trooped along all around him, all locked in noisy conversation. He kept his head down as he passed them.

On occasion a member from a group would acknowledge him, in a mostly friendly manner. The boy would look up, smile politely, and go back to his journey. It was hard to discern why the interactions did not go further.

It could be because he was too shy maybe, but also social interaction appeared to be a burden. The boy was resigned to walk alone, though by every present sign he did not have to. He resonated with self-isolation and imposed burden, despite the small stature and care-free surroundings.

Death wondered if he thought he was not good enough. Or possibly he believed the people around him were not worth his time. Perhaps it was a mixture of the two.

He was getting too introspective, focusing on one pocket of time with no real context and trying to extrapolate an entire existence from it. This was never a good idea and achieved very little in the grand scheme of things. Death tried to move things along, whilst keeping with the boy at this current point in time since it probably meant something significant.

He hurried at an unhuman pace until he reached the door of a modest terraced house with a small front garden, slightly unkempt. He pulled a key from a specific pocket in his backpack rather than knocking. This showed a sense of responsibility and need for control. Logically, when this young Steve walked into his dwelling his mother should be somewhere inside.

He watched the boy be greeted by two enthusiastic dogs. The excitement of these animals over his return was something to behold. Death wondered if he should invest in the same kind of companionship.

They certainly appeared useful, especially if you attached pouches to them. The affection was a bonus. This was not the case with cats. Death had some dealing with these little beasts, mainly due to the Egyptians.

He was not a massive fan.

The Steve-boy began his routine of homecoming, putting his key back in his backpack, placing the pack on a hook and his shoes on the stairs neatly. During this mundane display Death witnessed a figure creeping up behind him. It was hunched and clearly did not want the child to notice the threat until it was too late.

As it moved closer, he found himself wanting to yell out,

to warn about the danger that was about to befall the boy. The futility of the act held him back. This was just an image of the past, it could not be altered no matter how strong the desire was. Whatever was about to occur, Steve came through it, no matter how harrowing.

Hopefully it would be character building.

The figure struck. There was a scream. Steve jumped back from the sudden shock of nails digging into his shoulders. The already tense small frame exploded.

"Damn it mum, stop doing that!" Faux outrage echoed off the tight walls.

The woman laughed in a delighted cackle before trying to prod him in the ribs. The boy drew back into a stance akin to a martial arts style. Although it was one Death did not recognise.

"My monkey style will defeat your tiger style!"

The boy moved his lips in a strange manner that did not fit with the words he spoke. Death was perplexed. The woman withdrew.

"Well, I'm not messing with that! You win this round, but there will be another. Oh yes, there will be another!"

Then she tried to poke him again. He dodged and cursed her before giving her a loving hug. She hugged him back and said she was going to check on the dinner. As she walked away Death made a note of her features, highlighted by the smile she wore.

As delightful as the scene had been, Death felt no need to stay around. The present was calling to him. He tried to search his vast database of those he visited in their passing, limiting it to the last few months. He saw nothing. Although in all honesty he could not know if this was due to her passing being after the events began, or if it was because of his waning powers.

He pulled himself out of the vision with some trouble and gave Steve a disappointed shake of the head.

"I could not see either way. Sorry Steve."

He and his new friend let out matching sighs.

"To be honest my powers are not what they once were. I worry that they may run out altogether at some point."

"Ah well, it can't be helped I suppose." Steve shrugged in a far less belligerent manner than Death expected.

With an intake of breath Steve went to add something to his half-hearted reaction. He was used to disappointment. The reaper braced to receive a delayed backlash of frustration.

"So, do you have a timer thingy like Spawn then?"

Death blinked a couple of times.

"...I do not know what that means."

"Never mind." Steve smiled.

He was content in the relative obscurity of his allusion. It was better than any short-sighted chastising he could come up with. Confusing those who irk you with an unknown reference was the best type of passive-aggressive venting.

"Well...I suppose I must be the spawn of something. I do not know what that something is though." Death said, rubbing his chin with a wistful look on his stony face.

Steve realised that he was dealing with a character more disconnected than he was. Even obscure references didn't work to bring him back down to earth. It was a disturbing experience to meet a powerful figure such as this and realise they had no direction.

It was a shame because you'd think a zombie apocalypse would be Death's time to shine. He evidently had not chosen his appointed purpose to begin with. Now he didn't even have that to fall back on.

While humans held no control over their initial existence, at least they were only expected to serve for generally less than a century. Death, as Steve understood it, had been around for thousands of years doing the same thankless job. That was a pretty harsh hand to be dealt.

This realisation made the lack of answers bother him less. He hoped his mum managed to move on before she passed. He would hate to think she was shuffling around somewhere with the dead outside.

Then there was a faint calculation in his mind. Despite the previous apparent teleportation, what if Death came here in a less 'magical' way. You had to think defensively to survive.

"Did you phase through anywhere else to get here?!"

Death looked confused.

"You know, like how you managed to appear right bloody behind me in the kitchen, scaring the piss out of me. That's how you got all the way here right?"

"Hmm I did become non-corporeal to get through the last house, yes. I did knock first though."

"Well, that's nice to know." Steve said, trying not to get distracted with sarcasm. "So, you didn't break down any doors or barriers or anything? I worked hard securing this place. The last thing I want is some stony-faced bastard leading a bunch of undead straight into my living room for tea and biscuits!"

"You don't have any biscuits." Death said with affront.

"You know what I mean!"

He was unsure why the human became so irate. He was telling him exactly what happened and what needed to be said to satisfy this line of questioning. Maybe reciting facts was not what he wanted. Death attempted to be more obtuse.

"You are safe as long as they do not read smoke signals."

"What is that supposed to mean?"

"Well, that is how I found you. There were puffs of smoke coming from one of the windows. I saw it between the houses."

"Goddamn it, Dave!"

Steve pinched his brow in frustration.

"Are you saying I should not have come here?" Death said pensively.

"Yes! I mean, no. I...uh, I suppose you are welcome here. I just...I thought the street was secure." Steve sighed

"Well, this is not a very warm welcome. I do not want to bring any harm. I took care not to break down any fortifications for that very reason." Something in his brain twanged, but he was caught up in a rush of still uncommon emotion and Death brushed it off. "Maybe it was not enough. Perhaps I should not have come at all."

"No, it's not like that Death. I just don't want to lose this place, that's all." Steve collected himself. "I don't know what you know of pop culture…"

"I am aware of bits and pieces. Although measuring the exact time and culture is difficult." Death thought on this. "The new thing is the motion pictures, is it not? Sometimes a person departs in what they call a cinema and I get a nice treat. I never did feel right watching the television box thing in the home of a client though, it seemed a bit morbid."

"Wow, so you've probably never seen Bargain Hunt then? Or Come Dine With Me?"

"No, I am not aware of these. Have I been missing out?"

"Not really…Anyway, if you saw any survival movies you would know most of it is people finding or building a place of safety before inevitably getting overrun. It's something to do with the subconscious need for change and the conscious will to keep things the same. An encapsulation of the struggle to hold on to what we have while existing in a constantly flowing universe." Steve explained, getting lost in his usual musings of his former life before catching himself. "That and the fact that a plot needs to move forward, and the needless destruction of an apparent haven is the easiest way to achieve this. The Walking Dead would have been buggered if they couldn't hop between various versions of strongholds."

Death looked lost.

"The point is that this isn't a story, and we are not slaves to that type of predictable pacing. There is no real need for this place to get overrun. We are safe here and could remain that way for the foreseeable future." He pulled himself out of his spiral. "You are welcome to stay here. I just do not want you to be the catalyst for a dramatic and tragic series of events that result in most of us dying and the few survivors being forced to flee to an uncertain future."

For some reason the grim reaper began to sweat. He did not know he could even do that. It was perplexing.

CHAPTER FOUR

Jenny Concord could not figure out how she came to be in this situation. A couple of months ago she was just a schoolteacher. She didn't really see it that way; however, she knew that is how a lot of people around her described it, especially her mother.

Now that life was gone. In its place, she was precariously dangling from a ladder. She was trying to construct a sign on the roof of her house looking for help. The undead had started pooling below, drooling over her ankle flesh.

Unlike the other side of the terraced street, her row had mostly open back gardens leading onto a road. She had already boarded up that side of her house completely to keep her safe. This of course didn't stop the shambles from wandering around back there from time to time. It was no great loss to Jenny; she paved her garden long ago, not wanting the hassle.

It did not help her sense of restricted freedom, however. She had been stuck in this ramshackle fortress for far too long. Unfortunately, she had missed the opportunity to leave and now this desperate plea for help was the only thing she could think of. Helicopters were not frequent in the illustrious city of Coventry, but there was always a chance. Although at this point the amount of peril that she was in made the idea seem less reasonable to her.

Jenny reflected that perhaps she should have asked for assistance from one of the others. She had a lot of trouble with that sort of thing though. She assumed Dave and Steve could have been quite handy here but was not sure how they would handle her wanting to leave the street. There was a sense that if it was something they wanted to do they would have done it already.

She hated wasting her breath.

Jenny could never get on with people enough for them to follow her lead anyway. There was something about how she came across that made others dismiss her out of hand. At least with the children she taught there was structure in place where they were required to listen to her, on a good day at least.

Before now she had only wanted to live her life and meet some nice people along the way; it never really worked out like that. Rather she turned inwards. Books and study occupied her world as she grew up. She wanted to impart what she learned onto others. This was troublesome because of how no one took her seriously.

Being alone was unsatisfying. Trying to bring people into her sphere was frustrating. Sometimes the entire world felt like it was stacked against her.

She did not want to give up the hope of discovering those who she could have an instant connection with. There were the Newsagents' daughters. Jenny had been talking to them a little since things went further to hell. But their age and attitudes did not entirely match. It was mostly a matter of conversation for conversation's sake.

Additionally, their father was one of the worst people she had ever met. She was not the type of person to often use the term 'mansplaining' as it was rather reductive. Still, if there was ever a person it applied to then it was him. She had often been forced to listen to his comments whenever she needed to pick something up after work.

He constantly commented on her appearance or inquired about her relationship status without any prompting. She could not fathom why she would care about his opinions when only after a pint of milk. If she tried to offer a retort, he would only fob her off or act offended that she did not simply accept his irrelevant views on her life with a smile.

Jenny had considered finding another local shop, but the convenience of the top of the road after a busy day generally outweighed the irritation of the comments. She tried to put up with it and be generally pleasant. Still, there are only so many times you can hear "So when's a pretty girl like you going to get a boyfriend then?" before you want to tear your hair out.

The worst thing was everyone would downplay it, like she was silly for taking issue with some stranger interjecting their beliefs onto her life. One time he started insisting she needed to be having children at her age. His exact words were: "No one wants a sandwich when the bread is mouldy." She was buying bread at the time. The entire thing was far from innocent chit-chat she was being too sensitive about.

Horribly, this was pretty much the most male contact she had in her life, over the age of eighteen at least. There were no male teachers at her school, plus it was almost all just mums at parents' evenings. If she did see a couple on the rare occasion, then it was always the wives that did the talking.

On a day-to-day basis, outside of the radio, the only male voice she heard was that of the Newsagent. Also, she supposed the sporadic 'too-big-for-their-britches' bloke on the street who would feel the need to yell comments at her as she cycled past. It wasn't the best representation of men in general.

Therefore, while Jenny did not exactly have an aversion to Steve or Dave, she found it hard to warm up to them. When you are bombarded with the same representations every day it is hard to have an open mind about these sorts of things. Ah well, just more in a long list of people who she considered 'not her type of people'. At this point the list was so extensive that she might have to rethink her strategy.

As it stood, she believed she would be better off moving on to somewhere else. Part of her felt like it never really made a difference; it didn't stop her wanting to try again though. The problem was more pressing now if anything as most who could turn out to be her type of people were probably dead.

Jenny spent so long in her youth hanging around with the

wrong people. She now wanted to devote her time to those she thought might be good for her. It would have helped if there was a better support system to advise her about avoiding this at the time. However, the likelihood she would have listened to such guidance was slim.

These reflections wouldn't really matter if she was about to die from being distracted. Jenny cleared her head and tried to straighten herself up. This action actually caused the ladder to tip and start to slide off of its precarious perch. A desperate scramble ensued where she made the split-second decision to go for the roof instead of the window.

She grabbed onto the shaky tiles and through sheer force of will managed to pull her way up to safety. In the process of her life flashing before her eyes she swore she could see the robed figure of Death on the other side of the street. She shook it away, the last thing she needed was to pay heed to delusions caused by fear and adrenaline.

Before she could fully focus Jenny heard a sickening thud. She looked behind her to see the fallen ladder had impaled two of the shambles below. One had taken it right through the face and slumped to the pavement, unmoving.

The other had somehow gotten it stuck halfway through its side. It was otherwise perfectly fine if a little off balance. It continued to stumble, now dragging both the ladder and fellow cadaver in a terrible drunken embrace. This was reminiscent of the city centre after the clubs shut. Jenny would often witness these scenes as she made her way to work at ungodly hours.

She turned away from the ghastly sight and towards the more practical problem of how to get down. She couldn't drop from this side. The Chuckle Brother zombies were not the only ones in the vicinity and the fall alone could kill her. There was no part of her that wanted to risk becoming another player in this morose skit of 'to me-to you'.

She thought Steve didn't realise the exact level of danger lurking so close to their little sanctuary. Sure, the windows and doors were all reinforced, but you couldn't completely shut out the outside world. Then again, she already determined Steve as someone who wanted his little space and everything else could go to hell, so he might not care either way.

A certain amount of her acknowledged she was the same. At least in that she did not want to be bothered by the general tangle of other people's problems. The only difference was she did not ignore obvious situations occurring around her. Staying on the street meant they would eventually run out of food or be penned in. Then they would be done for. It wasn't enough to simply sit back and wait for help to arrive. They had to actively seek it out.

When things needed to be done and everyone else was content to let it slide, Jenny would always take it upon herself to do something. Of course, this thinking led her to be stranded on this roof. Potential irony aside, she couldn't fight her innate instincts. As per usual, a voice in her head kicked in, demanding her to be proactive.

She started to work one of the loose tiles free. It came off in her hand. Not a good sign for the construction of her house, yet useful in this situation.

Jenny hefted the tile to check the weight and get a good grip on it. She readied herself to chuck it over the roof onto the street, where it would make enough of a noise to garner some attention. She checked her positioning and once confident she was stable, let it go sailing. It made a satisfying smash on the pavement below.

Hopefully Steve or Dave heard it, so she wouldn't have to suffer any stupid comments from the Newsagent bastard about her inability to do anything. Any day without that type of thing was a blessing. The worst thing about people like that was their hypocrisy.

If you couldn't do something alone, they would insist you were weak for looking for help. On the other hand, if you didn't ask then they would call you stupid for trying to do it yourself. It wasn't even necessarily a sexism thing; with ignorant people you're always damned either way. It was exhausting.

She spared another look towards the mess down below. The gore leaking from the ladder sprawled on her paved garden in indiscriminate splotches, mixing with the rotting brain matter to create a chunky soup. The disgusting sight made her nearly add her own contribution.

The effort to fight back the urge to vomit nearly made her lose balance. There was a wobble along with a shudder, but she managed to contain herself. Jenny tried to settle in and wait.

Despite what people might clumsily discern by casually observing her existence, she was not very fond of waiting. Her patience was in fact razor thin. She had a habit of snapping at people when they dithered or didn't understand a point clearly. It made her teaching classroom an explosive affair.

She wasn't really angry with the students when they got things wrong. It was more a frustration over the clunky nature of the language in explanation and interaction. No matter how much you know or learn, expressing it to someone else can be the hardest thing in the world.

Jenny had tried to better herself in this regard all her life, yet conversations remained cumbersome. The points conveyed were never clear and took ages to reach with any semblance of real understanding. A lot of times you could see when people gave up trying to comprehend each other and simply feigned recognition. Or else they started screaming at each other.

It didn't help that she often thought in a pessimistic way, despite her proactive nature. It could be fine if the person you are talking to had the same mind-set. However, Jenny believed most people were not like this.

Tragically the only time she seemed to be able to strike up a pleasant conversation with someone was when she was drunk. The alcohol didn't act to aid the speed of her brain. In these cases, instead of giving out some observed witticism, she would inevitably come out with something massively obvious and banal. The worst part of engaging with a new person in these situations was watching the light in their eyes die as they mentally noted that you weren't all that interesting.

There wasn't a night that went by where she didn't wish for there to be social alternatives to drinking. Everyone could be forced to sit in a room for a couple of hours and get to know each other. Possibly a cinema without the film to distract you. Sometimes she wondered how good her ideas really were.

The same applied to her tile notion. It had been several minutes since she slung the thing and there had been little sign of anyone coming to save her. All it had managed to do so far was attract more shambles to the paving below. The lack of any human presence meant loud noises travelled a great distance.

Jenny peered over the rooftop again, still nothing. Then she noticed a movement out of the corner of her eye from the top of the street. It was a little hard to make out, but it looked like the window above the newsagents. She vaguely perceived what was someone peeking out at her through partially closed curtains before quickly disappearing behind them.

She cursed the man in that house. She presumed he must have heard the noise and forbade his daughters to do anything. Jenny understood the need to protect your family but surely it was short-sighted if something truly was wrong.

Take for instance; hordes of undead breaking through the barricades and pouring onto the street. Then shutting them up in the house would only serve to trap them all to await a slow death. There was no helping some people.

"That's right, turn a blind eye!" She yelled in frustration.

Feelings of annoyance gave way to a driving purpose, and she resolved herself to finish her sign and get herself away from this hostile environment of passivity. She set to work again and began to shout out her displeasure. Jenny was aware the noise would attract more zombies to join those lurking below. At this point she wasn't too concerned as the tile would have done the same job. The act of protest was both self-actualising and self-destructive.

She hammered nails relentlessly. The thin wood cobbled to the tiles firmly, spelling out the message: 'ALIVE INSIDE SEND HELP'. Jenny resisted the urge to add something slightly pithier like 'NEED COMPANY'. She would not want to get things off on the wrong foot.

She was working so furiously that it took her a while to hear her name being called. It was Dave, joined by Steve and a figure she could not understand. There was something very off about his skin and style of dress. Still, he looked like he could help her out of her current predicament.

While from this distance he looked to be attractive in a classical way, his pallor was quite off-putting. He looked like a fashion model from beyond the grave. He could almost blend in with the pavement. It could be some type of crude camouflage. Jenny's head became a maze of questions, wondering how this strange figure had gotten here and why.

Maybe he was a kind of zombie superhero, out to protect the world from the same fate he once suffered in some tragic origin story. Then again, he might be a xenophobic yet clever ghoul, who hated the presence of humans and just wanted to watch one die by preventing the others from rescuing her. Or alternatively an undead prince, wanting to broker a peace with the last living human beings now that the war was all but won.

There was the insane possibility that he was the literal embodiment of Death, come to meet her. But then why was he hanging around with those two first? Whatever the case, the important question was whether he was indeed real. She had been starved for male company for quite a long time, but it felt strange for her to conjure up such a figure to objectify at a time like this. Surely no one would choose to represent themselves in this vain form.

"What are you doing up there?"

Jenny was brought back to reality by the frustrating banal question asked by Dave.

"Oh nothing! I'm just hammering a few things out!" She replied briskly.

She knew it was a bad line, she did not care. The whole situation was too absurd to devote valuable quipping energy to. All three looked perplexed, even the imaginary one.

Jenny found when a woman was sarcastic or pithy; men had a hard time following, as if they expected everything to be on a base level. It was as if anything resembling wit shouldn't exist in a woman's diction. It made sardonic observations about the world a real chore.

You'd try to break the ice by saying "Wow, this weather, eh? Who could ever tire of the sky being cloudy and grey?" and they'd look at you like you were mad. What's worse you'd then watch them do that very male calculation of attraction leading to agreement. Then somehow, they would reply how they also enjoyed the constant shroud of grey that covered the Midlands, saying something akin to "It's predictable at least."

Yes, as predictable as they were.

Actually, come to think of it, it was everyone, the women she talked to were no better. The only difference here was that they stopped at the 'looking at her like she was mad' point and then it went no further. Maybe Jenny had far too high a regard for the capacity of those around her, at least until they let her down anyway.

She tried not to get too discouraged. At least in this case she managed to throw off her own imagined figure of death. It was possible that simply baffling the grim reaper could get her out of this situation.

She carried on putting the finishing touches to her sign as the three exchanged looks. Then the new one remarked "I think she was making a joke." The other two nodded as if this was a good and knowing observation. Jenny would have slapped her head, dumbfounded, but the gesture risked her slipping in what was already an unsafe environment.

The positive reinforcement of the others encouraged her delusion. He called up "Excuse me miss, what happened here? We heard general commotion in the vicinity."

Who was this guy? In some ways it was nice that he was so well spoken, but there was certainly something off about it. It made him sound a bit like a git in all honesty. Why would she dream up such a fantasy character?!

"Don't trouble yourself!" She called out. "I'm just doing a spot of busy work! No need to take my soul or anything!"

"What?!" Steve bellowed back.

"I don't do that anymore." The stranger replied strangely.

"What?!" Dave shouted, possibly echoing Steve, possibly questioning the other.

Jenny wanted to ignore them. To carry on with the task at hand, but her interest was piqued. Plus, despite their appearing incompetence, she did need someone to help her.

"I need to get down!" She replied, making a mental note to interrogate this new figure after he came to her aid.

"I thought you said you were busy up there? Why would you want to get down?!" Steve cajoled, almost certainly being aware of how annoying this was.

"Well come down then!" Dave added. "We'll wait!"

Jenny scanned this reply for joviality. There was none. He was truly being that dense.

"I do not think she knows how." The third said, as if she couldn't hear him in the amphitheatre that was the street.

"How did she get up there in the first place?" Steve said, egging them on.

"Can't she just go down the way she came?" Dave asked.

Jenny had heard enough of this.

"The flipping stupid ladder slipped alright!" She called out in exasperation. "And that bastard did nothing!"

She gestured up the street to the Newsagents.

"Come to think of it, where have you been all this time?!"

Steve stepped forward reluctantly like a messenger giving a negative report to a feared superior.

"Sorry Jenny, we were dealing with a little situation that arose at Dave's place."

"Well, I hope it was important because I've been stuck up here for ages!"

Steve looked to the others, seeing no help.

"Uhh, it was pretty important. But we are here now. How can we help?"

"How can you help?! Bring me a bloody ladder!"

She realised she should be more polite to those about to help her, at this point it was hard to keep that in mind. Steve's explanation implied there were more important things than her safety. She took offence to that. Maybe she should not hold her life in such high regard. But as was evident, if not her then who would?

Dave appeared rather upset by this request and hurried away. Jenny hoped to fetch a ladder. She felt slightly bad as the man toddled off apprehensively. Then again if that's what was needed to get her down then so be it.

Steve and the unbelievably toned stranger continued to stare at her.

"You were making a sign?" Steve asked abashed.

Jenny sighed, knowing this wasn't going to go down well.

"Yes, I was. We have to think about long term rescue!"

"No, I get it." He said pensively.

"And by sign you mean a message to other people, yes?" The stranger chimed in.

"…Well, yes. Obviously!" Jenny called back.

"And this message is somehow a bad thing?"

"No!" Jenny shouted down with a certainty.

"Judging by the tone of Steve that is inaccurate."

Steve shifted uncomfortably but didn't protest.

Who was this guy? He spoke perfectly good English, yet he appeared to lack basic understanding of human interaction. He didn't grasp the unwritten rules of conversation, such as not highlighting a clear source of conflict and contention. Maybe he was simple, like a well-spoken Lennie Small. Jenny realised this was a terrible thought and tried to dismiss it.

"Why did you not use a ladder to position yourself in the first place?" He inquired further, adding weight to the thoughts she was attempting to cast off.

She took a breath and considered whether to give credit to such an inane question by answering it. She looked to Steve. He shrugged in amusement. No help there.

"If you weren't listening, I did use a bloody ladder! It's on the other side of this bleeding house, stuck inside two walking bloody corpses!"

"Oh no, sounds like a messy affair. I hope they are not too bothered by that."

Definitely simple. Perhaps she needed an interpreter.

"Steve, do you have anything to say?!"

"Yes, I think that you use the word bloody too much." He replied with a smirk.

He was enjoying this far too much.

Jenny's brain stormed a mental tirade while trying not to use the word bloody. Or else one using the word exclusively. At the same time Dave came running back out of the yard with a comically long ladder.

There was a secret hope this would lead to one of those classic moments where the guy clouts the other two chumps over the head repeatedly while looking for a place to put the ladder. However, there had already been enough slapstick for today.

She heard him call up that he could come up and help her out if she needed. This was a clear case of someone trying to be helpful overall causing more hassle logistically. Now she had to break her concentration to shout down a definite "No!" as she made her way to the ladder. It almost certainly made her look very ungrateful.

You could not win.

She would have to say thank you a couple of times once she reached solid ground to make up for it. This was irritating because they had not been there to aid her until now. Although any assistance was good in the end she supposed.

Mustn't grumble.

All her attention turned to navigating the ladder on her way down. It was sturdy enough being held by Dave. Steve and the stranger continued to spectate on the side-lines. She tried to keep her focus on the task at hand, rung over rung until she put a foot to the pavement.

Once she was firmly planted on terra firma she did indeed look to Dave and say thank you. The other two she was not so sure about. They really did nothing to help her besides offer wry comments. Then there was the Newsagents, she had thoughts to go storm the place and try to shake his world up.

"Hello there. Pleased to meet you Jennifer, I am Death." The stony stranger said with an outstretched hand before she could continue her machinations.

She regarded the hand.

No matter the truth of that introduction and its possible connotations, there was little else she wanted to do less than touch the grey flesh. When she looked up into his eyes though, somehow cold yet warm, she felt a weight of certainty that this would be what she would have to do to progress the situation. Her resolve weakened and her hesitance eased.

The polite, unassuming demeanour of his greeting was disarming, even if he did call her 'Jennifer'. She took the hand and tried to produce a friendly smile. All she could muster was a hesitant half-grin and a faint "Hi".

"Her name is Jenny, not Jennifer." Steve piped up.

She gave him a questioning look. Why was he coming to her aid now, as well as wondering why he was so sure this was the case. He shrugged. Jenny was of two minds about him.

"Terribly sorry." Death said, removing his hand. Her palm carried a little chill after the shake was over.

Instead of vocalising, she gave Steve another look, asking about the validity of this man-thing being Death himself. To her surprise he gave a definite nod. From her brief interactions with Steve, she knew he was never usually sure about anything.

Things started to become a bit awkward as she processed this information. She became compelled to lighten the mood.

"Not here for me, are you?" She said with a laugh.

"I cannot know. I do not believe so. There is a possibility I was drawn here considering the general danger you were just in. That and David...Dave here. I have been out of sorts recently and I do not know if I even have a purpose anymore. Let alone how it might work if I did."

His reply did not help.

The direct response to her offhand comment baffled her. When someone made a jokey throwaway comment, you were supposed to make one back to signal your agreed need for an easy conversation. She did not like the rules, but it was hard to process when they were not being obeyed.

It was a breath of fresh air if she was honest with herself.

He was polite, but it was not to keep others at a distance. It was how he tried to engage with those around him. There was a genuine interest in people coming from behind his words and attitude.

She realised Death, if he was indeed so, must have gotten on with Steve. He was the same when she tried to involve him in shallow chit chat the first couple of times. They occasionally crossed paths going in or coming out of their adjacent houses.

These interactions consisted of him either saying next to nothing or something far too earnest. She decided he must be really shy or simply did not want to talk to her. But then he had continued to make the effort to say hello on multiple occasions when she had given up trying to be pleasant.

It was not necessarily a bad thing, just unusual. When you take pains to fit in with the general gabble, meeting someone who didn't was unnerving. She could have seen it as refreshing, since they only saw each other in passing it was easy to dismiss as weird.

"I have to say you are taking this much better than Steve. He fainted when we met." Apparently, Death also experienced Steve's 'all or nothing' approach to social greeting.

"That's because you evaporated right behind me!" Steve blurted out defensively.

"Evaporated?" Jenny asked.

"It means…" Death began.

"I know what it means!" Jenny shouted. "But I also know how boarded up your house is Steve. How did that happen? It makes no sense." She could not resist picking at inaccuracies, even in this type of situation.

"I know! I know! He's magical or something!" Steve said, indicating towards Death in confusion. Jenny realised unless he was extremely good at play acting, he really did see this man as the grim reaper.

"Well okay. Still, the use of the word 'evaporated' makes no sense. Unless you mean he went from a liquid to a gas and took the form of steam...right behind you." Jenny could see Steve was getting noticeably flustered. It was enjoyable.

"There was boiling water involved somewhere I believe." Death contributed.

"Is that what the smoke was? I saw some a bit ago while on the roof. Do you disparate and appear in large plumes of smoke?" Jenny inquired.

"I think it was more to do with the tea." Death replied.

"You came out of nowhere and scared me half to death!"

"Was that a kind of pun or fun word play?"

"If it was, then it didn't make sense." Jenny added.

"I was legitimately asking. I am not sure I fully understand word play at this point." Death said, confused.

"So, why does he talk like a robot? Surely he has been around longer than anyone?" Jenny asked, turning to Steve.

"I honestly don't really know." He shrugged. "I think he is still getting used to human interactions."

"A little like you then."

Jenny marvelled at how freely the words came out. It was the type of comment you thought to yourself, not blurted out directly to the person. It also distracted her from the real lack of explanation given to her previous question.

Steve continued to look agitated but tried to take it in his stride. He gave her a smile to show that it was alright. Then he took a deep breath and faced Death.

"The point is my fainting was related more to the way you came into my house, not your actual appearance. I think in the circumstances I handled things exceedingly well." He said with emphasis.

"I am sorry about that." Death said. "I did make you tea afterwards."

"Well, that's nice at least." Jenny consoled. "Wait, where did you get the milk?"

"There wasn't any." Steve said solemnly.

"Oh." Jenny replied, bowing her head.

During this time Dave had taken down the ladder and put it back away. He was being extremely helpful for some reason. He came running up to everyone, asking if they were alright. He was fine with the presence of Death among them. He grasped him by the hand in an earnest manner when checking if he was okay. It was bizarre.

Jenny wondered what happened while she was stuck on the roof. More importantly though, she wondered why she was stuck with this awkward gathering of misfits. At least her sign was up now, even if it caused her a near death experience.

***

A short time before Jenny found herself stuck; Dave was about to find his own life in danger through a similarly self-interested bid for freedom. The thing was that he always attached a lot of importance to his smoking. It was more than addiction or habit, it was ritual.

If he wasn't able to do it exactly the way he wanted it was almost pointless, still he was not about to stop. In fact, he had already had a cigarette out his upstairs window a bit ago. It did little for him to be honest. He never wanted to smoke there. It was something Steve insisted on for safety. Dave didn't really understand it.

Leaning out the window felt wrong. It was almost as if he should be ashamed for doing one of the few things that made him happy. He liked Steve, but sometimes he could be a real tit about things. This last time had been one ruined cig too far and he set to pulling off the boards nailing up his kitchen door.

Dave had protested when Steve hammered them in "for

his own good". They were mostly sure the houses on the other side were either secure or empty, and his garden wasn't exactly exposed. Maybe there was a little hole in one of the walls, but was that so bad?

Standing barefoot on his lawn puffing away felt good, like justice. Dave wasn't one for rule breaking. At some point you just reached the age where you cannot be happy with anyone dictating how you live, especially not now.

For the most part working with Steve was alright. He kept himself to himself and did what was asked of him. He could even be a bit of a laugh if you caught him in the right mood.

Dave didn't ask for much, just let others get on and don't cause too much trouble. Do the job to the best of your ability and you were golden. Steve understood this before, but things had changed a bit.

Now he was all in people's business, telling them where to go and what to do. Dave was relieved he wasn't the one who needed to get everything together. At the same time though he thought it was a bit much, things being monitored down to the last detail.

He maintained people were fine to mostly go unchecked. Unless of course you've got giant hoops in your ears or spikes coming out your forehead or something like that. These things were unnecessary ornaments, like you're a Christmas tree.

Dave liked the season, just not all year round. He did not wish it could be Christmas every day. He knew everyone would be complaining it wasn't snowing on Christmas, every day.

Could you imagine having to put up with that in July?

Nightmare.

Yeah, it was since this all started to go down, Steve had become a lot more proactive. He wanted people to do things, or at least not get in the way while he did them. This was not the kind of management style Dave could get on board with. He wasn't a massive fan of being asked to do things. He disliked feeling like he was in the way even more, ever since he was a kid.

Growing up he was the third of five children. He was born

too soon to be the baby and too late to be a thing of wonder. He was a classic middle child. He felt like a burden, a mistake.

There had been just enough years after his older brother and several after him for his sister. He guessed his mum said enough at three, and then changed her mind when the rest of her brood stopped being cute. His last little brother he couldn't explain, if he was an accident then he wasn't treated like one.

Dave on the other hand always found himself underfoot, trying to stay out of the way to not get a smack. To him, being invisible was an achievement. He lived his life trying to find little comforts in the background.

That was becoming increasingly harder as responsibilities piled up and resources grew thinner. He still had plenty of cigs though, that was a blessing. Somehow in a time where so much else could kill you, no one seemed all that interested in 'death sticks' as a commodity. Maybe the thrill was gone.

Not for Dave though, oh no.

As Dave was narrating to himself, he heard some shuffling behind him. He paid little mind. It was probably a squirrel, small bird, or even a rogue hedgehog.

With less humans around there were bound to be more and more of the little critters pottering about. Not to mention the rats, surely they would thrive now. The streets and houses were filled with rubbish and rot and there was no one left to stop them. Even if the dead were interested in rat meat, they were no doubt too fast for the shambling buggers to catch.

Rats or not, the noises seemed to be getting closer. They weren't cautious and scampering. Dave continued to puff away, desperate to complete the ceremony.

It was only when he saw a hand reach out for him that he reacted. He dove forward, narrowly escaping the thing's grasp, dropping his cig in the process. He cursed his luck as feelings of fear took over.

One of the ghouls was right beside him and another was clambering over the small hole in his wall. How the hell did they get over that? Did one give the other a boost?!

He tried to backtrack to the backdoor and tripped over his own feet. He may have been drinking a bit before this. He fell awkwardly on his arse with a "Fucking Christ!"

Before he knew it the shambles was bearing down on him and he was struggling for his life. He didn't know how long he wrestled with the thing; seconds felt like hours. He started to get tired and accept the inevitable, especially seeing as its mate was approaching.

Just then a dark shape came from above and pulled the snapping corpse off him. He heard the thing say, "Terribly sorry about this." as they flung the bag of bones halfway across the garden. Even with all the confusion he got the feeling that the figure was addressing the zombie and not him.

His surly mind understood he was being saved by some ghoul-loving superhero wannabe. But then the image of those gnashing teeth came back into his head, and he was just glad they were no longer there. No matter who saved him, he was grateful.

Still prone, he saw Steve rushing towards the other ghoul and much less politely chop its head off with an axe. He was panting from the effort but seemed only a little bit worse for wear. Dave hoped there wasn't too much mess; he knew Steve would hate that.

Then he was being pulled to his feet to meet the steely eyes of a ghastly jacked giant. At least they were smiling. This could have been unnerving, but Dave found it oddly comforting considering how they saved his life.

"Hello there, my friend. I do hope you are alright. I think you took a tumble there for a second."

The person's manners were disarming. Dave struggled to find words as Steve came over panting.

"What...the hell...are you doing out here Dave?!"

"Well I...'

"Were you smoking in the garden again?!"

"Well..."

"Have you been drinking?! Did you really need to smoke so

badly that you had to take the bluffing boards off?!"

"I just..."

"Also, didn't you have a cigarette like half an hour ago?!"

"I mean..."

It was at this point in the berating process that the grey man interjected.

"Forgive me Steve, but I am sure this man has learned his lesson." He gave a laugh that sounded more like a notification of humour than the actual feeling. "To be honest I find it highly amusing that one pursuit that hastens demise nearly led to the same!"

If Dave thought that Steve was a bit peculiar, this guy was on another planet.

"He was breathing in one cause for concern and quickly felt the breath of another! It is the height of merriment!" Again, there came the boom of what was meant to be laughter.

It was genuinely hard to be afraid of someone so goofy. He was almost doubled over in apparent amusement. Then he suddenly caught himself and straightened up with a cough.

"Of course, this also acts as a sobering lesson. By the way, I am not too sure we should be dispatching them in such brutal a manner. I acted out of necessity, and maybe too harshly still. But was that act of decapitation truly required Steve? Maybe next time instead a casual dismemberment of limbs to render them harmless, no?"

"Shut up Death!" Steve was fuming.

He settled quickly though. It was his way.

"Oh yeah, by the way, this guy here is Death. Never mind about the smoking, I suppose I understand...a bit. I'm glad you are alright. Just be more careful, you nearly got munched!"

"I...I'm sorry Steve." Dave resigned himself. This was all a bit too much. "I didn't think the shambles would be able to get in. I thought the gardens were safe."

"So did I, but this guy also got in somehow. So, I suppose not." Steve gestured to Death.

"Hello." Death said, waving cheerily.

"To be fair he is a special case." Steve sighed. "Still, it pays to be careful Dave, even if it seems inconvenient. It's better to be inconvenienced than to have your neck bitten off by some drooling ghoul."

"I suppose so." Dave said, feeling like he was at school. Steve was still a bit of a self-righteous dick, even if he was there in his time of need. Unfortunately, he was also probably right. It was annoying.

"It is my view that humans rarely put caution over safety, on the whole anyway." Death chimed in.

Dave gave a resigned shrug. This was not helpful.

His foot was on fire.

The dry grass acted as kindling for the dropped cigarette and no one had noticed. Now the spreading blaze had caught onto Dave's shoe. Both he and Steve began to yell and stamp about. Steve wanted to stop the fire spreading and Dave to put out his own foot.

Neither was all that coordinated and the whole song and dance worked to fan the flames rather than douse them. There were a good couple of times where they each stamped on the other's feet. This mainly amounted to a lot of hopping.

The bloke known as Death hadn't moved. Dave presumed he was confused by the spectacle, but in hindsight reckoned he was just trying to work out the outcome. It stood to reason he was used to watching from the side-lines, this probably came naturally to him.

Without a fuss he whipped off his cloak and dashed the flames out. First, he patted Dave's leg before moving on to the rest of the grass. He expertly avoided Steve's own wild flailing, coming to a standstill holding a smouldering robe and a decent sized grin on his face.

"Well, it looks like my reflexes are getting better in this physical form."

He was of course naked, completely starkers.

"What took you so long?!" Steve shouted, unfazed.

"I did not want to interfere." Death said, with his nob out.

Dave, rather traumatised by events, felt almost removed from his body. Seeing the titanic form standing proud in front of him served to bring him back, and he started thinking about the desperate position they were in. These people he was with were now all he had in the world.

He had not really worried about those around him since his wife died. Now this thought sat in his mind like a grinning demon. There was a promise of destruction if he was not very careful. He needed to pay attention. His actions nearly literally burnt everything down.

Maybe he couldn't commit his smoking ritual. He should be grateful he wasn't out there fighting for his life on the daily. Counting small blessings and keeping others close, that's what he needed to do right now.

He saw Death staring at his robe, as if it should magically appear back on his body. After a few seconds of contemplation, he went to put it back on. Not before looking back to his nude form, as if considering whether that alone might be the way to go.

Dave was at least somewhat glad he made the decision to re-clothe. One life-altering revelation was enough for now. He didn't want to be provoked into finding more.

Meanwhile Steve was back in his face.

"Now that this minor emergency has been taken care of, what was that loud crash?"

This confusing accusation threw Dave.

"Loud? Crash?"

"Yeah, we heard it when we were on the way to see you. I thought you'd broken something upstairs, but we spotted you and those undead bastards out here before we could look. So, what happened?"

"I honestly have no idea mate. I didn't hear a thing what with nearly being eaten and all...Wait, how did you get into my house in the first place?"

"I used the spare key."

"Spare key?"

"Yeah, you gave it to me years ago. It's not a new thing."

"I don't remember that but fair. Wait, why did you use it without letting me know first?"

"We did knock." Death interjected.

"Yeah, this guy here then volunteered to pass through the door, but I thought that would be a bit intrusive, so I used the key instead."

"Well, that makes sense. Wait, why did you have the key to hand? Seems strange to me mate."

"I have all my keys with me in case of emergencies. It just stands to reason." Steve said blankly.

Dave let this disturbing development slide. He supposed in a way this made Steve more trustworthy since he could have entered his house at any time for years apparently. The three continued to ponder the possibilities until they decided to find Jenny.

Cut back to now. Mystery solved, and Dave wanting to do whatever he could to protect those around him. This was why he was so quick to get the ladder for her.

She was ogling Death with huge interest. Dave thought to himself that she would have been even more fascinated if she had seen him in the garden minutes ago. Standing as proud as he did now, only more naked.

She accepted his existence as fact and began complaining about Michael. Apparently, he hadn't done a thing to help her. If this was the case, he would need a stern talking to. There were only six of them, well seven now, in the whole street and they had to stick together.

To Dave, especially these days, it was all very well to say; "I look out for me and my own", but that depends on what you mean. Do you mean yourself, your close family? What about extended family? Family and friends? It just didn't fly anymore.

Or is it more based on location? It could be your house, or street, maybe even city, or country? In the end the statement generally relied on whoever "me and my own" was against.

The way he saw it, right now it was the living against the

dead. Other divides didn't matter. "Me and my own" were the whole human race. Anyone you let die became one of them. When the world was that bad, splitting things any further was a balls-up waiting to happen.

Michael couldn't just hold himself up in his Newsagents with his daughters and leave the rest of them out there to fend for themselves. Well, he could, it wasn't a sound way to handle things though. It couldn't be allowed to stand.

Dave wasn't exactly adept at 'man to man' conversation, but it might have to be what happened here. Of course, having Death looming behind you might help. It'd certainly make the inevitable confrontation easier.

It would probably frighten the life out of him.

Jenny was insisting they needed to do something about it now. Steve hesitantly accepted that it was the only move, and Death was just happy to meet more new people. He liked the appreciation for socialising, even if it was a little simple.

It stood to reason that you'd have to be at least a little interested in people's lives if you were Death. Still, it probably wasn't something you could pursue much when you were on the job. It'd be like working in a cinema and only catching the end of movies when you were going in to clean up.

You'd always be finding people at their worst, so you'd have to remain a bit removed. Dave could relate. Construction supply was also hard like that.

He couldn't count the times he'd been speaking to some stressed out customer about their clearly doomed project. No matter what, he sold them what they needed and went on with his day. You'd do yourself no favours by getting too invested.

Now Steve on the other hand could never let that type of thing go. He was always double and triple checking things to make sure they were absolutely correct, even if the customer told him to leave it. He needed everything to be precise and perfect because if it wasn't his brain would pester him until it was put right.

In all fairness, he wasn't like some people, who looked for

mistakes to smugly hold it over you. He was checking for only himself. Steve might be annoyed if something was wrong, but it was never anything personal.

When he had helped him build the gates at the top of the street things were a little heated. He would be constantly over his shoulder to make sure it was to his liking. Arguments about what material to use, sizes and shapes, it was all very fussy for his taste. Better than that Michael though, who hadn't lifted a finger, even though his gaff was right next to it.

CHAPTER FIVE

Michael sat in his grizzled armchair in the middle of his flat and thought about all the times he'd probably been robbed by little shit-stained urchins coming in his shop. Not much of a problem anymore, still it pissed him off. Security was always an issue.

Fact was, short of banning anyone under forty, there was little you could do. Anyone worth their salt remembered when a chocolate bar was 15p, not the lofty 85p it was now. Before it was a cheeky thrill, now it was grand larceny. Not that he was complaining about the price of course. He didn't even feel bad about it, inflation and whatnot.

On the other hand, this raise in price could turn even the most respected customer into a common thief. You never could trust people not to sink to the lowest of the low if the incentive was good enough. He always believed that if you gave someone the chance to disappoint you, they would.

It wasn't like there weren't any good people in the world. It was just they were kept honest through rules and instruction. Otherwise, people were animals.

If he could, he would have locked him and his girls away from all of them a long time ago. His home was his castle, his nice little slice of the world, carved by his own graft. Only now he didn't have to worry about the hassle over bills, or noise or whatnot. No ruddy salesmen coming to him with their hands out neither. It was a perk of the situation you could say.

They had food and entertainment and a good view of that

bloody great gate keeping everyone else out. What more could you ask for? Nothing, that's what.

Despite this his daughters were restless, ungrateful. They had far too much curiosity over the pratting about of others. He remembered their interest in the men who went out to look for unnecessary supplies. His eldest almost managed to volunteer to go too. He put a stop to that quick smart when he clocked it, you'd better believe.

She whined about "needing news of the outside world." Rubbish. He schooled her that they had everything they needed right where they were. Admittedly the telly was on the fritz and the newspaper trucks weren't delivering. But you could get a grasp of current affairs by reading the old papers.

It all came around again, nothing really changed. He was sure in a couple of months this would all be only a weird little episode. It'd be a funny story and nothing more.

That had been a couple of weeks ago, but it still held true. Maybe it was taking a little longer for things to get sorted out than he first thought. And maybe those guys who went looking for supplies hadn't ended up returning. But his family were still doing fine.

If anything, it showed how right he was. He'd stopped his daughter from disappearing without a trace. With him keeping a firm eye they would be safe. Safe as houses, they were.

There was no way waiting this out wasn't what to do. The only difference between now and before was he wasn't being bothered by anyone asking for supplies. Everyone on this street seemed to think just because they needed stuff and he had it that he should share. Well bollocks to that!

He closed his doors sharpish as soon as he got a whiff of this. The only thing he lost by doing this was the frequent chats he'd become accustomed to. He would take peace and quiet over pleasantries. Even though they were what made the world go round when you got down to it.

Of course, there were those out there still in dire straits, suffering and whatnot. It wasn't really his problem. There was only so much you could do for people who wouldn't take care of themselves. Sure, the construction around the street by that weirdo was part of what made them safe, but he was sure they would have done alright.

The world was full of people trying to convince you to be grateful for things you didn't even ask for. He would rather pay his own way and know he didn't owe anything. Now that might make him unpopular, but at the end of the day it didn't really matter.

Family was the only thing to justify giving a damn about those around you. Aside from that it was the law of the jungle. Survival at any cost, anything else was so much guff.

With the undead knocking at your door, you didn't worry about anyone else. You couldn't be worried about what your daft neighbour was doing on their roof. Arsing about when they should be keeping to themselves. It was infuriating.

To be fair he wouldn't have minded so much if his eldest hadn't been so interested. A few months away at Uni and she came back with all these wild and stupid notions. He seriously considered banning his younger daughter from following suit. Might not be a problem now though.

Still, he hadn't paid nine grand to turn his daughter into a subversive. Come to think of it he would be a bit taken aback if fees stayed the same. Hard to justify the need when there will be more practical jobs. It was true before, but even more now. He couldn't imagine bloated middle management culture being around after this.

Now sure your fat cats would have their secret bunkers. Plus, the good old working class would probably have hunkered down and survived through sheer grit and strife. But those soft middle-class twits, who never did a real day's work in their lives and got paid far too much for it? Nah, he couldn't see it.

More likely they all died already during outbreaks in their fancy coffee shops. If the walking dead targeted trendy wine bars they were buggered. Pushing papers didn't prepare you for keeping hordes of corpses out of your glass fronted fortress. He hadn't fought off any ghoulies himself, but he was sure he could handle himself if the need arose.

Not that it would if they stayed put. No, he would see this all through from the comfort of his own couch thank you very much. The only thing he missed was his Daily Mail and maybe the good old BGT on a Saturday night. Bah, telly was all rubbish nowadays anyways.

As a newsman he knew that if he wasn't being updated by reliable sources then most likely no one else was. He did not need 'breaking news' from his daughter that the silly tart from down the road was safe and sound due to the emergence of a ladder brought by jokers across the street. To him it would not have made much difference if she had slipped off.

Good riddance in his opinion. He scolded her again to get away from the window. She obeyed, which she should.

He leaned back in his chair and unwrapped another Mars bar from the box resting by his side. Life was good.

***

If there was one thing Lucy learned from her time away at Uni it was that her father was a fat headed idiot. She knew though that there was no point arguing. He thought he was right in all things and the only way round it was to accept it, ignore it, and then do what you wanted when he wasn't looking.

If the woman from down the road stayed up on that roof any longer, she would have snuck away and figured out how to get her down. Luckily the guys from the other side of the street discovered her first, so she didn't risk his ineffectual wrath. She knew it would only amount to him complaining for a couple of hours, still it was something she'd rather avoid.

Her father was not a violent man. The days of the shadow of the patriarch were all but gone in her opinion. Most men of his age didn't have the tendencies of their fathers. She knew when he grew up punishment through physical means was an accepted practice. A father who did hit their children then was not necessarily a violent person either, only following standard protocol. Times change and now a man who struck a child was not fit to be a parent. When society shifted to call something abuse, it was abuse, no matter what came before.

One had to move with the times, and this worked both ways. His moaning at her to get away from the window was enough alone to make her think twice, because who wanted to be lectured and patronised for an hour. This distraction meant she hadn't gotten an entirely clear view of what transpired.

She could have sworn there was someone else with them. Jenny was the only one she really managed to have a discussion with recently. If there was a new person around then Lucy was desperate to meet them.

She would have to wait until her father fell asleep to find out for sure. Ever since the others didn't come back from their last scouting mission it had become near impossible for her to find excuses to leave the flat. Before, there had been enough people and activity for her to come and go without her father kicking up too much of a fuss. He was too busy trying to appear social, like a big man to all the local lads, despite them having very little interest in him beyond his shop.

At this point, every time she wanted to go out, he would complain there was no good reason to go talk to the "weirdos" at the end of the street. She did not know what was so weird about them. Jenny was lovely, and the other two seemed nice enough. One was simple in a working man way and there was something about Steve she liked, he was a bit different, and she could only see that as a good thing.

The problem with her father was he believed that anyone who didn't think exactly like him wasn't "normal" and therefore should be sneered at and avoided. That small-minded mentality of someone who never left their hometown, it was the chronic condition of localness.

What she was really worried about was her sister taking on these qualities, especially now her future of going off to Uni was in question. Joyce had always been a little more akin to her father. Before her mother left, she told her on one of her more drunken evenings that her dad always wanted a boy. Joyce was the next best thing.

Lucy always suspected this. It was nice in a way to have it confirmed. It'd been two years since their mother left but Lucy could tell it was coming long before that.

Around the time she turned thirteen her mother started going on nights out without their father and it was all downhill from there. They barely said a word to each other or appeared in the same room, a difficult feat in a relatively small flat. Lucy always wondered if something concrete happened or if it was a natural drifting apart.

This was one thing she could never find out as her mother exited before she could give a further confessional. Her father wasn't going to say anything. He'd let nothing slip if he thought it might tarnish his "manly" image. He'd rather eat and drink his problems and pretend they weren't there.

Lucy suspected that things got too real for her mother once she reached fifteen. It was one thing to bare your soul to an unjudging child. A teenager who had their own feelings and problems was something else.

In the year before she left, Lucy often caught her mother staring at her with a look best described as a wistful sneer. This had bothered her and she spent a long time wondering what it could mean. She concluded it was a contradictory mixture of her mother's own longing to be young again and a concern that her daughter would turn out just like her.

When Lucy told this to her best friend Tracy at school, she called her a pessimist. This was the type of labelling Lucy hated. She wasn't a pessimist, far from it. In fact, she liked to see the best in people whenever she could. But that didn't mean she couldn't see what was staring at her right in the face. Tracy was most likely dead now.

The truth was her mother was a deeply unhappy woman. While Lucy was sad that she was gone, at least she managed to escape her situation. It would have been nice if she'd taken her daughters with her, however.

She gathered from the easily overheard snippets shouted down the phone by her dad that her mother had met someone new. They didn't have room in their life for kids. She suspected her mother tried to hold out until her girls were both moved out but couldn't last. Lucy could understand.

Again, it wasn't like she was leaving them with a monster. Her father was not evil, just an insufferable small-minded man with no capacity for empathy or change. There are much worse people out there in the world. But he was still a pain to put up with, especially when you couldn't simply up and leave.

Lucy vowed she would not turn out like him, or like her mother. She longed to see the world and experience more than marrying someone who she met in secondary school and let his existence define her. She was determined to engage with life fully. She wanted to give every person a chance no matter how different they were.

Still, she could not understand people who met their best friends and partners when they were in the first fifteen or even twenty years of their lives. Maybe in this vast planet they found their soul mate and those who could understand them the best out of everyone they could ever see in their entire existence in this short amount of time. It seemed unlikely.

It was much more probable these people clung to the first agreeable person they encountered so as not to be alone. They gave up on finding something better early on and then lived to regret it. There was so much out there, and Lucy wanted to see at least a good portion of it before she settled.

The potential of having a new person on the street played on her mind. She wanted to know everything. They could have news from the outside world, or brought supplies and support. Or she could be imagining things, either way she needed to find out.

Lucy resolved to sneak away at the soonest opportunity. There was a good chance her dad would pass out any minute. That was his fifth Mars bar in an hour and the sugar rush would soon give way to the inevitable crash.

She figured out in her first term that sugar was more of a drug than people gave it credit for. The same went for coffee and carbs. It wasn't like she completely stayed away from all things like that. She was simply more mindful of the potential chemical imbalances they could cause. The way your body felt could change drastically with the slightest nutritional shift; she tried to keep hers in check. It was a question of discipline.

Lucy usually kept these things to herself. She knew most people didn't like to be told what they were doing was wrong, even if it completely was. Her sister Joyce had already lost her patience with her since she came back.

Let alone what her dad would say, being a man for whom chip butties were a thrice daily practice. She may as well let his bodily neglect work for her. It was only a matter of time until the inescapable occurred.

Part of her thought she was being nosy. It was a nagging remainder of her former way of thinking. There was definitely a small-town mentality of 'don't concern yourself with the doings of others' that pervaded her mind. However, at this point there really was not any excuse not to care. In dire times you had to involve yourself in the business of others.

It would be accurate to call these times dire, and vital to have concern toward your fellow man…woman…people, fellow people…and animals, animals were people too. She found it ironic that her father was so dead set on not being involved. He himself went on about a time when you could go next door for a cup of sugar or some last-minute babysitting. It was possible this had all been a one-way street.

Or maybe it was to do with the type of people her father saw the others out there as. He unquestionably held a divide in his head between "good" and "bad". It had nothing to do with moral action of course. It was much more discriminatory, not that he would admit that.

Lucy found there were those, especially her father, who would deny anything that appeared to be negative about them when suggested by an outside party. It could be said without judgement, something even they brought up themselves from time to time. But from someone else it warranted an automatic defence. There was no reasoning with these people.

She learnt in life that people refused to play fair when it came to conversation. They manipulated social conventions so they were always right and could not be questioned. To do so would make them appear to be in the wrong, and that was the worst thing ever apparently. With these people you had to, at best, agree to disagree and then rule them out as incapable of being fair or rational. Lucy liked to be challenged, but there was a difference between an uphill battle and an impassable gorge of ignorance.

It was pretty obvious that her dad's small-minded nature drove her mother away. However, it was this very attitude that kept him unaware of this self-knowledge. Instead, he blamed her and whatever external source he could think up at potential times of self-reflection. He was destined to never realise what he needed to do to become a better person. Lucy hesitated at using the word "better". The term was problematic.

In this case what she meant was; a person who did not stay on a path leading eventually to anguish and loneliness. The fact was she would leave home at the first chance. There was only so much intolerance one could take. It made her sad, but she knew it was inevitable.

Her sister might not see it this way. Lucy didn't want her dad to be completely alone. Still, she couldn't resign Joyce to a life with him either. This is exactly why these types of unmoving attitudes are so toxic; they mostly affected those around you. It was a harmful and weak way to be. Again, the term "weak" had unwanted implications, but it was hard to think of another way to put it.

All she heard when interacting with her father was fear. Fear of inadequacy, fear of change, fear of his failings as a dad. Tragically, these very fears were what made them real, it was profound. If people like her father could be braver and expose their weaknesses, they would be accepted. Instead, they were only tolerated until you could get away.

Lucy looked to her father. His eyes were already drooping as he began to nod off. She hoped Joyce wouldn't give her any trouble. Maybe she could even convince her to come with her. She must be getting a bit restless.

She didn't completely know how her sister felt about the others on the street. They were more growing distant recently. Maybe this adventure would give them a chance to bond over something new.

Her father was now slumped completely in his armchair, fully asleep. There wasn't going to be a better time to make her move. She edged towards the door leading to the shop below. Once through she would leave the house and hoped her sister would follow.

***

Joyce sat with her colouring book, giving a cartoon Santa a jazzy yellow jacket with crimson furry trim. Reverse Flash style. She knew some people thought her simple for amusing herself with 'childish' activities. Joyce did not much care. It was no one else's concern.

Her mum always struggled to compromise and look what happened. Her dad insisted on everyone seeing things his way and was the loneliest person she knew. Then there was Lucy, who wanted to 'fix' everyone, an impossible and thankless task. All were bad examples of how to be, so much for role models.

In her mind the only thing that mattered in life was being happy with yourself. As someone with little responsibilities and outstanding mental issues, she chose to spend her time doing supposedly trivial things that brought her bliss in the moment. Joyce knew this state wouldn't last, so why not enjoy it.

As she grew older, life would demand increasing sacrifices of her. End of the world or not it would be a constant struggle of contributing while keeping hold of some semblance of true self. Having the ability to know what made her feel fulfilled was important.

Of course, she had aspirations. They were vague but they were there. Lucy would say it was leaning a little bit into gender roles, but art and fashion were her passion. It wasn't as cool or sexy as being a doctor or scientist. Joyce never really connected with any of that stuff though, so why pursue it.

Admittedly, this could be due to an underlying subliminal influence from media and western society. To her mind though everything everyone did was programmed by the surrounding culture to some extent. Whether they were going along with or against it, it was all just a reaction in the end.

Besides, the fashion industry was arguably one of the few places where female designers can get significant power, sway and say. Sure, you needed to be in a certain position before this was true, there were sacrifices to make. She couldn't think of a single pursuit where this wasn't the case though. She loved so much about it; the designing, crafting, photography, organising shows. Hell, even the modelling looked fun in certain lights.

Lighting was also another area of interest, not to mention filters and photo-shop. There was also a secret part of her that wanted to be the judgemental person with the big catalogue all the models walked for on go-sees. In her mind there was time for all this later, right now Santa needed to look peng for some penguins and heat up the North Pole in his snazzy jacket.

The colouring book was full of various interpretations of holiday scenes, all customised with her array of fancy felt tips. Some now wore artistic designs, sharp lines masking cartoonish outlines. Others were given the colours of recognisable comic book characters when Joyce was feeling in the mood.

Often, they were the pattern of villain costumes. She took a special glee in making smiling figures reflect a hidden menace connected in their clothing. Images of evil elves were especially pleasing, as if they were the henchmen to the jolly big bad. Not that Reverse Flash needed backup, but why play fair.

There was certainly an appeal in being able to cover the

world in the space of an evening. What super villain wouldn't use that power to their advantage? Not to mention their sway over children. There was no way Santa didn't have some sort of evil machinations. As Joyce grew older, the fashion designs had become more frequent and started to outnumber the villainous patterns. These in turn greatly outnumbered her initial practice of filling in figures as heroes.

The whole thing started with her dad refusing to buy her a superhero colouring book as a kid. He called it unsuitable and stupid. This way of thinking never made any sense to Joyce, but it was popular at the time. He had conceded to buying her the generic kind, and her eight-year-old mind used its imagination to fight back.

Joyce was aware her continuation of colouring books was probably partially some kind of rebellious action, but it was also practical. She'd never been great at proportions, having trouble sketching figures for her designs to go on. She held no illusions of becoming a graphic novel artist. She had almost zero skill in the department. Colours and tracing, those she excelled in.

All of this might be pointless wonderings since the entire world was pretty much screwed. An apocalypse was not kind to the dreams of an aspiring fashion designer, comic book artist, or any creative pursuit decided upon really. Mad scientist was probably the closest she was likely to get.

There were weirdos out there who prayed for the end of modern society and longed for a simpler time of survival living. Joyce wondered if they were non-creative types, or maybe just idiots. Go on a camping trip and let everyone else be.

It would be hard to put effort into writing, composing, or designing a cool piece of clothing if you spent all day foraging for food and fending off the living dead. Joyce honestly did not understand people who hated on modern society. The ability to live comfortably and pursue passions outside of the basics was in her mind a great freedom.

Some people said, "in my day" and "our ancestors didn't need." This reductive thinking got in the way of progress. While there was a place for remembering past struggles, it was mainly an effort to not to have to go through them again.

Her sister talked about giving up her worldly possessions and the plight of others. This was especially grating considering where they currently were. Joyce knew they were lucky to even have a place to stay right now; she didn't want to give that up.

Her dad would say people who didn't have what they did deserved it. She didn't really like this way of thinking either. It wasn't anyone's choice to be born where or how they were.

Mostly these views came from a lack of nuance. She knew in the end he just didn't like the idea of people expecting him to give more than he was willing to. He was a severely flawed man, but he was still her dad.

He'd only been asleep for a minute and already Lucy was getting antsy. No doubt she was going to try something 'daring and defiant'. She'd been peeking out the window on and off for the last hour, giving pointless updates like they were important. "Look, someone is on a roof. Oh, now they are down. Look, one of them took a breath."

Her sister infuriated her with how reactionary she could be. Like, why did she have to wait until he was asleep? If she wanted to, she could go over and see what was going on. Sure, he would moan, but beyond that what was he going to do?

He'll only be more annoyed when he wakes up. Then she will have to hear about it until Lucy got back. Then would come the inevitable protests and justifications. It was all so long.

Her phone and laptop were toast so there wasn't even a way to drown out the sound of irritating people trying to draw you into their bullshit. When stuff like this happened before, and it did no matter what either insisted, she could blast some music and get on with her own thing. Now Joyce had to act like she actually gave a damn. Or pretend to ignore it, which took as much mental effort as actually taking part.

Her sister made for the door, and she decided she might as well go too. At least then she could temper things when they got back. She could give an actual account rather than going by

Lucy's interpretation. Also, she would not have to listen to her dad's impotent rage up to that point.

Lucy stopped at her movement, looking like a frightened shrew. A devilish smile then crossed her sister's lips, as if she was doing something utterly forbidden. Joyce shook her head at how cool she clearly thought she was.

Then she cursed herself, knowing her sister would take this to be a disapproval over her actions. It would only add fuel to her so-called rebellious fire. She would never grasp Joyce's genuine disbelief at how lame she was.

"I'm going to check on the people down the road." Lucy declared with a conspiratorial hush.

"I know. I'm going with you." Joyce said plainly.

For a second Lucy looked deflated, like she was expecting a rebuke against 'the dangers of the outside'. This then turned into an equally stupid smile. She looked as if she'd won some kind of great battle or something.

To her, joining her was a sign that she was completely in the right. Like somehow it was a moral imperative that almost no one could ignore. She would have slapped her if it wasn't far too dramatic.

Lucy pulled her close and hugged her in a weird embrace. Then she dashed off, a woman on a mission. Joyce shrugged in resignation.

She tidied away her books and pens. The evil speedster Santa would have to wait to have his look completed. She gave a last regretful look to her dad, wishing things with them could be different and headed out the door to the stairs.

CHAPTER SIX

Lucy and Joyce came out of their house as Jenny and the others were making a move to visit them. Dave was in the lead and his look of determination gave way to relief when he saw the pair. He waited until they were within earshot and then called out.

"I'm glad to see you girls. We were about to come over to ask what the blazes was going on."

"I'm sorry." Lucy said abashed. "Our father wasn't happy with us getting involved."

Joyce rolled her eyes, bracing herself for the inevitable.

"Doesn't surprise me at all." Dave huffed. "What changed his mind?"

"He didn't. We snuck past him when he fell asleep." Lucy said with a conspiratorial tone.

Joyce sighed. It was nothing more than she could expect. It would have been so much better for everyone just to pretend he sent them out to see what was going on rather than painting him as this menace that needed to be fought against. She never understood why people were so willing to act as instigators just because they weren't the target. It was as if they didn't see that everyone was connected in some way.

She was reflecting on how her sister needed to grow up when she noticed the towering figure standing past Dave with Jenny and Steve. You'd think it would have been the first thing she saw. It certainly was all she could see now. They looked like something straight out of a painting, well before art had been forced to go all Meta anyway.

The muscular form woven in flowing black robes stood proud amongst two people who looked decidedly regular next to him. They were talking to him in pleasant conversation, as if this wasn't remarkable at all. They gave off the same vibe as those charity workers who stopped you in the street and tried to act as if you were best friends. The demeanour set her on edge, all she could think about was what exactly they wanted to sign them up for.

Joyce heard a gasp and knew her sister must have noticed them as well.

Lucy had never seen such an impressive person in all her life. This guy, whoever he was, was the tallest, most handsome man ever. She felt a kind and friendly presence from him that instantly put her at ease.

She breezed past Dave and went straight up to him to say hello. He greeted her with a warm smile, his marble features beaming. He spoke in a very cordial and gentlemanly manner, clearly a caring individual. She was instantly more grateful that she found herself in the company of this group. Lucy was sure he was there to help and keep them safe.

Dave smiled as the girl ran up to Death. He'd worried his new friend would cause some distress. It wasn't something you encountered every day. He was also a little disappointed since part of him wanted the joy of rolling up to Michael's gaff with Death behind him unannounced.

He could imagine it scaring the bejesus out of him. That'd serve him right for his lack of community spirit. The fact that these girls had to sneak by him to get out of their own house didn't sit well. Something had to be done. He would have to say his piece before Death introduced himself, because as soon as he talked in his polite manner the ruse would be ruined.

After his introduction, Lucy had embraced Death in a full body hug. He stood awkwardly holding her weight, but he was not upset by the over-familiar greeting. It was possible this was normal; he was not entirely up to date on the social greetings of young females in the current era.

Steve and Jenny exchanged glances. This led to their own socially awkward moment at the warm way they smiled at their mutual bemusement. They both got nervous and looked away, accompanied by a couple of ill-timed half-glances from each that did nothing to ease the situation.

They equally wished the other would do something to break this cycle. When neither did, they mutually had the same idea to look towards the younger sister to see her reaction. She was clearly much more uncomfortable with the appearance of Death. This was understandable, and arguably more reasonable than Lucy's reaction. They again realised they were thinking the same thing. Identical thought processes repeated, which led to more disharmonies after being so much on the same page.

Anyone watching them would have thought they were a classic TV couple who everyone in the audience was rooting for to get together. They were realistically more infuriating since in fact these types of apparently obvious romantic entanglements had the habit of not being realised. More likely these feelings of awkwardness would go unresolved and overtake any unspoken feelings to breed a genuine dislike for each other. Both would remain reserved rather than push invisible boundaries. If they were to get together it would most likely be the result of some outside factor.

Death became confused. The girl was still in his arms. This had to be irregular at this point.

Was this supposed to be romantic? Was he supposed to kiss her now? Something told him this would be inappropriate, but he was not sure why.

Perhaps it was because he felt more like a mother chimp holding a baby rather than a man embracing a lover. If a person were to describe this physical interaction it might come across as sexual. After all, the female had her nether regions clamped to his hips, but it felt like anything but.

Should he have an erection? Should he try to create one? Death did not know what to do.

He decided against it, erring on the side of caution, and settled for simply standing there. He felt the grip of her thighs loosen and he eased his grasp so she could dismount him. She was smiling when he looked down at her face, so he concluded that he made the right choice. He wondered what would have happened if he had conjured up an erection instead. Probably best not to think about it.

Whatever the case Death was glad to meet more people. Even if one was glaring at him and the other got a bit too close for comfort. It was quite a lot to take in. He was trying to tailor his behaviour to fit with each individual. With contrasting ideas of what was socially acceptable for a first meeting it was quite a challenge.

He reflected that this was perhaps the cost of socialising. You could never really know if you were doing the right thing when it came to new people. He also supposed friendship was the acting force behind how this could be remedied.

True rapport, Death hoped, did not come from checking boxes and getting a perfect score. Instead, your hesitation and errors were accepted because of how you were perceived in someone's mind. This arguably could be governed partially by the things you said and did upon a first meeting. But more likely a person would make initial judgements mostly based on their own experiences and feelings. It was something outside of who you were, or even who you were projecting to be.

It was something nearly impossible to predict unless you read their mind first of course. There was a thrill in this risk of first meetings. The lack of control could lead to a reward in the relationships that grew to last beyond this confusing beginning.

Friendship was two differing elements clashing together until they either bond or drove each other away. It was messy. In such a process there was only so much credible analysis that could be done.

Death decided to just go with it. He could try to delve into each of their minds, but that felt against the spirit of things. If this person could accept him despite his abnormal appearance and without judgement, then he owed her the same.

He looked down at the girl and smiled. She beamed back at him. He turned to the other girl and gave her the same smile with some slight exaggeration to try to bridge the apparent gap between them. Her glare only intensified.

The grim reaper was confounded again.

Any feeling of freedom and contentment faltered, giving way to further fruitless analysis. Why did one action work for one of these two, but not the other? They were of roughly the same age and gender, clearly related. It would stand to reason there would be some cross over.

There was a moment of silence between everyone before Jenny took control of the situation. She walked over and made motions to introduce the new arrivals to each other. She could sense there was a strange dynamic, but sometimes unabashed persistence of an outside party did wonders. It would also serve to alleviate her existing social predicament with Steve, so that was a bonus.

"Lucy this is Death. Death, this is Lucy."

Jenny's introduction of the literal embodiment of human mortality raised only a slight look of scepticism in the girl. This quickly gave way to a warm grin. She embraced him again.

"Cool!" She said, appearing to be satisfied.

"No need to worry. He's not here to take any of our souls or anything. That avenue has dried up apparently." Steve piped up from behind.

"Oh, interesting!" Death perceived this to be yet another possibly strange response from the girl. "I like your robe!"

"Thank you. I made it myself." He made a slight sweeping motion to show the fabric off. It came a little too close to being more revealing than intended.

"Where's your scythe then?" Came the incredulous voice of Joyce from beyond Dave.

"Ah...well, I dropped it somewhere. I believe it makes the wrong impression anyway." Death gave a glance to Steve.

"Yeah, someone might take you for a threat." Joyce shot

back.

"You are certainly correct in that regard. Regrettably we already had an incident of that sort." The stony eyes of Death bounced around, trying to assess reactions.

"We don't need to talk about that." Steve chimed in.

"There was an axe involved..." Dave said, digging deeper.

"It was a simple mistake!" Steve protested.

"Well at least I know I have a good level of invulnerability now." Death said, trying to keep things positive.

"You're invulnerable?" Joyce weighed her options.

"I never had to worry about it before." Death stated. "But times have changed, one cannot be sure of anything anymore."

"I suppose it makes sense. The dead are coming back to life and eating people. So, the rules are kind of all up in the air." Joyce concluded.

"Precisely." Death gave a nod.

There was a look of understanding between the two. A statement of affairs had taken place. Almost everyone else was standing uncomfortably.

"I think it's awesome!" Lucy cried with glee. "Well, not all the shambles...zombies...living impaired I mean. Not that they might not have some type of valid existence maybe. They are being quite problematic though...Whatever, how often does a person get to meet the actual Death?!"

"Usually just the once." Death said. "Although there have been occasional repeat visits, mostly medical students trying to play God. It does not normally work out well for them."

"What's he like?" Jenny asked.

"Who?"

"God."

"Oh...I do not know. I have never met a one above all so to speak." He felt suddenly inadequate. "To be honest I do not know what is in charge of things. I am quite certain something created me and assigned me to my role. But outside of that I am in the dark."

Jenny and Joyce exchanged glances.

"Wait, so in all the time you were doing what you do, you never really knew who you were actually doing it for, or why?" Joyce said incredulously.

"Nah, a job is a job after all." Dave said in understanding.

"Well, that's one way to look at it." Steve speculated.

"No holidays though." Death revealed.

"Probably no pension either." Dave added.

"I do not believe so honestly. There was no discussion of what came after." Death gestured around. "Unless this is it."

"There cannot be much appeal in immortality if you don't get to enjoy it." Jenny said.

Death looked taken aback for a second. He contemplated this thought and his face clouded over as he realized she was right. It was depressing.

"Well, if this does count as your retirement, now you get to hang out with us all you want!" Lucy declared with relentless optimism.

It worked. Death's smile instantly returned.

"You are right Lucy. I can make the most of what is before me. Even if I am disconnected from the purpose I had before. Whatever I was tied to, the contract seems to have expired."

"Well now you are a free agent!" Lucy encouraged.

Simplistic or not, it was hard not to appreciate the remark and its positive nature. Death realised that he was doing what he wanted already. To truly interact with real living people of all different mentalities and personality types.

In his vocation as Grim Reaper he saw the world several times over and witnessed the many wonders of nature. He had met all kinds of interesting and famous people, mostly at low points in their existence but still. Death was present in every time and location, but from an outsider's perspective.

He was not able to get involved in any real way. Not only did he lack a true investment in past experiences, he also never controlled where or when he would have to go. He just got this feeling, like a buzzing in the brain, and this would compel him onto the next place and person.

He was a tourist. He might have a good conversation, or a moment of enlightenment through an interesting idea shared, but nothing lasted. This was an intrinsic part of his life at the time. Forming bonds would not have been healthy or possible.

This also meant he had no one to miss or share with. Now he was meeting people he could get to know on a personal level. This potential permanence was important to him.

There were already great poems, songs, and works of art, even serious philosophical and scientific theories dedicated to him. In terms of leaving a lasting impression on the greater world he felt like he had pretty much achieved that. To have real friends though, people that cared about him and held him fondly in their mind.

That would be a wholly new experience.

What with most of humanity seemingly being wiped out, there were not a lot of places Death could find this. Despite his optimism, there was a good chance anyone he came across would have been hostile. This group was different, outside of the initial axing of course. They were not gruff or ruthlessly out for themselves and yet they had managed to survive for over a month. It was an extremely lucky discovery by all reasoning.

It could be surmised that much of this was down to Steve. Death already found him interesting. When he looked into his mind, he saw how the man thought. His world view could boil down to the philosophy; "Well, I can see that point of view, but I feel like it is wrong." This stance delighted few and infuriated many.

This was also why he could be trusted to make decisions. He was removed enough from situations to assess what should be done while factoring in the feelings of others. If he thought the best thing was to stay in one street and shut them off from the rest of the world, then he would aim towards that.

Death ascertained that currently he would leave anyone behind who thought differently. It was both a great leadership quality and a terrible one. Steve would always have a plan to execute, but he might end up doing so alone. Some would call this confidence others would say it was sociopathic.

Having gotten past these introductions without the help, he thought maybe it would be alright to delve into the others. He would certainly like to know how all these different people saw themselves. As well as finding out how they all related to each other.

"Right, so I'm thinking to just go pay a visit to your dad. Give him a piece of my mind." Dave said, interrupting Death's musings.

While the reaper was not a fan of this type of aggressive posturing, it sounded like there was another person to meet. It was important for him to have a grasp of everyone present so he silently decided to go along with the proposal. Perhaps this older male would be a figure of retiring understanding.

Both sisters looked perturbed for very different reasons. Joyce was irritated by the continued confused characterisation of her dad, and Lucy really didn't want any interaction with her father to spoil this amazing circumstance. If her father caught sight of Death he was liable to flip his lid and tell him to sling his hook, which would be bad for all of them.

On the other hand, maybe it would be good to confront him. Shove the massive figure of Death in his face and see if he could deal with it. That would teach the delusional patriarch his real place in the world.

Lucy looked up at Death's steely grey eyes with her best beaming smile. She hoped her positive energy would transmit to the towering figure and bring him on board with her agenda.

"Could you please come with us to smooth things over with my father?" She cooed.

He returned the smile.

She got good vibes from him.

"Lucy!" Joyce hissed at this.

An unspoken conversation took place between the two via various intensifying glares.

"Of course, I would happily accompany you." Death said magnanimously. "Even the sternest of men have reconsidered themselves when I have paid them a visit…admittedly by then it is often too late for them to actually do anything about this, but at least the idea was there."

Lucy looked confused.

Joyce looked concerned.

Steve and Jenny let out dual sighs of resignation and Dave gave a nod of approval as he started making his way up to the Newsagents.

Death found himself a little out of sorts at the different reactions. Before he knew it, he was swept off in the direction of the gates. For a moment he was concerned they were about to escort him out. He realised it was only his own insecurities as they were simply following along to the shop door at the top of the hill.

Dave's hard rapping on the glass rang out through the streets. This was far too theatrical, not least because the shop was not actually locked. The noise carried across a large area devoid of human life like a dinner bell.

He knocked again, there was no answer. He looked up to the window to see if he could spot a face peeking out but there was nothing. He heard a couple of groans from behind the edge of the gate and returned them with a mocking accuracy.

Steve was not impressed by any of this. He was caught in the logical bind of not wanting to be confrontational, however in doing so was allowing a hostile situation to arise. He was also aware that if he tried to talk Dave out of this he could be seen as cowardly. With him seeming to make headway with Jenny, they exchanged a couple of looks after all, he couldn't afford this.

The irony that he was being cowardly by not wanting to look like a coward was not lost on him. Life is complicated and this could not be helped. At least that is what he told himself.

As for Jenny, she knew this might not be the best course of action. It was probably better just to leave Michael to wallow in his own crapulence until she could find a permanent way out of this place. However, there was a nagging urge to see him get a telling off for being a miserable and insufferable bastard. He had made life awkward for people and she wanted him to feel at least a bit of the same.

After another few seconds Death volunteered to phase through the entrance. Needless to say, Lucy was impressed and wanted to let him do this. An exasperated Joyce, who had been stalling, reminded everyone they could simply go inside.

"Ah, door handles." Death remarked to the bemusement of everyone else.

It was typical. Not only had her sister's daring escape only lasted all of two minutes, but it also led to the exact situation she was hoping to avoid. Great.

It occurred to her that if she was a more dramatic person, she might have made some kind of protest. She could shout at them to leave her dad alone or slap her sister before storming off maybe. Instead, she just pushed the door open for them.

Joyce slumped through the entrance and gave her own mocking moan at the noisy gate zombies set off by the shop's bell. She was resigned to let events unfold as they may. It was hard to muster up any kind of resistance when people felt so righteous.

"Is that offensive?" Lucy asked Death in response to her sister's taunting.

"I do not believe they care." He replied. "So it would only be as offensive as you find it."

The concept fascinated her.

Dave, being swept up by all this action stormed through the shop up to the apartment. Steve thought about how he really needed to inventory this place. He'd been having his own problems with Michael in that department already. Hopefully this confrontation would lead to a productive resolution.

They found Michael where the girls left him, slumped and sleeping in his ratty armchair. Dave coughed and he gave a stir. He awoke from his nap with a start to see his daughter and that dopey jobber from down the road cockily standing in front of him. He saw by his her crossed arms that there was some beef to settle.

He immediately went on the offensive.

"What the bloody hell are you doing in my house?!" He demanded.

"We've come to have a word with you Michael." Dave said, bolstered by the backup present.

"Oh really? About what you puffed up little chump?!"

"About how you treat other people dad!" Lucy blurted out, cutting off Dave's ire and robbing him of all his righteous momentum. He stumbled and chose to remain silent.

"I treat people the way I see them! And right now all I see is this bugger in my house uninvited, presuming to tell me how to live my life!"

"He's just worried about us Dad!" Lucy sobbed, getting far too worked up about the whole thing.

"Oh, don't give me that, we barely know the guy!"

He was getting as over-excited as his daughter.

"We are part of a community dad! It's terrible that you can't see that!"

"Community?!" Michael scoffed heartily. "What, with this bunch of scrubbers?!"

Dave found his voice.

"Listen Michael, we might not have much here, but we're all that are keeping each other alive. So maybe you should get some perspective and stop how you're acting before you do some real damage."

"Do you think just because I want to protect me and mine and not rush over to help out some wobbly tart that I'm some kind of monster? Do me a favour you bloody idiot!"

What this situation needed was calmer heads. Steve and Jenny, milling about in the doorway until now, started to make their way into the room. Just behind was a dejected Joyce, who did not see any of this going well. They had also been partially blocking the entry of a certain large grey addition to the group.

"Well, speak of the silly cow now! Here comes the bloody cavalry, I don't think! Somehow you roped my other daughter into this! Bloody marvellous!"

Joyce wanted to tell her dad to calm down or tell them to get out. Or tell everyone to stop being such idiots. Instead, she could only muster a "Hi dad." This had very little effect on the situation.

"By other daughter don't you mean *favourite* daughter." Lucy spat out.

The venom came unexpectedly. Her father looked taken aback. He stuttered. His eyes darted from person to person and his red face swelled. He needed to shift focus.

He grabbed a Mars bar from the box and turned to Steve.

"Is this what you want is it?!" He held it in his hand like a triumphant detective brandishing the murder weapon after a stunning reveal. "You won't get anything from me!"

He unwrapped the chocolate and took a big bite.

"Wait…What?" Steve was perplexed by how this turned on him.

Michael was a shade of beetroot now.

"Oh yeah." He shook his finger. "I know, I know!" He said between accusatory chomps.

"This makes no sense." Jenny sighed.

It was at this moment Death's head popped into view.

Michael turned at the movement without truly seeing, still looking for other targets to lash out on.

"And who the hell is this?! Another bastard looking for a hand-out?!" His purple hue intensified.

This last point didn't really make much sense, but he was too far gone now. The only option was to continue. The figure stood up and the full towering effect of the Grim Reaper met his gaze.

He choked.

"Hello." Death said cheerily.

Michael choked again. He didn't stop choking.

He tugged at his collar and the room started to spin. He fell backwards and the world was darkness.

He became one of the few humans to see the genuine Death right before he died in over a thousand years.

The significance was lost on him.

***

There was screaming. Death was used to this. It was almost his calling card, a wailing siren alerting him to a job well done.

This was different.

He often came upon rooms full of people stretching their lung capacity over someone who just passed. For the most part, the screaming had not been caused by his presence. This was after all why he stopped being corporeal in the first place.

In his job it would be a bit of a problem if when someone dropped dead, turning up caused another couple to go as well. It would also make conversation afterwards awkward. So, this was in some ways a familiar worry, as well as a somewhat new experience.

A worst fear realised some might say.

Admittedly he had appeared to a few people throughout modern history before their deaths. For instance, there was a man in Germany who made his existence rather busier than he would have liked for a number of years. He gave him a piece of his mind before he went, so he would not have peace of mind when he did. Death considered it a perk, but this was far from that.

Both girls were huddled around their father sobbing. He never had any connection to anyone around a deceased party before. Death was not sure what he should do here. He could say a few words, but he did not know the man beyond "he was shouting and appeared to have a fondness for confectionary." It might be fitting, but more than likely not appropriate

As he was pondering this, Lucy turned to him with a face of nothing but anger and accusation.

"Why?! How could you?! Why didn't you say anything?! You evil...you monster! You killed him! You...you..."

The rest gave way to incoherent sobs.

Death wanted to protest but he could not. He did not know

if he had any right to. He knew that people died all the time, of any number of culminating factors.

Did his appearance end his life, or the consumption of so many unhealthy calories over the years? Medically these could have weakened his heart to the degree to be overcome in that moment. There was a biological argument, yet not something that entirely exonerated him as his appearance could still be the trigger.

If someone was assassinated, was it the person firing the gun that was responsible? The person who hired them? Or was it the victim's own actions that necessitated the hiring? It was a philosophical debate that would not go down well during this moment of high human emotion. Even Death had the sense to know that.

Joyce was comforting her distraught sister staring daggers at him. Yes, definitely not the right time to bring up the merits of what constitutes responsibility in the situation of a person's passing. Suddenly Lucy was running towards him. She started to pummel his massive frame with impotent rage before Dave managed to drag her away.

Death was taken aback. He looked around the room.

Dave was panting with effort restraining Lucy. There was the angry face of Joyce promoting a constant state of hatred. Jenny was looking in silence at anything but him, and a resigned Steve simply stared at the prone figure of Michael.

He realised he was out of moves. His shoulders slumped in defeat. He saw no other path. He would have to leave.

Trying to take a step Death noticed he could not feel the floor underneath his feet. More precisely this was because they were halfway through the floor and falling. It became apparent that he was involuntary turning non-corporeal and his body was slowly sinking through the carpet.

He had gone almost completely before anyone else really noticed and they certainly did not see his expression of surprise as he went. To those looking it would have appeared to be a completely intentional move. Death wanted to struggle, to claw his way back up and plead his case. But he could not muster up the will to do so.

Being around people was even more difficult than he had thought. No matter how desperately he wanted friends, Death could not fight the emotion in that room right now. Maybe it was for the best that he just faded away.

As quickly as these feelings took over there was then an unpredictable shift in mood. For some reason melancholy gave way to a self-righteous anger. The change was punctuated by the solid ground hitting the soles of his re-materialised feet.

He was in the middle of the deceased Newsagent's shop. Was this a kind of existential self-defence mechanism kicking in to stop him ceasing to exist? Or was he entirely unstable in this unfamiliar circumstance to the point that he could not control himself?

If he had been thinking clearly, he might have given a sigh of relief for this change in feeling, as who knew where he would have ended up? As it was though he only felt like lashing out. Why was he always to blame?!

Looking around, Death saw the boxes of chocolate bars that the man would constantly scoff. At the stacks of papers, he would clutch with hands shaking in fury over anything he did not see as right and proper. He had a clear picture in his mind of the man's life, and it made him angry. He tried to overcome this rush of emotion and managed to get a hold of himself.

He attempted to reach equilibrium through introspection. He drew upon several millennia of hindsight and realised that whatever the truth of the situation, it was better to move on right now. There was no point losing himself and he could not control, change, or rectify the feelings of others in any healthy manner.

Instead, Death needed space and time, hopefully to find a group who would not hold him responsible for the passing of a loved one. He resolved to leave the street. He truly hoped this experience would not affect them too adversely. He wished he could make the phrase 'having a brush with death' relate to something positive.

Despite this regret, the grim reaper was more in control now. Not wanting to cause a scene he phased through the shop door rather than risking ringing the bell. The grey Coventry sky greeted him, and he tried to see it as a comforting blanket of potential, rather than a stark void of nothingness.

He braced himself against the firmly constructed gate and spared a look back up to the window of the flat where all his new friends were. He faded to nothing for a second and the thought drifted past that he might never return. He did though. He passed through the gates with no problem, as if they held no significance.

When he appeared on the other side he was surprised to be greeted by Barry amongst a host of the undead. Despite their short time together he was glad to see his bloated and drippy face. Death smiled at him. Barry gave back his textbook vacant expression. He knew it meant he was happy they were reunited as well.

He silently made his way from the settlement. His resolve was reinforced by the thought that if some people had survived during all this, then surely others would have. He would find them.

The rest of the clustered shambles looked to him as he passed, but only that. They did not follow him, and all turned back to the gates as he left. They too had abandoned him.

There was one shuffling pair of footsteps, however. It was Barry. He followed him despite the promise of a fresh meal. He slowed his pace to allow the overstuffed figure to keep up with him. Death went to put his arm around his chum in a gesture of camaraderie. Barry stared up at him and let out a low moan of comprehension.

He spent the trip outside of the area explaining to Barry why he had to leave. Death hoped his friend could understand. He seemed to. Barry even stumbled when he got to the part about the shopkeeper having a heart attack. Death guessed his companion could relate. He conjured his scythe to steady him.

He could at least keep one portly fellow upright today.

CHAPTER SEVEN

Death was at a bit of a loss. After a few hours of wandering his unyielding optimism was starting to wane a bit. It was easier to picture a positive meeting with a group of keen and welcoming survivors before he stumbled upon some.

He began to worry that no matter what other steps he took he would have trouble. It was hard to see what he could do to make things go smoother. The thought of assuming a more regular human stature did not occur to him.

Instead, he had the idea that he could become a kind of zombie shepherd, forsaking human company altogether. His mind went to what this could mean for him. Where would he be leading them except to devour any remaining people? That would be a bit too anti-social for him, even with current events notwithstanding.

He had a rapport with the dead, although the others did not follow him while there was the potential of food involved. The notion of classifying those inside the street as edible gave him a pang of guilt. He would have to return in the future to see how they were, if he made himself known to them while doing so was another matter.

Again, he felt frustration at his lack of ability compared to how he used to be. Having a wide knowledge of events and unlimited potential to traverse the Earth was completely lost on him while in his vocation. It was a functional existence. Now he was at a loose end and could really use these capacities for scouting. It was like being a leaf on the breeze as opposed to one on the branch.

Death thought this was a poetic and fitting metaphor.

He realised he was back in the town square. Barry was staring up at the Godiva statue that sat in the middle of the shopping district. It was a strange symbol of naked abandon amongst the consumerism of banks, restaurants, and clothing stores. Not as awe inspiring while overseen by a monstrous Primark, but Death was not to know the nature of this.

He joined his companion in looking to the figure on her horse, slightly rusted in blue and grey. He compared his own skin. Was he to become like that statue? A figure of neglect, whose meaning and purpose will be forgotten over time. His flesh appeared to reflect the thought and shimmered with a ripple of decay.

It freaked him out.

The constant shifting of his physical condition in relation to his mental state was very concerning. He would need to try to stay positive to keep his own existence in check. There was something perverted about being exposed to both emotional and physical hardships and be forced to bear them with a sense of cheerfulness.

He understood now why some humans brought their own lives to an end quicker than they would naturally occur. Or at least risk them unnecessarily to make them more meaningful. Sometimes being passive could be the worse fate.

Sheer will drove everything. If you exist without any kind of aim or goal you might as well give up. The proviso here being there is always something else to achieve if we just look. Even if you did reach where you thought you wanted to be, there was always another step. Life kept going.

In this process it was like a pebble leading to a landslide. It is not necessary to possess the drive to reach your objective, only enough to get things rolling. Then you simply keep going with initial momentum.

This is of course easier when you have some other stones

rolling with you to speed up the process. To him this extended metaphor explained the want for social interactions in the first place. Death needed to find more pebbles.

He remembered it was around this area that he saw an interesting canine weaving through the undead a few days ago. The mysterious dog had a very definite purpose, a 'someone' to get back to. He wondered if he could get involved in that.

What he needed was a way to locate the canine again. He pondered over instructing Barry how to track them. Not that he knew how to teach such a thing. He would have to learn how to be a good teacher first. It was a pickle. On the other hand, he had nothing but time, so it would be a welcome distraction.

They spent the next few days looking, his undead friend slowly falling apart during this time. There was neither hide nor hair of the animal, so they then began to hunt for the nearest pet shop to find something to entice it. Death was aware dogs ate treats and required their own specialised versions due to an aversion to chocolate. Households who made this mistake were never very pleasant to visit.

Their search was successful. After all dog treats would not be the highest thing on the list for most looters. They found a shop, set any remaining rodents free, fed the fish and loaded up on supplies. He was walking the streets, laden with a host of biscuits and a couple of squeaky toys just in case.

Death was rustling, honking, and generally making quite a clamour with abandon. Much of the dead had ceased looking at him with reverence and mostly treated him with disinterest. He heard what he thought was one of the toys gradually depressed from squeaking. The shrill noise persisted. It became clear that it was the sound of a child shrieking in the near distance.

The reaper abandoned the bags of treats, letting them fly through the air. A couple of the packets were already open, he had gotten curious. The contents spilled all over the pavement. One bag hit Barry, who trailed behind him, helping to garner his attention.

His friend had been getting less responsive. Chewy treats

from the open pack became embedded in his bloated flesh. He would make the perfect piece of dog bait if the need arose. He could still serve a purpose, even if he was becoming sullen over time.

He raced through the street and barrelled into a group of four zombies who were bearing down on a girl. She was crying out for someone named 'Tess' with her eyes shut tight. Part of him felt reluctance at destroying these feisty dead, but there was only so much he could do in the situation. The girl looked helpless and there would only be more on the way. Death could not simply let her get eaten.

Of the four, two were standing after his initial dive into the group. He grabbed one by its gaping maw and yanked down hard, pulling the jawbone clean off before shoving it right back up into the skull. He swivelled the jagged implement, shucking out the insides of the thing's cranium and caving it in from the inside out.

Simultaneously he clasped the second by the back of its head with his other hand, bending it over. Then Death drove his knee hard into its face with a devastating quickness, destroying it utterly and crushing everything but the scalp. The efficiency of this left him with a skullcap kneepad that was as gruesome as it was garish.

He had no time to shake it off as the two that had been knocked down were beginning to stagger back to their feet. He kicked at one and meant to take the head clean off. Instead, the thing let out an accusatory groan and his foot went all the way inside its mouth. His toes continued their momentum and came out of the things now vacant eye sockets.

The impact sent the skullcap on his knee travelling down his leg at an alarming speed, colliding with the thing's forehead. The skull-on-skull collision sent fragments everywhere and the previously wailing mouth was now rendered silent. The owner's grey matter well and truly scrambled. The eyeballs, popped out by the impact of the toes of Death, rolled around on the ground like marbles mixing with the sprinkles of cranium in a kind of snowball effect.

They were then squished by the remaining undead, who was now fully upright. The thing looked puzzled as it gawked at Death, as if deciding how to handle the situation. It seemed like the innate desire for food took over whatever sense of survival could exist in the already dead thing. It lunged for the little girl, who remained frozen with her eyes closed.

He called for her to get out of the way as he struggled to dislodge from the booted husk. The force of the kick had been such so that its teeth managed to sink into his stony flesh. He doubted this would lead to any kind of infection since his whole vital system was of his own design. However, it made things a bit awkward right now.

He could not even apparently phase his foot through the dental catastrophe, which was fazing for Death. He had before been perplexed by the expression 'putting one's foot in one's mouth'. Maybe this was the meaning of frustration behind it.

There was pain where the teeth broke his skin, unable to heal while the rotting splinters remained lodged inside of him. He struggled towards the final ghoul, dragging the other along as he did so in a completely ungainly hobbling motion. He was hoping that the hopping would help dislodge his foot and save him some time. However, to his annoyance the movement only drove the spikes of bone deeper.

He felt a flash of anger. The urgency rendered him unable to enjoy or analyse this sensation no matter how new or novel. Death was not about to let this little girl get eaten because of his own incompetent error. He channelled his frustration into strategy.

Planting his free leg on the ground, he gathered up all his strength and delivered a full roundhouse kick to the shambling thing before it could reach the cowering girl. The zombie was hit by about two hundred pounds of putrid tissue and organs. They smashed together with such force that both bodies were what could only be described as 'pulped', collapsing into an unrecognizable heap on the ground.

The momentum left Death spinning. Still tangled in all the bone and body parts, he ended up in a heap amongst the soup of gore he created. He felt a mixture of cold and warm sticky fluids soak up into his robes, coating his body like the frozen centre of a microwave ready meal. He never needed to eat, but he did have a certain obsession with food trends. This came both from an occupational standpoint, and as a general morbid curiosity.

He looked up from a pile of skin and sinew to be greeted by a snarling dog, standing protectively in front of the girl. This canine happened to be the very one he had been looking for. This was indeed fortuitous!

The girl cried "Tess" again, this time in glee. She wrapped her arms around the Collie in relief. The dog did not move a muscle, still staring at Death with murderous intent. He tried to bypass the situation by appealing to the girl.

"Hello there, my name is...Steve. I mean you no harm."

Even he knew that you should not say "hello my name is Death" to a frightened child, let alone their guardian. He was in enough of a messy predicament as it was. The girl did not look up. She continued to cling to the dog with a quiet whimper.

Death tried the unorthodox action of shaking like a dog himself to dislodge some of the caked-on gore. This move only succeeded in spreading it across the area and causing the girl to further retreat into the fur of her canine protector.

Tess let out a viscous bark of warning.

"Miss? I really do mean you no harm you know. Would it be alright if you told this to your dog as well?" Death had to persist with politeness above all else.

The girl peeked at him for the briefest second with an expression of muted fear and wonderment. She spoke another "Tess", this time with a soothing tone. Clearly the girl had been through a lot. Death hesitated to look inside her mind however, having already had second thoughts about the invasiveness of the practice.

Instead, he tried to press on unheeded. He turned to the snapping canine. They had calmed slightly from the command of her name, but not entirely.

"So, I gather your name is Tess. Hello Tess."

He gave a wave and thankfully the dog stopped snarling. The animal instead fixed him with a hard stare. Death was not overly familiar with canine behaviour, but this seemed strange. He thought they generally had the reaction of curiosity to their name, a raised head, or a perked ear perhaps.

The look said "That is my name. I do not know what you think repeating it is going to do however." She then gave him a cursory sniff and let out a growl. He responded with a nervous chuckle, thankful that he had not chosen to be made of bare bones in this moment.

"So, is it just the two of you out here?"

Death instantly realised his mistake. The question came across more predatory than concerned. It was funny how trying to sound caring could come across as creepy and threatening in certain circumstances. He balked and began to backpedal. He was a force of nature talking to a child and a pet, but it felt like he was in front of a hostile inquisition.

"What I meant to say is that I was watching you before and it looked like you were hunting stuff out. Looking for things for someone more vulnerable perhaps?"

This sounded just as bad when it came out of his mouth. While neither of them could articulate it, he could almost feel the question of 'watching me before?' hang in the air. Let alone the 'vulnerable' comment. He almost cried out that he was not *watching* anyone; he only happened to spot the canine and his eyes were drawn to it!

Death tried to detach himself from the situation, to press on from his viewpoint as a timeless being, but it was no good. The current climate of reading too much into things had seeped into everyday conversation too deep. Either that or it was all in his head. It could be that his giant stony visage alone in a world of slouching ghouls put the much smaller figures on guard.

Who could tell?

Death was not getting anywhere. Still he felt the need to

persist. Apart from these two, the nearest living beings blamed him for the passing of one of their own. This was somewhat factual, yet it seemed rather unfair. He was being typecast.

The dog wore the same incredulous look as before. The stance of the girl had softened, although she remained behind the scruff of her hairy protector. It was a start at least.

Just then, another corpse lurched towards the trio. Death saw an opportunity and summoned his scythe, which he only now realised he instinctively dismissed when he heard the girl. It was a piece of him that would always be awkward to show those he first met, no matter how essential it often was.

He cleaved the thing in two with ease.

Minimal splatter.

Death turned with a look of triumph, expecting some mild praise. Instead of this the girl recoiled and the canine bared its teeth. Before he was a grim towering stranger, now he was still all these things, but with a weapon.

He was trying to act as their saviour. It was not so easy to assume the role. There was a trust to be earned first, especially with ones so susceptible to outside harm. He needed to figure out how to do so and he was not sure he had the words.

He stashed his scythe behind his back. Even at his height it was difficult. It was a moment of panicked reaction. He could have simply dismissed it, but he made the wrong decision. Also, there was probably a part of him that did not want to abandon the familiar item again while so uncomfortable.

He tried to shift its weight without looking and ended up fumbling the handle between his hands. It overbalanced and he dropped it. He attempted to pivot around to make a grab for it, but he had second thoughts about re-arming himself in front of the two smaller figures. Unfortunately, he committed too far into the pivot and could not turn back in time.

His feet caught on his robes as his fingers met the handle. There was an awkward moment where his body was turned in three different directions. He fell once again, scythe in tow this time. His twisted mass met the pool of shredded ghouls.

It was just a disaster.

This time, however, he heard a sound almost completely alien to him. It was the laughter of a child. He looked up at the girl, who was almost doubled over with glee. Tess even stopped growling. Somehow the first fall did not cause hilarity, possibly because she felt too frightened. This time though she found it hysterical.

He staggered to his feet, trying to sort himself out. Death realised that in the fall the long blade had travelled through his abdomen and pierced several large chunks of zombie. He stood there, looking like a ghastly shish-kebab, and the little girl just giggled. This was all very gruesome, even for him.

Tess was giving him a look saying he was the most stupid thing she had ever seen. Imagine the look a cat gives you any time it realises that you do not have food. There was something off about this animal. At least she no longer seemed to regard him as any type of threat.

The girl rushed out from behind her canine shield and ran towards him with her arm outstretched. Despite the apparent reassessment of him, Tess gave an instinctual bark of warning. Death himself was at a loss for what to do as it was not the best time to receive any type of embrace. If the girl avoided being impaled, she would at least get very mucky.

With little other choice he shut his eyes in concentration. If this did not work, things were going to go poorly. In this case the urgency helped him to focus. The scythe faded away into nothingness, allowing the pieces of rotting flesh to drop to the floor. He opened his eyes again a couple of seconds before the girl reached him. Stepping over the gore he stuck his hand out to meet her.

She took it and shook it.

"Hi! My name is Anna, nice to meet you slashy-man!" She declared obliviously.

Tess was pensively pacing, eyeing him with suspicion. The look reminded him of the younger girl from the street before. They barely had a conversation, but the scepticism radiated off her. And that was before he killed her father.

Everything was happening so fast. He was not prepared. Reflecting, perhaps he should have peered into her mind when they met. He was still struggling with the moral implications of the practice but doing so might have prevented the proceeding tragedy from occurring.

He decided it was probably better if he did try to read this girl Anna. She might have several family members waiting with weak hearts. Who knew what other factors could alienate him from this new social outlet before he really got settled.

He already attempted to ask them directly and it did not go down well. Since he had made some progress with them, he did not want to have it spoiled. Anna looked up at him with big brown eyes of innocence. Death locked onto that expression and could instantly sense a hidden trauma.

Death saw a house and a woman intrinsically tied. He felt a warmth of safety emanating from this memory. It mixed with a sense of childhood anxiety over abandonment.

The woman must have been Anna's mother. He could see she was dressed in a nurse's uniform. She looked to be rushed and frazzled, glancing around, and packing things into her bag in a haphazard manner.

"Takes care now Anna. I'm sorry...I have to go. You'll have to be a big girl and check in on nanny. If anything happens the number is on the fridge!" He heard her say from a doorway.

Then flashes of play and distraction. Running around and television in the background. Stuffed animals and army tanks, an interesting combination.

A tether of importance kept him in the moment. This was a mystery to him. Then there was a loud thump from upstairs.

It was the sound of thunder to the girl. It brought her out of her current occupation, and she remembered her nanny. A fear of responsibility filled her. If her nanny fell out of bed, then her mummy would be mad.

She rushed upstairs, making herself big and brave as she did. There was no idea of what she was going to do when she reached her destination. She had to keep moving forward.

Her tiny legs scaled the stairs two at a time. There was no hesitation now. She reached the goal of nanny's room, kept up her steely will and opened the door.

She should have knocked. What she saw in the room was scary. Her nanny was gone. No nanny on the bed, no nanny on the floor.

It was confusing. If her nanny wasn't on the floor that was good. But she was not in the bed either and that was bad. Her mummy told her nanny was extra sleepy and it was normal for her to be sleeping lots. So why wasn't she in the bed?

Anna wanted to go back to playing. Still, she was worried her mummy would be mad if she didn't find out where nanny went. She called for her. There was not any answer. Where had her nanny gone?

There was heavy breathing. Her nanny did breathe funny. Mummy said it was from being all smoky. It didn't make sense to her, but Anna needed to trust her mummy.

It was coming from the bathroom. Her nanny must have had to go. Anna felt bad. Nanny couldn't go on her own and she wasn't there to help her.

Normally her mummy would be there. She was gone, so Anna should have been there. She didn't know what to do, but she could figure it out. Anna was a big girl now and she wanted to help.

Then she saw her nanny.

She was sitting by the sink.

There was something bad. Her skin looked weird.

Nanny always had strange blue lines on her skin, now the lines were grey. Her eyes were weird, and she was making scary noises. Something was wrong and she needed help.

Anna would have to be a brave girl and take charge.

She shuffled over to her nanny. Reaching out, holding the dress mummy got for her birthday. It was special, there were flowers on it. Nanny had flowers on her dress too. Nanny didn't smell good though and she was very still.

Anna trembled and hesitated.

The glassy eyes of the old woman snapped open as the girl reached for her. There was some movement and screaming, feelings of a struggle. An overwhelming feeling of terror took Death out of his trance-like state.

He was glad the intense emotion brought him out of the experience. His consciousness had drifted away and felt like it was taken over by the raw mental state of the child. He was left with a sense of dread burrowed deep inside his being. Death was present for many traumatic scenes, but never experienced such intense feelings directly.

It was unpleasant to say the least.

He was not sure he wished to read into someone again, no matter what the potential benefits. He did not know how to handle this level of anxiety. It was all very foreign to him.

Death felt like he was infected. He tried to rationalise this by thinking about it as part of understanding the deeper human experience. Whether that was a good thing had become a little debatable. Part of him still longed for his role of observing from afar, even though it only ended a short time ago.

He could not guess what happened next to Anna. Despite how harrowing it was, she had managed to survive somehow. This girl must have a will of steel despite the timid demeanour he first witnessed. Every time an obstacle appeared she found the ability to meet it despite her young age.

It was enough to make one re-evaluate what was meant by the phrase 'only the strong survive'. This tiny person of little experience got through such harsh and damaging circumstance. Millions of others had died. At this point willpower becomes a much more concrete definition of what was important in life.

Death could relate.

Anna was looking at him with her head cocked sideways. She studied him with an intense curiosity, any feelings of fear towards him having left. Seeing he had shaken out of his stupor she began to lose interest and turned to Tess.

"I'm sorry I ran. You forgot your coat. I wanted to give it to you. But the monsters came, and I dropped it. I couldn't see you. So, I lost it." She looked forlorn at the admission.

Tess gave a sharp bark, somehow conveying the message: "Never mind about the coat. I'm just glad you are alright. Never do that again!"

Anna perked up. "We should see if Mr. Benjamin is okay. Come on!" She said cheerily.

She started toddling off. Apparently presuming the dog and the reaper would follow. Tess gave him a withering look. He shrugged at the incredulous dog and they both turned to accompany the precocious girl.

It was nice to be included at least.

All Death could surmise was that the girl felt safe in his company. She undoubtedly learned to trust quickly once initial barriers were overcome. This was presumably a necessity right now.

It would be foolhardy to blindly trust anyone you met in desperate times. At the same time, you could not get anywhere in this world without help from others. Existing trusted friends and family were in short supply after all.

Meeting this girl made him decide that what happened in the newsagents was overall a good thing. This duo of Anna and Tess looked to be in more need of his help and companionship. Plus, it taught him to not have any philosophical hesitations to killing the undead.

Not when it meant the preservation of the living anyway. It might be unfair to choose one over the other. Then again, these creatures had been given a turn at life already, they had no right to take away someone's first go-around prematurely.

Death was already at least indirectly responsible for one human fatality since re-entering the physical plane. He needed some way to prevent that total from going up. Having a vague argument about how the walking dead were no different from humans was not going to achieve that.

This way of thinking was how everyone ends up undead. Where would he turn for conversations consisting of more than guttural moans if that happened? That low drone was already a constant soundtrack to this new world.

He realised some of this noise was coming from behind him. It was Barry. He had completely forgotten about him up to now, what with the meeting of these two new individuals. It was very well and good having an undead chum following you around while on your own. However, what if that chum tried to make chum out of your new chums upon meeting them?

This could be a problem.

Then again, he was not making any effort to attack them. Unlike the others Death encountered back there Barry was still not hostile at all. Instead, he held the same melancholic gaping look as always. It was as if his brain recognised the reaper and believed he could be his saviour.

Anna, and more importantly Tess, had not noticed that he was following them yet. He needed to decide what to before that happened. His living-impaired friend might not be a threat, but they would not know this. Death pondered the precarious notion of making introductions. Perhaps he could pretend Barry was a wandering ghoul that he was keeping at bay instead.

Images of pantomime battle sped through his mind, filled with lots of shoving and hits with the dull side of his blade. He could let Barry get his mitts on him and phase through, sending the rotting behemoth sprawling to the floor. This would help to make him look less like a threat and Death could come across as a hero.

But then, what came next? He could not bring himself to end the second existence of his companion. Nor would this be enough to truly placate any potential hesitations from the pair. Maybe they could outpace his friend, claiming they were being pursued and needed to run for their lives. This seemed a bit too alarmist, as well as being far too duplicitous.

With all this pondering Death missed his opportunity to make a choice in the matter. A waddling Barry meandered into one of the collections of rubbish bags littering the street. The resulting din not only alerted the others to his presence, it also scared the heck out of the former shepherd of souls himself.

In a flash Tess turned round, noticed Barry and gave out a low growl, taking an attack position. Anna saw the stance of her canine colleague and sobbed at the sight of the massive zombie sloppily trying to remove itself from a pile of black plastic. The whole scene was a mess and Death faltered.

Tess felt no hesitation as her snarls gave way to vicious barks. The noise confused Barry and he began turning this way and that in the pile, tearing the bags and spreading the weeks-old waste around. His rotting mass mingled with pungent ooze as he writhed around in the sludge, forming the ghastliest snow angel in history.

Within the horrible show, Death noticed his bloated body was still dotted with dog treats. If he was not careful his friend would become a disgusting chew toy. He tried to appeal to the canine.

"Oh, no. No. Bad food. Not for you."

Tess gave a quick series of aggressive barks chastising him to say: "I was never going to eat him you idiot! I am trying to protect my friend!"

He could relate to this, the tone also hurt his feelings. He needed to do something before the situation got even worse. There was the worry that he would offend someone no matter what he did, even though Death himself was quite perturbed at this point.

He finally took some initiative, luckily that the stench had kept Tess at bay until now. He grabbed Barry by one flailing arm and used his own colossal strength to yank him to his feet. The sudden strain on his decaying frame resulted in several terrible gases being released. Death instinctively removed his nose. He seized the opportunity to play peacemaker.

"Bow bee bere Barry." He said all bunged-up. "Bit's bot bice boo battack bun's briends. Bou batter bot boo bat bagain."

Barry gurgled, hesitated, and then turned to the others. His gurgle intensified.

"Bo Barry!" Death said with more command in his voice.

He was unsure of what the noise meant, or if his undead friend could even understand him in this state.

Despite the pronunciation, the tone communicated some massive intimidation. Barry turned and almost cooed, cowed by the chastisement. Had this somehow worked? It was the same tone he used to announce to only the most stubborn souls that they had departed the mortal coil. Perhaps it reached beyond the lack of a nose to a primal part of the decomposing brain, compelling it to take heed.

Death conceded it was better to test out the boundaries now with an awareness of the risks, rather than assume safety due to fear and awkwardness. Doing so could eventually get the girl killed if the wrong situation should arise. Humans had a terrible habit of putting off the possibility of the worst in favour of a silent hope that it would just not occur.

It was the opposite of 'A watched pot never boils.' The reality was more like 'If you do not watch the pot, it will over-boil and send scolding water all over your hob.' But that would not make for a catchy turn of phrase.

Death improvised. He brought back his nose to aid in any possible communication. Then he conjured up his scythe again, positioning it around Barry's neck to act as a restraint. This way if the worst happened then it would be his shambling comrade who was at any real risk, not the little girl. This was not his first choice, but he was in a bind. It was better than the alternative of Barry being ripped apart by Tess, or vice versa.

He felt more than a little cruel, still it had to be done. He put some slack on the scythe and let his corpse companion get a little closer. Anna, understandably, moved back a little. Barry, possibly feeling judged, let out a growl. Tess answered with her own.

This was not going to work. There was simply too much instinctual distrust to overcome and no way for parties involved to reach a peaceful accord. The only answer was to part ways.

Despite this, he could not let this result in the separation of Barry's head from his shoulders. He pulled his stinky pal back from the duo and set him down as tenderly as possible on the ground. Feeling bad about putting him back in the filth he had created.

"You best stay here for now good fellow." He implored in a soothing tone.

His friend stared up at him vacantly.

Death turned to leave, shooing the others away as he did. However, as they began to proceed on their journey, he heard rustling from behind. Barry was trying to get himself up out of the rubbish.

"Barry, stay!" He commanded, trying not to turn back.

His unsightly acquaintance continued to stir.

"I said stay!" He whipped round and with a flash of anger knocked Barry back down into the heap.

The effort was painful, Death felt like he had been struck himself. Who knew that bonds so quickly formed would be so hard to break? The husk of a man stayed down this time, which was probably for the best. But he could not help feeling a sense of regret.

He searched for a better solution but found none.

The only thing he could do was turn his back and keep walking. The others were confused by how this interaction had taken place. No questions were asked though, them being glad to get away from the pungent pile of flesh.

Anna skipped ahead with Tess trotting along beside her. Death followed with footsteps heavier than before. He resolved himself that this was indeed the right course of action. Even so, he could not shake the feeling of sorrow caused by abandoning his fallen comrade.

CHAPTER EIGHT

The group continued, ducking through back streets and alleys with little incident. The others knew where they were heading, and Death was putting his faith in them by following along. He had thrown his lot in with them and there was no going back.

This feeling grew as they moved further away from town, in the opposite direction from the street where he found Steve. He hoped they were all okay, considering he turned their lives upside down within minutes. Then again, he had helped to save Dave, and was at least present when Dave helped Jenny off the roof. Something you could not say about the Newsagent.

Not to speak ill of the dead.

He would make sure things would go better this time. For one thing he would announce himself first in a normal voice. He also thought about taking on a more traditional appearance to fit in better.

Then again, this may feel a bit too much like lying. Where might this practice end up? Would he have to look completely different? He had only just got used to his body as it was. What if he coincidentally ended up looking exactly like someone else, then would he come across as a kind of pod person? Plus, Anna and Tess already knew him in his current form, so there was an inherent confusion there.

Death knew he was coming up with excuses for not doing what should be a completely logical step to adapt to the human world. Creating this physique had been his first active choice in a very long time. It was a marker of new-found agency and he had already grown attached, despite the relatively short time of existing like this.

It was difficult to create attachments when you existed to arrive at the end of things. This melancholic thinking had taken Death away from the world. He did not notice as they came to a stop outside a lone shop on the corner of a suburban area.

It stood out like a sore thumb, a gaudy green and black as opposed to the whites and browns of the surrounding houses. The name Band On The Gun was emblazoned in a lightning font above pulled down shutters blocking the contents of the shop from view. He wondered what the title entailed.

Clearly this was the destination of the rag-tag group. With the front locked up Tess led them round the side to a grate. The girl Anna worked it free with an easy familiarity and Tess went straight in.

Anna paused and looked to Death.

"I forgot! I don't know how you're going to get in! You're too big!" She cried, putting her hands on her head and pulling her hair in an overblown expression of frustration.

"Do not worry about me dear girl, I will be able to get in on my own." Death smiled.

"Good!" Anna exclaimed, not seeing the need to ask any follow-up questions.

"You run along inside now. I will sort things out."

He shooed her away, almost feeling fatherly in the action.

"Okay, see you. Bye!" She was already leaving.

She waved before disappearing into the grate and letting it close behind her. Death was not sure, but he thought he was handling talking to a child quite well. You just accept that they took things at face value and could tell when you were trying to be deceitful.

Death nodded in understanding and braced himself to let his physical form drop away. At first nothing happened, he felt a panic begin to grip his mind. Before it could fully take hold, he disappeared through the brick with a start and nearly fell to the floor. He was stopped from landing on his face by a sharp jerk, like he was tethered to something.

Craning his neck to look backwards he saw what caught him, his own leg. Somehow most of his physical form travelled through the wall unscathed. Yet his ankle locked in the mortar like it had always been there. This was a pickle.

There was a thought to cutting the leg off and letting it grow back. If his head could seal up, then it should not be too hard to replace a limb. Then again there was a question of what happened to the initial leg afterwards. It might vanish, or else remain outside for a ghoul to chew on. Who knows what effect that could have?

A further wrinkle was the possibility that this fallen part may start to regenerate too. What if a whole other Death grew from it? This could be a perfect solution to his friend problem. But he had spent enough time talking to himself already. Plus, what if the other him did not like him or wanted to replace him. It was all too much trouble.

Glancing around he could see that no one was present to witness his faux pas. He calmed his mind and phased the rest of his leg through. He let out a sigh of relief over the successful transition. The faltering was a worry he filed away for later. The reaper distracted himself with the developing habit of studying shelves.

The first thing he noticed were the numerous guitars that lined the walls of the shop. Other various musical paraphernalia were spread around in a display fashion. Strangely along with this there were also a large number of guns and ammo.

Obviously there had been no looting in here because the shelves held unimaginable amounts of weaponry. Mainly of the hunting variety if going by the laws of this land. Contemporary geographical trends in arms regulations were something Death was closely familiar with. It was a large part of his former work after all.

Death supposed middleclass residents of the surrounding suburbs must have favoured food over ammunition, it was the English way. More likely they all had left the city before this has become an issue. Or else they did not even know the place was here. A faceless shop they drove past every day on their way to work, absorbed in the tasks of the day despite the auspicious nature of the establishment.

Having said that, none of the extensive armoury appealed to him. For the experienced wielder, the scythe was the ideal tool for taking care of the dead. Despite the shifting landscape he could not see himself truly taking up anything else.

To begin with Death chose the implement as a symbol to bring comfort. At the time the scythe was invented there was a clear divide between those working the land and those whose land was worked. As much as human history documented the passings of those in the high towers, those in the field died far more often. These were the people he wanted to cater to.

It was a familiar tool to represent the cleaving of the soul from a mortal plane. He thought it a fitting image to enlighten those who passed as to their position now on earth. They were being cleared to make way for the next crop. It was part of a cycle that they could understand and not fear.

Further, most other farming equipment could not deliver that much of an impressive aura when held aloft. Death tried to imagine casting as iconic a visage with a trowel, he could not see it. Maybe a rake would have worked, he was not sure. He thought about explaining to a soul how his hypothetical rake represented how one is pulled towards the grave to make way for new life. Somehow it did not come across as clear cut as the scythe metaphor.

While a possible solace to those who toiled, the symbol could also serve as a warning to those on top. It represented a reminder of their prosperity due to the sweat of others, as well as what they might have reaped in the hereafter. They would be cut down like everyone else, no matter their status.

He never could get to grips with the sheer arbitrary divide between humans. The modern world, before being a desolate place without a possible afterlife, had made more sense to him. A person could achieve great power and influence despite any initially low social-economical background.

If he was going to take on a new metaphorical tool for the new age it might be the handgun. It was both associated with sudden ends and also a means to seize opportunity. It reflected shifts in power, conjuring up images of highway men and their current day equivalents.

Then again in terms of comfort it did not exactly send the right message. Moreover, this change would only lead to lots of issues. While he did want to have conversations, Death already had enough trouble getting asked the exact same questions by everyone.

This was also why he did not adorn any kind of jaunty hat at any point over the years. He could not face all the potential 'What is with the hat?' comments. Explaining fashion choices at the same time as attempting to emphasise a soul's place in the universe was a hassle he did not need.

He tried to listen out for human activity. He could vaguely hear noises from the back of the shop. Upon further inspection there was a door standing slightly ajar behind a counter display containing both guitar picks and gun clips.

He edged his way towards the door, deciding to be extra cautious by announcing his entry.

"Hello anyone in there. Just to pre-warn you, I am Death, and I am coming into the room. However, I mean you no harm and I am not here in any kind of professional capacity."

That should do it.

He entered fully and saw Tess and Anna gathered around a figure slumped against the back wall. Judging by the state of him and the blood puddles on the floor, Death might have been lying about his last statement. If still working, this could indeed have been a scene he would visit. At least he knew he was not responsible for it this time.

The man's face was paler than his own. He was also gaunt and looked like he had not eaten in a couple of days. It did not look good. Despite this the man was smiling and he extended a hand in friendly greeting upon seeing Death.

"Hey there pal. The name's Jerry."

He took the icy hand and shook it whole-heartedly. Jerry had a twang to his voice. He was an American, which explained all the guns he supposed.

"This is my buddy Tess." He said, ruffling her fur lovingly. "And this little lady here is Anna if she didn't introduce herself."

He coughed hoarsely.

"We have met." Death said, looking to Anna with a nod. She nodded back accordingly in a business-like fashion.

"She usually don't say much, 'part from to Tess here. But when she came in just now, she was flapping her gums about ya more than anything I have heard since ma' here girl brought her in a few days ago."

Anna looked up at him and shrugged. The man coughed again. Tess gave him a look full of concern that he did not think she was capable of doing. This was not because she was a dog, but because of her general demeanour.

"I think she must've been living in the local area." He said through short breath. "Tess must've run into her on one of her scavenger missions. I ain't been up to it as of late."

He gestured to his crumpled state, highlighting what was already apparent.

"I see. Well, you seem in good spirits at least." Death said, trying to keep up with the light casual tone the man had set.

Jerry let out a wheeze. He thought it might have intended to be a laugh of accord.

"Y'all gotta be in these times doncha? So, what about you then fella? Seems like what with you being Death it would be a busy period for ya? Kinda like Christmas for Santa ya know?"

Death felt forlorn, saddened not only by the comparison, but also by the knowledge that Santa Claus did not really exist. He was only an amalgamation of different beliefs from various cultures and nothing like the very real figure of the grim reaper standing before him. He could not tell a dying man this though, it would not be right.

"You would think. But no, I find myself unoccupied these

days." He sighed, trying to remain cordial. He perked up a little. "As such I can volunteer my services to help you in any way I can!"

"Well, that's mighty kind of ya." Jerry coughed. "I reckon I could definitely use all the help I can get."

Death already decided he liked Jerry, he hoped he would be around for a while.

"Anna, could y'all take Tess to get some water please? All this excitement must have tuckered her out." Jerry said keeping up his wheezing, smiling demeanour.

The girl gave a curt head nod and led her out of the room, smiling at him as she left. She was definitely at least somewhat detached from reality. But Death knew there was a lot going on inside her head.

As for Tess, she also looked up at him. Then she looked to Jerry, and then back at him. Her eyes narrowed. She reluctantly followed the girl out of the room, the message being sent.

When they were alone Jerry beckoned Death closer.

"Alright, now the little-un's gone we can really talk. Man-to-man so to speak."

His tone shifted. Not unfriendly, only more serious.

"I have a favour to ask...In case I don't come out of this alright." He gave another cough signifying this could very much be the case. "Tess and Anna 'been taking care of me something fierce...I'd hate to not be able to repay the favour."

The confident facade fell for a second and the American's plucky demeanour gave way to a fearful spluttering.

"I may...I may need you to look after 'em when I'm gone. I don't know much 'bout the whole Death thing...but...but...you certainly are an imposing fella...I reckon that will help them if they gotta go at it without me for a'while."

Death was hit with mixed emotions. On the one hand this was a very flattering request. He was not exactly used to being asked to take care of life instead of snuffing it out. On the other he was looking for companionship, but this was like becoming a foster father. He did not know if he was equipped for the job.

Several potential eventualities flashed into his brain. Key milestones of a developing lady so to speak, how would he deal with any of them? Especially now?!

Yet Death could not refuse the request of a dying man. It was not exactly a code, but a practice he became accustomed to. It had been another reason he stopped appearing to people before they died. There was less chance for being tasked with a possibly daunting earthbound errand.

There were several accounts on this that existed. Some fictional, others told by those who actually used the method to temporarily escape their fate. Word got out and the procedure became far too commonplace, people were challenging him to games of chess or some such thing. Despite numerous claims, he was not the crack chess player he was made out to be.

This had led to a few embarrassing occurrences, so in the end he decided it was best to avoid the possibility altogether. The undue hassle of being entered into contests he had little idea of the rules on was too much. Plus, Death had little way of knowing when he was being cheated.

Above this concern however there was also the inevitable inconvenience of having to come back round to the person in short order. The unknown forces in charge of his employment were clearly not fans of the practice. After reluctantly agreeing to a bargain and then coming through on the reprieve, the soul in question would without fail meet with a far grizzlier end.

While he was not privy to the designs of life, it was clear that it could not be truly deviated from. No matter how clever, worthy, or conniving a person was, they could not escape their fate. There was a bottom line somewhere and it was not worth messing with in the long run.

All this meant it made sense to avoid the circumstances. It was much easier to deny a soul once they already passed. He was just doing his job after all and there was nothing to barter over anymore.

He was dealing with living people again now though and the habit was still in the back of his mind. Plus, this request was a lot nobler and less problematic than any bargain to save skin. Jerry wanted him to look after those he left behind, how could Death deny that? He did not even have his responsibilities in his role as Grim Reaper to fall back on.

"I understand Jerry. I will endeavour to do so if the event arises. I certainly hope you pull through." He said in the end, it was the only thing he could do really.

"Me too." Jerry smiled, and then he died.

Well, that was disappointing.

He found himself in another compromising position, left alone in a room with a man who passed. It would be suspicious for any new addition. Let alone someone with a name acting as a flashing arrow saying: "he is responsible for this!"

Just once he would like to not be the one around for this. There was not even a soul to guide here, concerning from both a personal and professional standpoint. When a vet had to stick their arm into a cow's anus there was usually a calf at the other end. If not, it was all just a bit shitty.

He knew Tess was going to come in to see her master and immediately blame him. How would Anna take this? Before she seemed to have warmed up to him. How long would that last now it looked like he killed the only adult she had contact with for what appeared to be quite a while. It was an all-around bad scene.

A banging from outside stopped his deliberations. Death decided it was a good time to make himself scarce, so he went to check what it was. Stepping out of the office, he realised the noise was not only coming from one source. It was coming from all over, echoing throughout the shop.

The metal shutters at the front were being pounded and the sound was intensifying. It was a mob, not some desperate individual. Death did not want to risk phasing into a bunch of bodies, living or dead. Who knew what the outcome would be? Instead, he looked for the way Anna and Tess had come into the shop when they arrived.

He could not see either child or dog and wondered where

they could have gone. He called out but there was no reply, this was starting to get frantic. There was no time to wait.

***

In all the commotion Steve had missed where Death went off to. Leaving the scene may have been the best course of action, but he didn't expect him to disappear completely. He hoped he was alright, however he had more pressing issues to deal with. Namely, what to do with Michael before it was too late.

He knew enough about this type of scenario from films to know that a recently dead man in an enclosed space is a recipe for disaster. Bringing this up to Michael's distressed daughters was another matter. He could not exactly say "Come on girls, I know you just saw your father die but we have to toss him over the barrier pronto!" Well, he could. He did not think it would go down too well though.

As a rule, he took a backseat in situations like this. He felt like he could generally manage things if the need arose, still if someone else could handle it instead that would be great. He saw that Jenny and Dave looked as lost as he was. Damn it.

Every second ticking by was a chance the old newsagent would rise from his supine position and take a bite out of one of the girls seated either side of him sobbing. Who knew where things would escalate from there? His thoughts compelled him to take charge. Yet he was frozen, paralysed with indecision.

While this drew on, the younger of the two sisters gave a sniff of finality and wiped her eyes.

"Come on Lucy." She choked. "We have to get rid of him."

Her sister looked like she had been struck.

"What?! No!" She flung her arms around the corpse and cried. "He's my dad! We're not going to do anything to him!"

Joyce touched Lucy's arm like she was radioactive.

"Do I really have to tell you why we need to move him?"

The calm tone gave Lucy pause. Her face wore conflicting emotions, her mind at war with itself. She sat up, then looked

142

down at her dad. Her lips scrunched up and her eyes squinted as if having to bite on something exceedingly bitter.

"I…I…I suppose I have to do what's needed…to keep you safe." She conceded.

Joyce now wore the same look of swallowing something distasteful for the greater good.

"Yeah, I need your help right now to keep me safe."

The two locked eyes in understanding. They chose to not fall apart. Lucy turned to the others.

"Can I please have some help getting my father into the bathroom?"

Steve thought to question this decision but bit his tongue. The bathroom was better than nothing. This could easily be one of those times where an error could prove fatal. It was hard to hold a completely logical stance on the matter when all these emotions were flying about.

They gathered round the prone body and helped the girls with the heavy load. Steve grabbed a leg, taking the lead. Jenny hoisted the other leg with a grunt after giving a silent glance of acknowledgement to him. He wondered if like him, part of the reason she took this position was so they could be as far away from that slobber-lined mouth as possible.

There was being helpful and then there was being stupid.

The girls had his shoulders and were gritting their teeth in determination and grief. They knew what they had to do but it didn't take away from the pain they felt. The physical weight of their father was nearly as much of a burden as the emotional. Steve kept this thought to himself.

Dave was the odd man out. Having to keep repositioning himself in the middle, partly shouldering the weight, but mostly trying to look busy and like he was helping. Steve experienced the same thing when required to help someone move, he was glad he had a dedicated leg. No one liked holding the middle of a sofa.

Together they managed to get Michael into the bathroom with only minor fuss. Steve wasn't sure what the plan was after that. Still, he felt better for shutting the door behind him.

Joyce pragmatically suggested that they should take him outside and bury him as soon as they could. Lucy insisting that they wait since they had no idea how this whole thing worked. Jenny mediated the idea to wait until a grave was dug for him. For now, it was safer to keep him in a closed room no matter what happened. Lucy started to protest at the idea until Joyce stated plainly that she already lost one member of her family today and she didn't want to risk losing another.

This all made sense to Steve. There was an argument for destroying the brain before he could even come back. But up to this point no one in the group had dealt with the reanimation process. He, Dave, and Jenny were all quite solitary people and Michael's family kept to themselves, so none of them had been there when a loved one died until now.

Whatever way you sliced it a botched job could cost them their lives. So, it was probably better to sit on it. Best to come back to it when they were more prepared.

It was certainly possible that without being bitten he was no threat. Steve could see how the girls wouldn't really want to bash his brains in unless it was absolutely necessary. Plus, even if this did mean dealing with a reanimated Michael, he wasn't all that spry in life. Could he really be that hard to handle as a lumbering corpse?

Perhaps this was wishful thinking. Whatever the case, he knew having Death on hand would have been useful. Steve had somewhat handled the shambles attacking Dave in the garden. But that was in the open, not an enclosed space like this.

Fundamentally, Death was always going to be the better prepared of the two, physically and mentally if Steve was being honest. He comforted himself in that he was arguably superior emotionally due to his general knowledge of human feelings. Although even here he held his own detachments.

The gardens themselves were another problem. First, the mysterious appearance of shambles out there was a worry. And second, everything was overgrown, and visibility was becoming an issue. A scythe wouldn't go amiss right now, also he needed to get his axe back. The whole thing was a bit of a headache.

He decided to make investigating and the cleaning up of the surrounding gardens his project in the following days. He dragged Dave along to help him out as well, because why not. After their tragedy, the girls moved their stuff to Jenny's place and set to digging a grave under her supervision. They chose to bury him in their own garden as they knew he would want to be close to his shop.

Dave filled his time playing look out with a cig on the go rather than doing any actual work. Steve wanted to grumble at this but was finding it harder to ignore the growing background noise of groaning from the surrounding streets. So, in the end maybe it was better to have someone watching out as he went about his tasks.

He knew the gates at the top of the street were secure no matter how many undead gathered outside. Steve made it with enough mass so that they required several people to open even when unbarred. This was something the others had complained about before they left. In his mind it was better to be safe than sorry. On the other hand, it was now impossible to open them for the remaining group. They had become more of a wall than an entrance.

There was a temptation to feel trapped. For one thing no vehicles could get through to rescue them if that ever occurred. Then again, there were always the side exits down the alleys at the other end of the street. However, outside of himself, it may be hard for the others to realise how to operate them despite the relatively rudimentary design.

It was a rope and pulley system, needing a strong grip to handle. It was inoperable by the living impaired outside of any possible mutations like what he thought he came across when he first saw Death. Overall things would have been easier if the reaper had stuck around, for him at least.

His mind kept buzzing with worries like this, but he tried to chalk it up to general paranoia. He calmed himself with the thought that he and the others were safe inside the street. Let the shambles waste their energies, he had to have confidence in his own efforts.

He'd clear up the gardens and figure out where they were able to get in from. The grave would be dug in a couple of days and then all they needed to worry about was moving Michael. He should check on him, but it would have to wait.

He took great pains to scope out each garden from above before venturing into them. He went methodically from Dave's upwards. To his surprise he found no sign of holes in the backs of any of them besides his own and Dave's. This was both good and annoying at the same time.

Steve planned to lay some mortar on the walls so the dips in each were smoothed out. Part of him also wanted to check the neighbouring gardens on the other side of the wall. But that was a big job and if there was a major gap it would need more than just him. Even with Dave's help it might not be enough to check them out properly.

He could hopefully ask the others when they were more up to it. He was leaving them to their business of digging. Steve designed his route so he would get to that garden last, hoping they would be done by then.

With Michael gone there was much less division between the group. They all came together each night at Jenny's place to cook and have a chat. It was nice, but he still felt a bit awkward around the girls.

In this time, he had gotten to know Jenny a lot better and what was fleeting glances were now becoming lingering stares. Any silences filled with intangible sentiments and their actual conversations alive with a noticeable spark. The others would share their own knowing looks between the chit-chatting and laughter, mostly Dave's. Conversations mainly concerned topics that were moot in this micro-world they built, but it served as a nice distraction.

Within the span of a few days the gardens were checked, and the grave was complete. There was no other busy work to prolong the inevitable now. Steve wished Michael was already in the ground. He did not have any attachment to the man, so he was simply an annoying obstacle to him.

In the back of his mind, he was waiting for Death to show back up to help him handle the situation but there had been no sign. He mostly understood the sudden exit. Still, it would have been nice if he told them where he was going at least. Even if it was only brief, his brush with Death was a big event and he felt a certain amount of attachment.

Steve was tempted to go looking for him, but that would have meant certain Death. He smiled at his shallow pun. It not the type of thing you said out loud, except maybe to the reaper himself.

It was something else to share his thoughts with someone like Dave. He would listen out of a general sense of loyalty, but not really understand much of what Steve was trying to get at. While his and Jenny's interactions were getting better, they did not mirror his actual stream of consciousness. Perhaps such a thing was not even ever possible.

There was a growing intimacy there. It was a stressful and tentative dance that threatened to give way to something more significant over time. Or else slip into nothingness if he put a foot wrong.

He was a bit confused by all these different types of social interactions. Steve was used to being direct with people, while keeping them at a distance. He still managed to maintain this demeanour with the two girls. Their age and outlooks created a comfortable chasm between them.

He realised though even this was a relationship he found pleasant, or at least something he was getting used to. He was developing an attachment to those around him. It was strange. Even now he chose to keep part of himself separate from them. His clinical thoughts wouldn't fly with anyone except someone equally as removed as he was, he believed.

These developing ties were what led him to volunteer to lead the expedition to investigate the bathroom when the time came. He told the girls to wait at the grave site so they didn't have to witness what might have to be done. They agreed with varying levels of reluctance. Dave and Jenny were supposed to be his back up, as well as for the inevitable burden they had to carry down the stairs when the job was done.

He had spared a thought to create a kind of rig to help get the body down. Unfortunately, Steve could not access the body beforehand to assess the state and heaviness of the load. Thus, doing so seemed too fraught with problems. If he couldn't do it right, he didn't want to make the attempt at all.

He was focused on the potential of a reanimated Michael. Being a generally fearful person, he prepared by scavenging all the protective gear he could find. This way if he was greeted by a slobbering shambles, he could still navigate the situation.

There would be no unprepared neck mauling for him. Nor any suspicious scrapes on the arm coming back to haunt them later. And most certainly no unintentional lip locking leading to them being torn off and spat out. This was his biggest fear.

He was decked head to toe in thick material. Wearing two turtlenecks owned by Jenny so they were super tight. One neck was folded over the other. On top of these he wore a buttoned-up shirt with a tie secured around the collar to keep everything in place. He then duct-taped an old riding helmet of hers over this neck protection and was wearing three of those face mask things underneath for good measure.

He had gone further and fixed a pair of Dave's swimming goggles to his eyes, with a pair of reading glasses over that. He had also shoved a pair of oven mitts over his sleeves and got the others to duct-tape those together. As a final touch, as well as two pairs of pyjama trousers for padding, he strapped on a pair of his own old work overalls. These were all tucked into his work boots with some old cricketing knee protectors he found in his closet attached for good measure.

He felt like Batman. He looked like a deformed turtle. And he smelt like a sweaty man under a ridiculous amount of ratty old clothing.

It was true he had almost zero neck movement and could barely breathe, but he was willing to compromise dexterity and fresh oxygen for safety. This wasn't how he had first envisioned things. There was a slightly unfortunate caveat in that the girls asked him to do as little damage to their father as possible.

Steve's initial strategy was clear in his mind. He wanted to burst in and deliver a series of heavy blows to the head as fast as possible, then quickly run away. It was the same approach as he took to killing spiders. If you were swift enough and used a large flat object to squish them, there was no need to engage with the threat any further. The only nasty bit was afterwards when looking to confirm the presence of a mangled and lifeless corpse.

His intuition told him the girls wouldn't like this approach. Besides, finding an object big enough to smoosh Michael's body whole seemed quite unreasonable. What's more he didn't think anyone would forgive him for the mess it would create even if such a thing did exist. So instead, he had to opt for caution and care over swift and efficient violence.

Still, Steve was not a fool. He retrieved and armed himself with his axe for the occasion and was hoping to blast the door open and score a direct hit to the top of the cranium of a prone body upon entry. The plan was for the whole thing to be as safe and painless as possible, mostly for him.

He approached the door decked in his apocalyptic fashion statement, axe in hand. It was a struggle, but he had managed to get a grip on the handle. He called out to Jenny and Dave to make sure they were ready. His outfit meant he could not really hear or look behind him to check on them. He heard a muffled response from behind him and took it as a sign to proceed.

Stretching out his gloved hand he tried to silently unclick the lock. It was like trying to thread a needle underwater. His mitted paw served to only jiggle the knob.

The noise set off a scuffling from inside. While Steve did partially hear this, it was obscured by other noises behind him. This was possibly a warning. Instead, it served as a distraction.

It was too late. The lock had clicked open in his continued

fumbling and a rush of adrenaline pushed him to press on. This proved to be another problem as despite his initial grip, his mitt slipped off the handle as the door opened.

Then it was a scramble. His mind raced as to whether he wanted to try again to fully open or try to close the door so he could compose himself. He could not decide. He leaned in to try to find a better angle, the noises from behind the door getting louder all the time.

He finally heard them clearly and jerked himself back. He overbalanced. Another slip on the handle as he tried to correct himself caused the door to give way and swing wide open as his weight fell against it.

The next moments were a blur.

He sprawled onto the hard tile floor.

The wind knocked was out of him.

A pain in his back, he had fallen on his keys.

A persistent wheezing came from somewhere above him.

A ringing in Steve's ears made the distance hard to gauge.

A faint buzzing sense of danger made him think it was not a good idea to be lying prone on the ground right now.

Steve struggled to get up as a shadow fell over him.

A tremendous weight was suddenly on his legs. He kicked and a feeling of lightness appeared before the mass came back. Heavier this time. Steve continued striking with abandon at the bulky encumbrance. It started to feel like being trapped on an upside-down bouncy castle.

He shook his head to unscramble his brains. The reading glasses flew off in the process and the drooling figure of corpse Michael became clear. It clawed at his padded legs, making his way up towards his torso. The gaping maw of the dead thing snapped at him with a vicious hunger.

Steve let out a guttural yell of protest at the sight, but it was muffled by his own mouth protection. He needed help. His oven-mitted hands searched for something to use as a weapon, but nothing came to hand. His axe must have gone flying when he did.

His goggles were starting to fog. A dread settled over him and he almost surrendered to it before finding a second wind. He fought against the Michael thing, stronger than before. He managed to get free by booting and rolling until he was side to side with the deadly behemoth.

He felt like he was looking into the face of consumption. In response he began pushing at that mug. Steve was thankful he was so bundled up. If he was to become the thing's dinner it would take a while to unwrap.

He kept the snapping jaws at bay as he tried to gain some distance on the tile floor. At one point his hand was completely inside the slobbering mouth. Luckily his mitts were safe, even if they got him into this mess in the first place.

Corpse Michael instinctually bit down and sank his teeth into the thick material. It felt like his hand was in a vice, even if there was no chance of the skin breaking. Steve braced himself on the bloated belly with his legs and other arm. He began to pull, wrenching his hand free and taking a couple of the ghoul's teeth with him as he did so.

Dislodging from this blockage made the mitt come loose. He took the opportunity to pull the thing off completely. Right hand now free, he made moves to get to his feet.

In his frantic escape he slipped again and ended up in the bath, knocking the precariously hanging shower attachment as he did so. The monster reared up as the metal head fell on the back of his skull.

The padding provided by the riding helmet let Steve keep his wits about him. He grabbed the offensive implement with his free hand and desperately turned the taps behind him with his other mitt. The water came in a fierce spurt. It sprayed into the cavernous mouth like it was a grotesque fairground clown.

The effect was purely aesthetic however and did nothing to stop the oncoming charge. Steve was not sure what he had been expecting. Maybe for the sudden pressure to force them back, or else the strange sensation to distract Corpse Michael long enough for him to get away. In his wildest dreams he could imagine the rotting thing melting away like the wicked witch of the west.

Instead, the stream of water did nothing except turn the ravenous groans into more of a peckish gargle. It would have been comical if his life was not on the line. Steve could see the remaining teeth gnashing at him as he struggled to breathe.

His head started to spin as he hyperventilated with all the stuff covering his face. Time slowed down. He swung the metal at the blurry mass. There was a solid connection and the shape fell back.

Steve's comprehensive face covering was causing him too much trouble. With all the exertion he was liable to pass out if he didn't do something quickly. He ripped at his facemasks and ended up tearing the whole of his head protection off.

With the sudden intake of air, he let out a guttural shout, if slightly high-pitched. Primal aggression took over and he dove forward. He beat into the forehead with the showerhead over and over. He didn't stop until there was nothing solid left.

Steve stood up, panting and exhausted but satisfied. His swimming goggles all steamed up. He couldn't tell what noises were Michael and what had been his own. It wasn't clear when the shell of the former Newsagent departed. The room covered in shards of bone and gore told a story with a definite finality. It was like ghastly confetti celebrating a job well done.

It was all a bit of a pain in the arse though as now he was faced with the dilemma of how to tell the girls things had not gone to plan. They probably wouldn't understand that he was alone and fighting for his life at the time. Speaking of which, he had no idea where Dave and Jenny had buggered off to.

They should have been there to help from the second he slipped on the handle. Maybe the whole situation freaked them out and they just ran. That would be a pretty crappy thing to do if that was the case. This is why you didn't rely on people.

If he was someone who laid there waiting to be rescued, he would have ended up being Michael's first post-death meal. He wanted to believe trusting others was the way forward. But at some point they let you down. Going all in on people was not necessarily the best option.

Whatever the case, he was alive. Clothes covered in gore and a bit banged up, but still breathing. Thinking about it, Jenny and Dave must have a good reason for abandoning him. They clearly weren't anywhere in the apartment, so at least weren't simply stood watching. There would have to be words though. He hoped his inner politeness didn't take over when the time came.

It was hard to truly tell people how you felt, especially if they acknowledge what they did was wrong beforehand. It was the worst thing. If someone let you down, you could have a go at them. If they apologised to you directly it was hard to press on. Instead, you often found yourself saying "it's alright" even if it really wasn't.

The funny thing was that society will always tell you that apologising is the right thing to do when you wrong someone. It's framed as if you are giving something up. Rather, frequently this was the best way to negotiate out of a tight spot without suffering any real repercussions. The number of heinous things people must have gotten away with because they came clean was astronomical.

We're supposed to believe denial is the best policy, but regularly it will come back to bite you. It's almost always better when doing wrong to say nothing at the time, then wait until the heat dies down and come clean. This way most people will let it go and anyone who doesn't is accusable of being petty or overreacting.

Steve knew the rules. He did not exactly like them. Life, it was a problem, also death to be fair.

He looked down at the mess. On the plus side, he was in the perfect place to clean up. So, it wasn't all bad.

CHAPTER NINE

Death was not doing well. Another individual had passed right after meeting him. This did not look good and left him with the worry of Jerry reanimating in the enclosed space. Not only that, now there was an apparent hoard outside the building.

He worried that they were drawn to him like before. Last time the undead had treated him with indifference. This might have changed and now he was acting as a beacon, dooming any group unlucky enough to encounter him to be swallowed up by the shambling masses.

Or it was a coincidence, who could say?

With all the commotion, Anna and Tess must have found somewhere to hide. He doubted they would have gone outside while he was alone with their friend. At least it meant he could deal with this without having to worry about them.

He needed to investigate outside, if nothing more than to stop the incessant banging so he could think clearly. Fearing the results of phasing, he had rooted around for the hole Anna and Tess had gotten in through. He found that crawling through the tunnel with his massive frame was almost impossible. He went in bare handed and crossed his stony grey fingers that he could summon the scythe back once outside.

Luckily the natural strength of his form meant he did not need much space to utilise his muscles in moving forward. The level of force he could exert with even his fingertips was huge. He tried to focus on making the rest of his bulky body soft and malleable. While it was hard to visualise properly, it must have been working as the progress was steady. He still had a burning in his feet, a concern that would have to be addressed later.

Death reached the end of the line, popping the grate off the opening as he did. He could finally stand up in the open air. He had not seen any movement directly ahead of him when he was in the tunnel, so he took the chance that the entrance was clear. Being that there was not anyone in his immediate sight he took a second to put himself back together.

He pondered over whether to try to conjure up his scythe right now. It was certainly a useful tool, but it had also caused him a lot of trouble. He decided against it since he was not sure what was waiting for him. The last thing he wanted was to be responsible for the accidental killing of yet another human.

The grim reaper carefully made his way to the front of the store. He peered around the corner, keeping close to the wall. What he saw was pretty much a scene from any zombie movie, not that he held an extensive knowledge of the subject.

It could be worse. Still, they might be shambolic but there were enough of them where it would not be a good idea to let them cluster like this. Even if Death himself was safe, there was a very real possibility that Tess and Anna would not be. Plus, he needed to find a way to dispose of Jerry's body. Being unsure about his ability to phase, he did not fancy attempting to take someone else along for the ride.

Rather than risk the potential molecular complications, it would be much easier if he could open the front shutters and walk out with the body once all the walking corpses were clear. He wondered if he could lead them away by manipulating their simple cognition. Or else use his strength to just toss them out of sight.

He took steps towards them, but before he got too close the lurching horde turned and came at him. This time there was more than a strange admiration in their eyes. They looked like they positively wanted to devour him.

One was on him before he could think to react. Gnarled fingers hooked onto Death's robe, encumbering his movement.

The grasping hands tried to navigate the twists and folds. The confusion bought him some time. Still, every second he spent in this embrace let the others come ever closer and that could be a problem.

He brought a fist straight up and through the thing's jaw, turning it from gaping to folded in on itself. The head flopped back, skull touching shoulder blades. Any muscles once holding it in place now stretched beyond any use.

The body would not let go of his robes though. It stuck on to him like a stubborn piece of sticky tape refusing to do its job. The number of fatalities that had been caused by disobedient adhesives was astounding.

The rest of the pack was closing in. Rather than panicking, Death took a second to clear his mind and imagined the flowing folds becoming liquid. The material responded and the hands of the undead slipped away as if they were clutching at a jet-black stream.

The stubborn corpse fell into his hard body. It was not a kind reception. He met the visitor with a resounding knee that rocketed into its chest and sent it flying in the other direction. With a stroke of luck, and a pinch of calculation, it collided with a few of the other zombies coming towards him. This cleared a path for him to get a little more space.

This breathing room allowed Death to conjure his scythe. Despite his earlier hesitations he felt better with the weapon in hand. He was quite interested in the manipulation of his robes and wanted to test them out. However, he thought best not to chance taking on this many opponents with experimentation. Better to keep a distance and hack at them safely.

As you might guess, despite being a passive observer, he had several lifetimes worth of deadly combat knowledge. While only recently being called to put this into practice, he held an intimate understanding of how to efficiently disable a body. He just needed the composure and drive to put this skill to use.

The nearest dead thing came at him, and he took its head off with a clean strike. He then shifted the angle of the blade so on the upstroke he cleaved the next one in two. The separated body hung there for a second before dropping with a satisfying squelch. There were about a dozen left advancing. Clawing and gnashing all the way.

The reaper repositioned and readied to execute the same routine again. The head of the next came off swiftly. However, on the one after rather than going straight through, his blade caught on some cobbled together armour. Obviously, it did not work while the person had been alive, still it certainly was an obstacle now.

He might have been able to manipulate his own clothing. The former persons makeshift shoulder protection was another matter. He tried to work the blade free as the torso attempted to grab him, despite now being almost entirely split diagonally. Death's efforts served to exacerbate this situation and the thing became a ghoulish piñata, spilling out more innards with every shake.

His scythe finally came free when he pulled it through the maze of guts running onto the pavement. The remaining parts began to plummet. With little ceremony they received a swift kick. His powerful left leg sent the husk flying off to who knows where.

Death was starting to worry that he was enjoying all this dismemberment a little too much. He needed to remember to maintain efficiency. He had thousands of years of detachment to draw from, despite this there was something visceral about all this carnage.

He did not want to become a savage. He needed to avoid being overwhelmed. Three had gotten in close and he did not have the distance needed to effectively cut them down.

Two were to his left and one was on his right. He hit the one on the right with a hard elbow to the face. His stony skin caved in the thing's fragile visage. Jagged shards of skull tried to dig their way in to his flesh and Death's mind started to race.

He thought to thicken his robe on his arm to ensure that the epidermal layer below remained intact. When this worked, he was pretty pleased with himself. Until he considered that he could have just made the cloak this hard to begin with and not risked any potential penetration from the blow.

Also, he could have gotten out of that situation before by making his scythe incorporeal. He needed to be more mindful. He would not have had to struggle to wrench it free when it got stuck in the first place. The notion was annoying.

He comforted himself by thinking about how his powers were faulty. He should not rely on them. This too was annoying.

He hit the two to his left with a sharp blow from the top of his scythe, the impact felt good as their heads rocketed back. The force knocked them to the ground, although they would no doubt be back up. In the meantime, he shoved off the shell to his right so he could have full range of movement again.

In a blink he imagined the soles of his feet being hard as granite and gave a mighty leap, connecting with the two heads. He was expecting a sickening crunch, but instead it was flesh on flesh, slippery and wet. This gave way to hard bone threatening to break skin.

He slid on the gore and ended up falling over backwards in a mess of robes and scythe. This had happened far too often. Sprawled on the ground and covered in blood he spent a few seconds staring at a spiralling sky before looking down towards his feet. They were covered in a thick brown slime and multiple cuts. There were several splinters of bone poking out in various places as well. It was gross.

This was the inconsistency Death was worried about. The manipulation of the robe might have been fine, but his feet had not solidified in the same way. He wanted something akin to a brick and what he got was more like jelly.

He took a second to pull out the large pieces. The wounds looked like they were sealing up so that was something at least. Although, it was not lightning fast like it had been several days ago. At least he should not have trouble walking like he would if the wounds had not healed at all.

More worryingly, if a bite was enough to infect a person

there was a chance that he too was now contaminated. It could have little to no effect. Or maybe somehow affect him worse.

What if the infection rotted into his brain and he became a slow-moving vegetable? Or what if he remained the same but began to crave human flesh, becoming a sort of super zombie? Would he be able to control the undead then, rather than the looks of admiration that turned to indifference and at this point aggression?

He did not have the time to further ponder. There were still several of the undead he would need to dispatch before he was safe. He had some trouble standing and there were four of a remaining seven closing in. He steadied himself for his grim work. It was getting less enjoyable now.

He went to one knee and swept his scythe across the legs of the line of ghouls. It was as he uncorked several sewer pipes as toxic liquid flowed out of the gashes and the four collapsed. He thought it would buy him some time, but somehow the lack of lower limbs did little to deter the writhing pile. They climbed over each other in a tangle of teeth and greedy hands.

He went to kick one and hesitated, unsure about using his still tender bare feet to deliver the blow. He thought for once in his existence he should have a kind of foot covering. For some reason all that came to mind was the ancient Japanese sandals with two wooden blocks on the bottom. With a little focus the Geta appeared on his feet. The next moment wood connected with cranium, it exploded.

Why did he have such control over manifesting inanimate objects, yet he was becoming so physiologically challenged? He would have expected it to be the other way around. Maybe his internal shifting feelings were being projected, in which case he should be careful when relying on anything that was not a solid object.

He affirmed his position by using the Geta to crack open the skull of another ghoul crawling towards him. If he could feel the wood beneath his feet, he felt he could trust in their ability. He hoped this was a sturdy hypothesis.

He booted the next nearest one in the side of the head to much the same effect. The last slithering corpse snapped at his ankles. Death glared at the biting thing with such intensity that its brain appeared to boil inside its head. Eyeballs popped and sizzled. It slumped on the ground, utterly destroyed.

Well, he had no idea he could do that! Paranoia gripped him. He would have to be very careful about how he looked at people in the future.

He would not want to commit a social faux pas in polite company when someone said something to cause such a glare. It is one thing to return a rude comment with a snappy retort, or stern stare. However, to melt the offender's head like a knob of butter in a hot pan would be seen as an over-reaction.

There was now room to experiment with only a few of the shambles left. Death looked intensely at one of the three remaining shuffling towards him. Nothing happened. This could be a distance issue, or else a recharge time, or maybe the right mindfulness. He had no idea.

More inconsistency. More confusion. Apparently, nothing he did could truly be counted on.

There was a scream from inside the shop. No more time for sullen contemplation. He dispatched the last three in quick fashion with beheading strokes since they were all spaced out nicely. Better to focus on immediate concerns rather than dwell on what he could not control.

Now the undead were cleared from the front, he went to raise the shutters. Death thought better of it when he saw the padlock at the bottom of the metal. He had no key and did not want to break the lock, or the glass for that matter. It would be foolish to compromise the integrity of the store in a temporary panic. Also, such wanton vandalism did not feel right. It looked like crawling was the only option once again.

He rushed round to the opening, discarding his scythe as he did so. His robe made the crawl slow going so he reduced its size, partially as a test and partly for convenience. He did not think of the risk of the material shrinking to a ridiculous degree and trapping him in the tight space until already through.

He breathed a sigh of relief as he went towards the back of the shop, where the commotion must have happened. When he got to the doorway, he saw why the scream occurred. It was Jerry and the inevitable.

Transformed from a nice wheezing wounded to a snarling predatory creature, it was dragging itself to its feet by pushing itself up against the wall. Advancing into the room, Death could see a frightened Anna cowering in the far corner. Tess stood in front of her yet was clearly confused by how to react to her former master in this state.

It was a complex situation that would only become more complicated the longer he hesitated. He made things simple by barging the Jerry-corpse into a set of shelves. He yelled for the two to leave as he began tussling with the spindly zombie.

The struggle was pantomime. Jerry was not really causing Death that much trouble. Instead, he was buying time for the others while padding down the former shop owner as he kept him at bay.

His reasoning was correct, and he heard a jangle from the ghoul's right trouser pocket. Now he knew where the keys to the front were, the only problem was getting him outside. He needed to get the post-Jerry past Anna and Tess without too much further distress. Beheading was not the way to go in this case. Moreover, his scythe was outside, and besides he was still trying not to wield it around the pair if he could help it.

Death thought about trying out one of the many hunting rifles in the shop. The noise alone made it a bad option. The last thing they needed was for another group of groaners to come sauntering up to the shop expecting to be fed. He could have tried one of the instruments along the wall, the possible sound created remained an obstacle. Besides, he never really did have any knack with that sort of thing.

In the end he went for the blunt force trauma option. He pushed back deceased Jerry, and then whacked him with both hands directly to the temples. That was all it took. The powerful and precise blows scrambled his zombie brain enough to shut it down completely.

This felt like an honourable send off. Jerry seemed like a good-natured fellow. It was only fair to not have his body parts dismembered all over his own store. He reflected on how every member of the undead was once a person, and who was to say they were not all as decent.

Death was so conflicted these days.

It took some nuance to get Jerry out of the office without any interference from Tess. Eventually she came round to the idea of him being moved when the reaper offered to bury him behind the shop. Surprisingly she understood the concept and approved.

With his immense strength it did not take him long. It felt good to work with the dirt. To put someone to rest by physical means rather than at the behest of an anonymous entity to go to a potentially spurious afterlife. It was the right thing to do.

After this he set to disposing of the other bodies littering the outside. Although this time he used the skip at the side of the building. There was not all that much soil to go about and using a mass grave felt worse. Plus, he could not have buried them all individually because there was no way to distinguish one body part from another due to all the dismemberment.

He explored the rest of the shop, along with the dwellings upstairs. There was only one bedroom, and the conditions were not great, nor the food situation. The only thing going for them was the relatively remote location and the extensive stock of weapons, which Death did not prize too highly. The arsenal did nothing to help him when Anna started complaining about her tummy rumbling.

Tess became lethargic after the departure of her master. She ceased going out to look for supplies and he did not really have the nose for it himself. With no real way to communicate clearly, their relationship was built solely on mutual concern for Anna. She was now not willing to leave the girl for a second. This contributed to her no longer venturing outside, despite the potential overall hazard to the pair. Dogs may not be the best at long term thinking.

As the tins of food became fewer, Death thought of Steve and the people on the street. While socially separated, they did not seem to have been wanting for cuisine. He remembered his walk of shame through those isles, stocked to the brim. Maybe it would be worth taking another walk.

He took the opportunity of Tess barking at him while he investigated a virtually bare cupboard to suggest they relocate to somewhere with more supplies. Anna said nothing. He could sense a hesitance from Tess herself since she stopped berating him, for the moment at least.

Death considered leaving them behind while he travelled back to the street. But then he would be worried about them staying behind with no food. Further, no one would be there to help them if for some reason he was unable to return.

Having connections was hard. There were so many more concerns than he could comprehend before he started building these relationships. Mainly these involved people dying around him, but there were other problems too. Death supposed the general philosophy when it came to these social constructs was based on how one got more out of them than they put in.

It was difficult to weigh out. One concern appeared to be replaced by another: loneliness for worry, feelings of isolation for hesitance of social actions. Death was unsure he was getting as much satisfaction out of the interactions as they were costly, to his ego at least, if not his sense of self.

Then again there was at least a sense of progress here. In the past few days Tess even started to warm up to him. She no longer kept her eyes on him when he entered a room. She did not even growl when Anna came up to him. As for the little girl, she had adopted him into her life fully.

There was no hesitation on her part when it came to the shade of his skin or classical stature. He appreciated this lack of judgement but was also aware this might have a lot to do with her age. Still, it made him feel welcome, and that was what he had been looking for after all.

Certainly, he would be sad if either of them starved. What if they were overrun? He also shared these concerns regarding the street he had to depart so quickly.

For all he knew these were the only humans left alive, so it was important they stayed living. He wished he could sense them. Unfortunately, this was something he did not seem to be able to do now. Either that or they were already dead.

Death could not afford another fatality on his conscience. He could not even give up and become non-corporeal again. He had people depending on him now, so at this point inaction felt like a purposeful negligence of duty.

He had no choice but to make things work for all of them. There were risks involved in the journey. To avoid this as much as possible he needed to be forward thinking and courageous. It was a chore, but it was part of the life he wanted.

This new outlook made some of the apparently needless deaths he witnessed over the centuries make a bit more sense. Before he could not see why humans would put themselves in hazardous position for those most likely beyond saving. Now he understood the equation a bit more. Life was full of stakes and peril. Otherwise, it was not really living.

***

Steve did not appreciate all this risk. He had come round from his former optimism. Now annoyed by continued absence from the people he thought he could rely on. The cleaning up alone was something he wanted help with, not to mention the literal bloodbath that had gone before it.

He created this sanctuary for the people around him. Not for any need for social company, but so they could all feel safe. He shouldn't have to be tangling with an obese festering corpse without at least a little bit of backup. He was beginning to think he should have just hunkered down on his own and let the rest of the world be damned.

The logical part of his brain knew that this was not a good strategy. Without a way to acquire sufficient supplies or obtain any information about the outside world, you were sunk. There were too many outside factors that one person alone could not account for.

There was no point sheltering in a bunker if you could not know when it was safe to come out. You might as well build a tomb for yourself and have done with it. It was impossible. You weren't secure in a remote location due to the lack of supplies. But a place with lots of resources would no doubt have a lot of people too, and people meant problems.

Basically, you needed to be an established farmer on your own island to have a proper shot at surviving. When things had gone down, Steve was logistically lacking in these departments. So, he worked with what he had available to him. Still though, it would have been good if the people he was left with could be a little more reliable.

He looked out the flat's front window. He could see quite a few shambles round the gates, but they seemed to be holding up alright. They should do, he built them.

Steve then went to the other window showing the rest of the street. The road was desolate. At least it had not become infested while he was distracted.

It would be more than a bit annoying if he were standing around being irritated about being left to his own peril, ignoring the danger others might be in. He heard a scream. Sod it!

Not knowing what to do he bolted out of the apartment and ran down the stairs. He burst out of the front door and was greeted by the still empty street. Any ability to quietly listen for any more clues as to where to go from here was drowned out by the sound of shambles.

His heart thumped, this only added to the distraction. The only thing he could hope for was another scream, and that was not something he should actively wait for. He decided to head through the shop and out the back to see if anyone was by the grave site.

He made his way through the stacked shelves and wished he appreciated chocolate and crisps more. Right now, he would give anything for a weapon or two. Some ammunition would be nice also, and steak, he missed steak.

Maybe he could have survived here on his own with these supplies. But he would have died of diabetes before too long. Michael was a fool, not to speak ill of the dead.

He passed through the back and glanced up the stairs to where the Newsagent laid in a pile of his own gore. No time to dwell. He did spare a look to the office door to the left of the staircase. How come this dwelling was bigger than every other one on the street?!

When he got to the garden, he saw the grave, shovels laid beside it and a homemade gravestone the girls had worked on. There was no one to be found. A rustling was coming from the other side of the back wall. To confirm this was the place to go there was another scream, this one slightly more masculine.

Steve sprinted across the garden, scooping up a shovel as he did so. His axe was still misplaced and there was no time to get it now. He leapt over the back wall into what could only be described as a shit show.

The garden was more overgrown than his own. Tangles of tall grass and weeds were intertwined with shards of timber, discarded appliances and multiple old bicycles. It looked like a massive dumping ground for the neighbourhood.

In the middle of this was Dave struggling with a shambles on a ratty old sofa. The wrestling duo was flanked by Jenny, one of the two girls and more than a few corpses scattered about. A little way removed from the scene was a prone figure, lying in a patch of grass covered in blood.

As bad as the scene was, they had been relatively lucky so far. Most of the shambles were held up by the general chaos of the garden, though they were getting closer with every second. Steve heard a rasping sound to the left of him and saw such an ensnared member of the undead clawing at him from behind a thicket. It was a good job the unkempt undergrowth was there, or he may have met his own sticky end in all the confusion.

He bashed at it with his shovel in agitation. The blow was mostly absorbed by the foliage and only served to dislodge it, forcing him into his own tussle. Fortunately, he still had most of his protective padding present. This gave him the time to push the gnashing carcass off him and deliver another blow. This hit splattered the mouldy head open to the grey sky above.

He heard a call from Jenny and made his way over, taking care to look out for other undead hidden in the dense jungle. He saw one getting close and gave it a swift clout to the side of the head, sending it down into the long grass. Steve drove the point of the shovel down hard into its skull, digging out a mix of brain matter and dirt below.

Another shambles got a kick to the knee, collapsing it. He didn't have time to finish it off. He hoped it was enough to give them some breathing room.

He reached the urgent scene and angled his shovel in an upwards arc reminiscent of his cricket days. He timed the swing just right to connect with full momentum to the zombie on top of Dave. Metal impacted rotted skin in a sickening 'thunk'. The head came right off and sailed some way across the garden.

Steve congratulated himself on his apparently latent skill. He definitely scored a cool six with that one. The decapitated body slumped on top of Dave and coarse black bile flowed out of the stump and onto his face.

That was not cool.

He choked on the vile liquid and threw up as he tried to shove the limp body off. By this time some shambles managed to get closer, and more were coming from some unseen place. Steve glanced around but couldn't figure out where their entry point was.

He had been so careful!

The figure on the floor began to stir. He hoped whichever one of the girls it was, was okay. He heard the other girl exclaim 'Joyce!', so it must be her then. Making the other one Lucy, he knew that at least. He saw Lucy rush towards her fallen sister and hesitated over whether to warn her about Joyce potentially being one of the undead.

He assumed she probably knew the risks and simply could not leave her sister. He understood this, but he wasn't about to throw himself into another dicey situation. He already had his own gamble to play. He shouted to Jenny for her to get Dave out of there as he attempted to cover their exit.

The whole idea bothered Steve to a degree. Somewhere in his brain there was a lecture about basic human decency and dynamics of bravery in the face of adversity. He tried to shut it out, but he could not. The situation seemed dire, and he could not abandon them when they needed him.

He wanted to rationalise his attachments to these people, they only ran so deep, and his survival was more important. He tried to decry them for whatever rash decisions had led to this predicament. What's more, not one of them appeared to have a weapon in hand despite the obvious danger.

It made little difference in the end. He was here, and they needed help. He was armed and able, they were not. It sucked, but it was life, and it was happening now.

Despite this, another hard truth was he could do nothing for the girls without dooming the rest of them. Unfortunately, they would just have to fend for themselves for now. Steve felt cold for this. It was hard to go against logical thinking when he was already being somewhat self-sacrificing risking his life for the others. He admittedly also had more of a vested interest in them as characters in his mind-play.

He called out and sprang into action, hoping they would be right behind him. He was going for space and distance rather than killing blows. He used his shovel to shove back the nearest shambles, clearing a path.

Jenny took Dave under the arms and dragged him off the sofa, using the decapitated corpse to cushion his fall. It was not a nice landing but there was little time to care. If they stayed in this garden much longer, they would all be dead.

Steve shielded Jenny as she struggled with the spluttering

Dave, who was starting to get his wits about him. He swept the legs out from an approaching shambles and clanged another on the side of the head, glancing behind him to check on the other two. They were nearly at the wall now and Dave was starting to move unassisted.

As for the girls it was hard to make out exactly what was going on. The movement of the three had attracted the ghouls who were not caught in the snares of the overgrown greenery. Still, the gap between them and a bunch of hungry corpses was getting thinner. In a few seconds there would not be anywhere for them to go.

He heard Dave and Jenny scrambling over the garden wall as he pushed back a couple of the closest undead. They were becoming one grey rotting mass at this point. She called out to him, and he trusted her enough to turn his back on the nearing horde.

He saw a hand offered from above the wall and he took it gladly. Steve spared one last glance back at the two girls. Their outlines were swallowed up by unfriendly hands before he was pulled to safety on the other side.

***

Death was walking with a purpose through the empty streets, Anna and Tess in tow. A day after he managed to pluck up the courage to ask them about leaving the shop, they had become much more receptive than expected. He had also noticed in this time that the shop name was actually a pun as he spotted an album cover with a similar title on one of the walls.

Anna said the place was starting to smell and being there was making Tess sad. There was no stubborn staying starving of hunger. Nor was the place overrun leading to a daring narrow escape. Thankfully, there was also no reluctant leaving the two behind to fend for themselves for the greater good.

Sometimes people just wanted to leave, even if the place felt familiar. Safety must come before sentimentality. Especially when what had originally made the place welcoming had gone, come back to life, and was now resting in a grave outside.

Body disposal was not really the job for a small girl and a dog. Admittedly Tess could have dug the hole for her master, it would have taken her a bit too long though. You could call this detached thinking morbid, but Death being Death did not really see it that way.

Despite obvious associations he had never really taken all that much interest in funerary rites. They were always changing with time and geographical location. Humans could not decide on one consistent way to bid farewell to their dead. Did it really matter how it was done in any one circumstance?

To Death if it was clean and did not garner any negative attention it was acceptable. Disposal should be more to do with the diseases that came with human remains, rather than ritual. Although, he could acknowledge some practices did serve both purposes.

However, so many corpses were littering the streets that there was little time for ceremony. He had not thought about it before. He was accustomed to things passing in and out of this world, but everything around him was rotting. The rubbish, the buildings, not to mention the undead. Even the sky seemed to be a decaying grey-brown right now.

His understanding of the human condition had improved. The several penetrating hits he had suffered added a physical vulnerability to his thought process. He was relatively sure that he was not about to get all snappy and crave human flesh. He still felt like himself, but also like he might come apart if he was not careful.

Whatever the case, the most important thing was to lead these precious souls somewhere secure. If something occurred with his mental state, they would need others to support them. He did not think Tess would agree. Then again, she was getting a bit less fierce now that her master had departed, and Anna needed her at full capacity now more than ever.

He worried he might be leading them to nowhere if the

street was overrun. If this were the case, he would just have to retake it. Faulty powers or no, he would do what it took to keep them safe.

He would give up his own existence for them if he had to. The thought of this was strange to Death, yet he knew it to be true. Despite knowing them a relatively short time he could not stand the thought of leaving them alone.

Due to circumstances beyond his control, he had become responsible for the lives of those around him. It was clear that the bonds you create with those you encounter become strong in desperate situations. He speculated this was due to creating an exaggerated responsibility through interaction in a constant state of danger.

Before this crisis, what you said and did could influence how people went about their lives, but only to a certain extent. There were so many other factors involved that you could only be partially responsible. Now the chance of a life ending due to your decisions was much higher, and so you had to care more. Or else you could act like an inhuman monster. Death was glad this was not the case for him, even though technically he could be described in those words.

When his main purpose was ferrying souls, he could not see how relationships held this much sway over someone. His only meetings were transitional, after their lives already ended. There was no responsibility to take on in this process.

He did not have any input on where or how they went. He just showed them the way. It was a lot easier, but also a lot less meaningful. Changes in circumstance brought things into focus. It was not only a job anymore.

Death started to notice some familiar houses. Even with the similar design of these terraced sprawls he could tell they were getting closer. Tess seemed strangely acquainted with the area as well. She was almost leading the way at this point.

They passed by the hodgepodge gates where he made his exit from the street. He probably should not have left at all, but at the time Death did not know how to react. Let alone how the others would treat him. Besides, he would have never run into Tess and Anna otherwise.

In this case Jerry would have still turned regardless. While Tess might have been able to fight him off, he was not sure that she would have been emotionally able to attack her master. So that probably would not have gone well for all involved.

That made Death glad things happened the way that they did. He hoped those on the street would be more receptive to him upon his return. He was beginning to realise he knew a lot less about how humans dealt with loss in the long term. Trying to recall exact details in his mind was like watching dozens of television screens all at once.

The information was present, but specifics were drowned out by the vast quantity of miscellaneous stimulus of thousands of years. The continuation of life never was his concern, and yet now it was so important. Especially since the deceased were no longer following the old set of rules.

Death peered above the gate to see if he could notice any movement. Maybe one of the girls would be watching from the window or something. Before he could get a good look though, Tess carried on down the road, Anna in tow.

Before he could say anything, several zombies in the front gardens started moaning and shuffling to meet her. He sprinted to catch up and got there just in time to cut the head off one who was about to bare down on them. He should not have let them get ahead of him in the first place and now they were in danger because of his hesitance.

The reaper would not let this stand. His scythe had come back to him on instinct. He was grateful for it.

He launched into a frenzy and cut down three clustering around the gate of the house Tess had run to. He stormed into the garden and slashed at anything in the relatively small space. His limbs were a blur and those who were in his proximity did not last long. He could not help wondering why so many were here, relative to how few scattered the surrounding streets.

Tess's continued barking drew his attention to something

that made at least some sense. In the corner of the garden was a passageway leading to a wooden door with an opening at the bottom. He saw in an invasive flash that before it had been big enough for a dog to squeeze through. It had now expanded so a crawling human would have a good chance of getting to the other side.

This in turn was no longer the case however as a rather large, bloated corpse was wedged firmly into the opening. The trousers of the former fellow had fallen so their backside was free for the world to see. He knew that posterior, it belonged to none other than Barry Williams.

CHAPTER TEN

A trail of guts smeared the opening that Barry had been trying to wiggle through. Unfortunately, this did not provide adequate lubricant. The chunky shambles just did not have the leverage or strength to force his way through.

He was caught, causing more damage to his already torn up body. Admittedly some of this tearing was Death's doing. He felt somewhat bad about this.

Barry must have been acting as a barrier to those in the garden when they arrived. A fleshy dam if you will. Once again, he came in handy even if he had not meant to. How they were going to get him out was another issue, it would be hard to free him without tearing him in two.

As he pondered this problem, Tess started sniffing around Barry and growling. Sensing he could in no way be a threat the canine left it at that. Anna stood beside Death and considered the marooned former man, seemingly not as scared of him as the others. It was hard not to look at that pinned down figure and regard it as anything but helpless. He was more of a threat to himself than anyone else.

An idea was knocking at Death's door, rather urgently and getting louder. While he was stuck in there, blocking a bunch of pests from climbing under, it did not mean others had not gone through beforehand. This was a problem.

Death was left with a dilemma, not wanting to take Anna and Tess into an obviously dangerous area. On the other hand, he needed to go and make sure those on the street were safe. He considered his position before a cry from the other side of the fence forced his hand.

These distractions happened too often. There was simply no time to truly weigh things up in the living world. One had to act before

Instinct took over and he ordered Tess to stay and guard Anna. He only hoped that she would not savage a prone Barry, who would have to wait until the potential peril had passed. As for himself, he was going to head right through the obstacle.

He approached the gate and straddled the bloated corpse as he prepared himself to phase through to the other side. He took a deep breath, closed his eyes, and leaned forward. There was a dull 'thunk' as his head hit the wood of the rickety garden door.

Nothing happened. His body remained fixed. He felt the vulnerability of his form as he stood there with his legs astride his undead friend. It was a compromising position.

Apparently, his luck had ran out completely and could no longer detach from his physical form. He had no idea what this meant for his other abilities, but he had to press on. Even if he could not become incorporeal or patch himself together after injury, people's lives were at stake.

He did not have time to try to fully detach Barry from his wooden prison to open the gate properly. Instead, he began to hack away at the thin door. His scythe felt steady enough in his hand and the wood chipped enough to create an opening from the top down so he could leap through.

He was somewhat frantic but tried to retain some control so that the effort would not further shred the ungainly undead. If he were a being of faith, he would have made signs to a god to beseech for luck and protection. In its place he simply took another deep breath and dived through into the garden. On the way his robe got caught on the splintered wood and ripped. He tried to summon some fabric to patch it up, but none was forth coming.

The reaper stood clutching his trusty scythe and surveyed the situation. It looked like everything he feared had come true and he was almost powerless. He was now only an immensely strong statuesque body, holding a reaping blade, with a burning determination to rescue his friends.

He saw a mass of vegetation and bodies, as well as what looked like the panicked figure of Steve. He tried to call out, but Steve jumped over the garden wall, disappearing from view. At least he was still alive. Death then saw two other non-shambles cowering on the other side of the sprawl of shuffling ghouls.

There was a moral quandary here. He could see Lucy was not looking towards the danger and instead turned away. Was she possibly acknowledging impending demise, surrendering to it? Was it right to meddle in something as human as this?

If she accepted her fate, should he stop it from coming to pass? Was that not as bad as being the cause? And perhaps he should let her save herself if the opportunity arose.

Death believed these to all be valid points, but in the end, he could not stand back and watch. Still, there was the problem that there was no time to cut down the ghouls in front of him. To save the girls he had to let go of the last piece of protection he possessed by dropping his scythe.

As the familiar tool fell to the ground it did not make an impact. It faded away into nothing. The former grim reaper did not witness this however as he was already making a dash for the fallen sisters. Although a part of him felt the loss.

He barrelled through the undead, scooping up the pair. If they wanted to chastise him for making the decision for them, they could do so later while still alive. The priority was to carry their burden for now.

The problem he faced, outside of the moral quandaries of the agency of those he wished to save, was that his hands were full. He already cleared a good number swarming towards them in his unarmed charge. However, this would not last too long. It looked like the path to the adjacent garden had been cleared somewhat, presumably by Steve.

He hoped there was a good reason for him leaving them behind. Maybe he had the same dilemma and decided on the alternative of letting them fend for themselves. He wondered if his friend could be that cold.

This did not sit right with Death. After all, why bother to fortify the entire street if he was only going to leave others to perish. The surrounding threat had become more apparent, but it had always been there.

It was another reason he needed to escape with Lucy and Joyce in tow. He would have to find out the answer. Otherwise, it would bother him highly.

With a relatively open path and time running out, Death settled on the strategy of breaking into a run before executing a flying leap over the garden wall. He could not gauge what the situation was on the other side, but he would have to trust that it was cleared for landing. Risks had to be taken, even when the outcome was uncertain. Especially in the case that alternative inaction would lead to disaster regardless.

He braced for the effort and then broke into a sprint. His huge thigh muscles bulged as he ran, the physical strain being noticeable but tolerable. Shutting out thoughts of surrounding zombies reaching out, he focused his energy into his legs as he prepared to leap. Death kept his eyes solely on the wall ahead, staying on the task at hand.

With a thought he was suddenly in the air. He feared that his physical being would not have enough power to clear the distance, especially with the added weight of the girls. He was pleasantly surprised when the gap between his feet and the ground seemed to be growing. This then turned to panic as he kept rising until he was well above the wall and still climbing.

Apparently he exerted too much force and now the scary part was going to be the landing. As he sailed over the mortar, he could see that the garden in front of him was at least clear. This eliminated one possible problem.

Now he just had to deposit them on the ground without incurring further injury to the girls or indeed himself. He could see a hole dug in the centre of the grass. It looked wide and deep enough to come down into successfully and hopefully the freshly disturbed earth would be sufficiently soft.

Death kicked at the air in an effort to control his descent. He managed to angle it so that he landed in the hole feet first, absorbing the impact before toppling over on his backside due to momentum and being top heavy. He lay in the dirt with his eyes towards the sky. Joyce and Lucy, clearly shaken, trembled in his gargantuan arms. But for the most part they were safe.

He felt himself losing consciousness, which was a strange concept for him. In his last thoughts he recognised he was lying in a freshly dug grave. Death laughed with a grim irony as the darkness swallowed him.

***

Steve rushed to catch up with Jenny supporting a spluttering Dave. Thankfully, this garden had remained free of shambles up to now. The nightmare on the other side would not stay there forever. He ushered the two into the house slamming the door behind them. A paranoid Michael had installed a fire door, so they were protected while it remained bolted.

He tried to shut out all that he had seen and done in the last half hour. He couldn't. It was all so looming and present in his mind.

Even the thought that this was Michael's house reminded him of the girls. How he left them. How they might be dead. He hated it but could not fathom what he could have done to save them.

There was no way they could have all made it out of there without some kind of inhuman effort. They could not even turn round all tooled up and mount a rescue. Dave was in no state and they had little to no gear to tool up with any way.

Then again, it's not as if any of them would have probably known how to use real offensive weaponry. It was very rare for anyone below a certain age to have even seen a real gun in the flesh. Outside of armed police or an upper-class shooting party in the country or something.

He was only about old enough to remember the ban and amnesty being put into place. He guessed Jenny might be just out of that age range. And, while Dave might have seen or even handled a gun, there was no way he could be trusted with one.

As with most things it was a question of the right hands. Of course, when it came to tools almost solely used for killing, the wrong hands were multiplied exponentially. It was a bit of a moot point. They had no access to any arms anyway.

He caught his breath against the backdoor, agonising over whether the shovel he still grasped could somehow be enough to save the girls. Was there still time? And what was that thud that came from somewhere outside?

Steve tried to tell himself that there was nothing he could do. Instead, he would check on his, hopefully, still living friend. Jenny had taken Dave upstairs and laid him in the armchair in the living room. He was mumbling and feverish.

Jenny gave him a look of sympathy and then unprovoked, hugged Steve. She sobbed into his arms. He held her there for a few seconds. He was helpless but tried to appear together.

He broke from her embrace and sat her down, still taken aback by the sudden show of emotion. He rested a hand on her shoulder in a gesture of comfort and asked her what happened. She began to pull herself together, glad to have something else to focus on.

"We were waiting in the hall, like we had discussed. Then, then there was a scream from outside. Me and Dave...Dave and I, rushed down to see. We saw...we heard...over the wall. There was...there was one of those things on top of Joyce. Lucy trying to pry it off." She stated, trying to remain coherent.

Steve remembered that he did in fact ask them to wait outside to back him up, rather than being in the flat with him. This probably was not the best strategy. But it wasn't the time to bring that up now.

"They must have...heard noises in the garden behind and gone to investigate. We came over to help. Suddenly so many." Jenny paused. "We did our best to fight them off, but we ended up surrounded. I'm pretty sure Joyce was bitten...And then you were there."

She looked at him dead in the eye. He could not read the look and pulled back. He was afraid she was about to hit him or something.

"Thank you for saving me. I thought I was going to die."

She broke into a sob again and wrapped her arms around him once more. Steve blushed. This was not the proper time to be getting these feelings.

He had known how to react to being thanked or praised. Instead, he was more the type to labour on in the background, satisfaction coming from knowledge of a job well done. He was never an attention seeker, or a 'go-getter' and it suited him. It also didn't make him all that appealing to most around him. It was undeniably part of why his fiancé had left.

Steve did not know what to feel. He wanted to be happy about getting to relative safety. It was like fixing the roof with one side of your house already caved in. There was a feeling of accomplishment, with a sense that the job was nowhere near satisfactory.

Losing the other members of his party was a blow and the two he had left were not exactly on solid ground. He couldn't lie, Dave and Jenny were more important to him. Still, Dave's status was questionable. Plus, he knew Jenny had been looking to leave a few short days ago, before the strange appearance of Death. Things had improved between them since then, but he was worried it would not be enough.

Before, with countless numbers toiling behind the scenes, you could live alone comfortably. Ordering online and talking to strangers on a forum if you needed some company. You could even throw out the odd video on the social medias if you really wanted to see yourself having an impact on the world.

Now only the people immediately around you were there to keep you alive and sane. If you wanted to be alone, the only company you would have was the voices in your head. Even for someone like Steve this was a grim prospect.

Could he offer Jenny the freedom she required? It was all very well staying in a room when you could leave at any point. When the door was locked from the outside it was a different matter. That was a prison. Is this what the street had become? How long was it before they all wanted to leave?

Steve wasn't optimistic about being the only person living in a tomb surrounded by shambles, even if he could exist in the security of the habitat he built. Not to mention questions over the level of protection this provided, since several times it had been compromised somehow. That was a puzzle he would have to get to the bottom of when he was more ready.

No matter how prepared he thought he was, something else always snuck up on him; from blindsiding personal losses to the dead coming back. Or a bloody newsagent's heart attack. Heck, the literal embodiment of Death appeared in his kitchen the other day.

Everything was becoming a shambles.

Dave was not looking good. As evidenced by Michael, he knew that if you died you turned. Popular lore held that a bite would infect you. However, the rules regarding contamination through ingesting blood and gore were fast and loose. He might just be sick, or maybe it was already too late. It was anybody's guess.

Steve was not about to be the one to make that call.

That was the problem with being sensible. You ended up debating over issues more impulsive people would tackle head on. Sure, you did not make as many mistakes. Still, errors were inevitable. You could not avoid every disaster, no matter how much you tried. Today was evidence of that.

Ideally a person could harness their cautious nature and make calculated risks. You could try to simultaneously prevent the worst while taking a chance every now and then. That was not how it worked though. Usually, you either expertly avoided pitfalls by staying still and achieving very little, or you rushed in blindly and let things fall where they may.

Right now, a mistake could cost you your life. So too any

hesitation. Frankly, the whole thing was more stressful than he knew how to deal with. In the end Steve had to be himself, and he was a careful person. But did that mean that he should leave Dave alone to see what happened, or take care of him now just in case?

Lost in thought, he didn't notice a shaken Jenny make her way to the bathroom. In her state she opened the door without considering what she might find. Judging by the bloodcurdling scream she was not prepared for the battered body of Michael lying where Steve had left him. At least he managed to kill the former newsagent before he went outside. If not, things could be a hell of a lot worse right now.

He rushed to her side, thinking to say that everything was alright. He knew she held no love for the man. Honestly outside of direct family it was hard to see who could. Still, it must have been a traumatic sight. Also, it was trauma compounded by the previous trauma. It was trauma squared.

He did not get to try to comfort her however as before he reached Jenny he skidded and tripped on a pool of sticky black blood. It was left from the struggle, which seemed so long ago now. For the second time that day he found himself staring up at the bathroom lights. His eyes focused beyond them to the ceiling above. Who uses Artex in a bathroom?

He pulled focus again to see Jenny looking down at him.

"Oh Steve, you are a mess of a person, you know."

She laughed. At least she seemed to be feeling better.

Often caring words would comfort someone. Sometimes gentle reflection could help. Then occasionally, falling on your arse will do. He sat up with a groan, fighting back initial feelings of defensive embarrassment and returned her smile.

"I see you managed to take care of our Michael problem." She said, almost hysterically.

There was a slight look of hesitance on Jenny's face as she realised this might not be the appropriate reaction to the sights of the gore-soaked bathroom. But then she doubled down.

"I never really liked him anyway."

Steve let out a laugh of his own, glad not to have to feign some unshared sentiment.

"No, me neither. He was pretty much a massive prick."

She helped him to his feet.

"What, did he also belittle and sexualise you unprovoked in the guise of inquiring about your relationship status?"

"Well, I'm not sure about the first part. But who knows?" Steve gave a hesitant smile. "I'm not really good at picking up on that sort of thing."

They shared an unease chuckle and glance, turning into a held gaze. They began to move closer. Then the door to the flat burst open.

***

Steve nearly shat himself before then tensing up. His bowels clenched, then his arms. He tried to get ready to face any new threat coming their way. He turned around to see Death in the doorway. His sphincter wasn't sure whether to be puckered or not at this point.

He was immediately distracted from his downstairs area by the sight of the towering figure clutching the prone but still breathing Joyce and Lucy in his massive arms. He hoped it was a good sign, the manner of entry indicated otherwise.

Steve wanted to appear strong while he still held Jenny. Judging by her previous reaction when he came to her aid, she was a fan of him 'stepping up'. It would be nice if that could continue. Then again, he was being confronted by a very recent anxiety and it was hard to deal with.

"Mister Carpenter, I have a bone to pick with you!" Death announced.

With all the violence and emotions flying about Steve was starting to feel a little removed from reality. He couldn't work out a serious response. So he fell back to the defensive stance of irreverence.

"If that was a joke then it would have worked a lot better if you were a bit more traditionally skeletal." He replied, with an uncharacteristic chuckle.

Death completely no-sold the jovial response, fixing him with a stony stare.

Steve noticed that despite his stern demeanour he was panting. That was concerning. Or else he was putting it on to emphasise the effort it must have taken to save the girls.

"How could you leave these two helpless souls outside to die?!" He screamed, almost stumbling with the effort.

Death was acting wild, nearly completely departed from the cordially polite being he encountered several days before. Whatever he had been through, it had caused a fundamental change. He had no idea how to react to this wholly new person. The data he had gathered from their brief first encounter was almost entirely erased.

All he could manage was a weak "I mean..." with a shrug before trailing off.

Jenny paid little attention to this fruitless confrontation. Instead, after getting over the initial shock, she rushed over to check on the two girls. It was hard to admit but she had already ruled them out as dead.

Despite her good intentions, Death looked down at Jenny with righteous fury. He was too caught up in his newly found feelings of anger to process a more measured response.

"And as for you!"

"No time for that now!" She cut him off, not looking away from the girls for a second. "How are they doing?!"

Death was puzzled by the direct inquiry and faltered. He was not used to feeling this level of indignation. Let alone how to cope when it was dismissed like an outburst from a moody child.

He thought of pressing on with his accusations but sensed this was a poor way to behave. It was all very new to him but defaulting to a demeanour of overwhelming politeness felt like the safest option. His shoulders came down and he shifted the weight of the two in his arms, looking down at them.

"Oh I am sorry. I cannot be sure. I am not really an expert on the health of humans…more the absence of it perhaps." It was as respectful as it was unhelpful, a truly civil response.

"Well hopefully that means they are still alive. Put them down somewhere so I can check on them." Jenny said, waving away his wishy-washy explanation.

Death stood there for a second not knowing what to do. He looked like a fisherman who yanked up his net only to find he was holding a shark. He was caught between the calculation of triumph and jeopardy. Wordlessly he set the girls down on the living room carpet.

Jenny went to look them over.

"More importantly, were you followed? Are we secure?!" Steve asked, having regained some of his senses.

Death shot him another hard look but then softened. This was all very confusing, and his heart was not in it anymore.

"I believe so." He sighed. "No hostile undead were behind me upon entering the building. I was forced to break open the door after you shut it behind you however."

His fury came back after Steve's eyes narrowed with his own internal accusations. He did not wait for a reply.

"I had my hands full at the time!" Death protested.

Steve brushed this off. The trail of blame was becoming too complicated to pursue.

"Besides, there was no door handle!" He continued.

"Never mind that now! We have to make sure everything is secure!" This was both true and acted as a great excuse to end the conversation.

He bolted for the stairs. Death followed on, again noticing that his emotions were bypassed by practical need. He was a little uncomfortable with this as feelings needed to be worked through. But he also saw that logical imperatives still existed in the outside world and they had to be observed first.

It made practical sense. Thinking in this way he drew up a glaring thought. He once again did not have his scythe to hand. They were both supremely under equipped.

There was no time to think. Steve was desperate to make it to the back entrance. This was made all the more difficult by the layout of Michael's house. Despite having made the trip several times it remained unfamiliar ground to him.

His mind, still full of noise told him there should be a path to the door through the standard narrow kitchen. Instead, he was greeted by a maze of doorways. Well three, but it felt like an endless number in every direction.

The question of why he took the lead over the immense figure of Death loomed in his state of confusion. His fear came up to bite him as a jaw snapped to his left. He realised that two shambles had indeed entered and were already bearing down on him.

He let out a yelp and leapt to the side.

Luckily, Death saw this and barrelled straight into them at full speed. The mass of granite crushed the two ghouls against the wall. There was little to fear from the mess left afterwards. Despite a lack of trepidation in the attack, he looked worse for wear from the effort. There was a noticeable difference in the way the reaper moved afterwards.

Although still imposing, Death was almost missing the air of invulnerability Steve had felt when they first met. He wanted to ask what happened, and more importantly where he'd been. The priority was to make things safe though.

Not having time to compose himself, rather than thanking him, Steve only shouted at Death to check and secure the other doors. If he had the time to contemplate, he may have thought better of it and shown some appreciation. What was before a sense of background responsibility shifted to an overwhelming urge to safeguard those around him.

This did not apply to their feelings apparently.

He headed through the one door he knew led outside and saw the garden was now filled with over a dozen shambles. He balked and tried to slam the door shut. It was no good. Death had managed to knock the usually sturdy barrier off its hinges with his daring rescue.

Steve grasped what was now a massive ungainly wooden board, which he had no time to put down. He had to do a kind of awkward duck-like shimmy to position the wood to block the opening. He managed to angle it so the entrance was closed, all except a little gap at the bottom where he had to tilt it to lean it against the frame.

He knew this would not be enough though as soon as he felt the first undead slam its grotesque pus-filled body against the former door. He grasped the metal pull-bar in the centre, as if it was the handle of some mighty wooden shield. Luckily, with him holding it in place, the weight of the barrier was enough to keep the hungry creature at bay.

The problem was that he couldn't move from the spot or the whole thing would collapse. Besides there was the worry of more shambles getting stuck in besides this one, as they were prone to do.

Groups, they were never a good thing in Steve's opinion. It all started out nice and then before you know it everyone in them is getting all loud and boisterous. They were supposed to lift you up, but with that support came more and more people looking for the same. Before you knew it the whole thing would be hijacked by people who don't even actually care about the initial cause, they just want to make trouble.

Despite this fundamental hesitation over group dynamics, he needed someone to help seal the entrance. This was how it always started. It was a slippery and unavoidable slope!

He yelled for the reaper and got no reply. His sweat was starting to run down into his eyes, making it hard to see. As he stood there, hands already trembling and blinking franticly, he began to hear scuffling noises from behind.

This was the worst case scenario for him. Steve called out for some kind of confirmation that he was not alone. All that brought was more noise from the other side of the wood. At least the shambles were being responsive.

The attention span of the undead was something he had no real idea about. He'd been lucky enough to be isolated from them for the most part, due to his own forethought it had to be said. It also meant he could not say whether the shambles now pounding on the door would forget about him any time soon.

They could no longer see him, although that might not be how they worked. It may be more to do with smell, or perhaps movement. It could be that they were just drawn to people by some ineffable factor of simply possessing life.

He was getting distracted, and he needed to stay focused. One slip of the door could mean the end for all of them. Even a few centimetres could allow one of those things to get a finger through. Followed by a hand, an arm, some teeth, and then you were dead. Whether they would lose interest at some point did not matter, they were outside now and they were hungry.

The scuffling was a worry though. If attacked from behind he couldn't keep anyone safe. However, there was no way to position himself with his back to the door to check what was going on. It would not have the weight behind it to keep what was on the other side out. It was a pickle.

Suddenly the subtly rising sounds became a cacophony of commotion. There was a crash, breaking bottles and scattering food packets. A lone pot noodle bounced along the laminate and landed spinning at his feet.

It was probably still perfectly edible.

He presumed Death was responsible. Either that or a new breed of super-shambles had thrown him through the shelves, and they were all shafted. If this were the case spilled food and holding a door shut would have been the least of his problems.

This fear was alleviated when Death came staggering out the doorway a few moments later. Steve really needed to stop thinking these things. It was not healthy for his heart rate. He had to concentrate on more immediate dangers, like nailing up this gaping hole for one.

He called to the grim figure to come give him a hand. He held up a stony finger, asking for a moment. Then he bent over to catch his breath, still a strange concept, before heading back into the shop. There were a few further crashes and bangs. No doubt more serviceable food was now ruined.

He came out after what felt like an eternity.

"I believe that is the last of them dealt with." He panted.

Just then another set of gnashing teeth came at him from the office doorway. Luckily, Death had the wherewithal to grab the thing by the jaw and nearly decapitate it with one upwards thrust, pulling out most of the spinal cord along with the head. The husk fell to the floor by Steve's feet. Despite their current predicament he couldn't help thinking how much it looked like a swing-ball set.

"Give me a second." Death said with a grunt.

He ventured into the office. Steve couldn't see round the corner apart from the edge of a filing cabinet. He had little else to do but maintain his grip in helpless anticipation.

A face plastered across the cabinet a moment later. The mouth was split open in a terrible grin that made him nearly let go of the makeshift shield. This remembrance of a visage was then fully obliterated by one of Death's massive grey fists.

"Okay, I think that is actually all of them." He said, wiping his gore-soaked hands on what remained of his robe.

The gesture was purely for show since the motion merely spread the mess around. It looked like he had been working at a grizzly potter's wheel. Death was an artist of the disgusting.

"Sure, fine. Good! Thank you! Can you bloody come help me with this door now?!" Steve yelled patience frayed.

"I am afraid I cannot Steve." Death stated with a far less reverent tone than required.

"What?! Why the fuck not?!"

"Because I need to go through it. I have people waiting on the other side for me...sort of."

"What?! Wait, what do you mean sort of...?"

"There is no time to expla..."

"I hate when people say that! You've taken this long, just clarify things fully!"

"I have to go." Death stated, ignoring Steve's request.

"Explain in the time it takes you to explain that you can't

explain dammit!" The door jumped as a shambles hit against it, the shouting drawing them closer.

"I can't. There is no time now." Death said firmly.

"But there was before?!"

"...Maybe."

Steve gave an exasperated sigh, nearly letting the barrier go from the sheer level of fed up he was feeling.

"Do not worry Steve. I will dispatch the undead outside. You tend to those upstairs."

As annoying as this all was, he was probably right. Death may be gassed from his tussle, but he was in much better shape to handle this. Also if he did not check on what was going on upstairs soon, the only people left alive could quickly become not that way.

He wanted to know what he was talking about regarding people waiting for him still. If he were serious about that they probably would need help. There had already been too much loss today.

Maybe Death could do some good, and he couldn't stand in the way of that. His mind was made up. He braced himself to remove the door.

"Okay, are you ready?"

Death nodded. No more words required. Steve pulled the wooden barrier back, trying to keep himself behind it as much as possible.

Death wasted no time by diving straight into the nearest zombie with a devastating kick. It went flying clear across the garden into a pair of his confederates who managed to clamber over the wall. He watched the enormous figure work for a few seconds before concluding that he probably had it handled.

Steve called out to him to knock when he came back and while he had some breathing room raced off to find something to brace against the broken fire door. He abandoned the idea of closing it off completely, but still wanted to be cautious. You should not simply nail yourself in and pray for rescue, but that didn't mean you couldn't also be as protected as possible.

CHAPTER ELEVEN

Tess was protecting her small friend. The tall, clumsy one had left them on their own. Humans, you couldn't count on them.

They were at her home away from home. They stayed here with the rest of the pack. When they were still together.

Where were they now? Where was Jerry? He could be inside the house maybe?

No, that was stupid. Jerry was gone. Tess knew that.

She whined. She had to hold back her grief. Anna could not know that she was sad.

The large pungent human was wriggling in her special entrance. It was too big now. But also not big enough.

The towering buffoon had shattered it. There was a split forming down the middle. The whole thing parting and falling.

Another wriggle and there was a crack. Tess barked to tell him not to continue. To stay still.

He did not listen. Only kept moving. Bad human.

She barked again. Anna cowered. Oh no.

It was hard to keep Anna from being scared. Everything was a threat. How could she not be?

She could hear movement from the surrounding area. Even above the wood cracking. Feet were scrapping closer.

All these humans moved funny. They had always been slow. But now they were ridiculous.

They were mean though. Humans were dangerous. Yet these days they were even more vicious.

She just wanted to be happy by her master's side. Have

comfort with the small humans. They were always nice.

The bigger the human was the less she trusted them.

This big one now was nearly free. He would have to be dealt with. He was falling apart, still a threat.

She barked again instinctually.

More noises coming. It was upsetting Anna.

The wood burst wide. He was free. He moved slowly.

This was not safe. She wanted to tear him apart. Tess readied herself to attack.

There were more humans. Some came from behind her entrance that was now gone. Others from all around too.

It was too many to deal with. She couldn't keep her eye on Anna and deal with all of these attackers.

She knew a way to escape. The big one approached. She called out to Anna to follow her.

The girl stayed still. This would normally be good. Now they had to move so it was bad.

Tess tugged at her dress to get her to follow. Anna cried but came along. She led her down the road.

There was a long tunnel they could go through. A route around the area. A special walk she remembered well.

Little feet were running with her. Both then and now. They would get away.

Slow moving humans followed them. They could never catch up. Too clumsy and stupid.

She looked behind and to Anna. Down the alleyway they went. The big human was following with a purpose.

Tess did not see the barrier until it was too late. Half way down the alley she realised they were trapped. There were too many pursuing them to turn back now and nowhere to go forward. Barry at the head of the line, lips lined with drool.

***

All this exertion was getting a little troublesome for Death. He had been running at full force for some time. Now he looked at the open grave that saved them from an unhappy landing. The freshly dug soil looked so tempting to just lie down in and have a little nap.

Mental energy was not enough anymore, he had to keep constant concentration on his physical exertion and the effort was taxing. None of others would be safe if he stopped here. All the activity was behind these houses so hopefully all the ghouls followed him, ignoring Tess and Anna on the other side.

Death found he still possessed enough strength to easily dominate any zombies stood against him. It was not unlimited though, and he was beginning to be seriously hampered by the laws of existence. If they started taking chunks out of him, he might not be able to recover before they overwhelmed, and ate him whole.

Therefore, he tried to balance expediency with efficiency. In his mind he would be bringing Tess and Anna back this way. So, it was prudent to make sure it was free from danger.

His hands were already caked in blood and beginning to ache. Death had the excellent idea of using the dead to damage themselves. It had already worked well in the shop, despite the mess. It could only improve out in the open.

He grasped the nearest corpse by the shoulders and lifted it off the ground. He swung the bag of bone around, letting it go after a complete rotation. The momentum sent it careening into another two on the other side of the garden. They all hit the wall with a satisfying splat.

The next nearest husk was used by him as a battering ram to spear three other bodies waiting there. The shells crunched and mushed together to form a sticky biting mess. They were no longer a threat, but they were annoying. Exhaustion causing him to lose all former notions of theoretical compassion.

Death ripped off the head of one of the few remaining by the wall. Peeking over the shallow mortar, he took aim to hurl the snapping ball at its nearest compatriot. He scored a direct hit, sending it sprawling to the ground. Then he repeated the process three more times, each getting a good result.

He was almost out of steam at this point, but there were only a few stragglers remaining. Most were tangled deep in the overgrown foliage and would be easy to take care of at another time if the need arose. It would do.

The human body could be so frail, especially when there was no working mind behind it. The subtle subconscious angles and arcs that the mind made to avoid disaster were no longer present. Nor the tensing of muscles at the right time to absorb impact. Without this a simple shove could spell calamity.

Once downed that was pretty much all. A crawling ghoul was a hazard if you stood staring at the sun for about an hour. But there was no real threat when you were on the move and kept your wits about you.

Death missed his scythe. Brute force was acceptable. Yet the sweep of the blade was a much more manageable means of dispatching these decrepit snappers.

The more he drew from his experience with humans, the more contempt he had for the undead. They were not life, just a mere imitation bent on snuffing out the real thing through an incessant hunger. Whether this was their fault or not, it did not detract from their status as an overwhelming virus that needed to be eliminated.

Death sneered at one of the few remaining shambles too deeply tangled to even move. He crossed the garden and made his way to the gate. He thought of how he would have to hop the wood again and the difficulty of getting Tess and Anna over the tattered body of Barry.

It turned out though he did not have to worry about this. The gate was destroyed and the bloated remains of Barry were missing. He should have seen this coming really since he all but shattered the door when passing through it the first time.

The problem was he had no idea where his charges were. While no trace of a struggle was good, there was no indication where they could have gone. He regretted bringing them here, he could not forgive himself if his choices got them killed.

The street was not beset with zombies, in fact he did not

see any in the immediate area. This was strange considering all those who entered under the gate and swarmed the garden. It was possible the wave was all there was, but it was unlikely.

Death spotted one straggler at the end of the road. It was moving with relative speed towards the alley close to Steve's house. It had a severe limp and was taking a long time to reach its destination despite its urgency.

His curiosity got the better of him. He went to catch up to the laggard. It was not hard.

As he got closer, he could see the straggler was not alone. There were several shambles at the alleyway entrance ahead of him. Maybe they had seen a stray cat or...or a dog.

He moved with some alarm at this thought. It got worse. He saw the group at the entrance were behind another cluster. In fact, it looked like the alley was jam-packed with the rotting bastards.

The horde was packed so thick he could not see down any further, so Death climbed the fence leading to the construction yard. A couple of the ghouls turned towards his direction for a second but were soon pulled back to the general thrall. He was worried they found another opening to the street. If this were the case, why would they be pooling together and not pouring onto the previously protected pavement?

He spotted what was drawing them to that area.

It was Tess and Anna, his greatest fear.

They were pinned down, yet somehow still alive.

Then he saw why. Instead of joining the horde, Barry had somehow opted to turn and hold them off. Even with only half his body barely hanging on his friend was struggling against the tide. It was a noble effort, but it was not going to last.

Death needed to figure out a way to get to his friends and help keep them intact. He started to shimmy across the railings. Again, some zombies paid him passing attention, but were soon distracted by the main target of their hunger.

Even when one of his Geta fell off they barely noticed and it soon faded from view. With one foot covering gone he let the other fly. They were not helping his progress at all anyway. The block toppled down towards the head of an oblivious ghoul but dispersed into nothingness before it could make an impact.

Death had a passing worry that he may have ceased to exist in the same way, and that was why they ignored him in his efforts. It was more likely though that all the barking, groans and screams of a terrified child were too much of a distraction for the beasts. They ran on instinct alone, he needed to not let his own analytical thoughts divert him from the task at hand.

The reaper gave in fully to his feelings of fear and rage.

He kept his eyes fixed to the spot Barry occupied. His bulk acted as a fine barrier, but it could not hold back the insatiable vermin who pressed in on him. Death went as fast as he could, still he was forced to watch as his companion was torn into by the pack. Before he reached them there was little left except a pile of miscellaneous flesh.

It had been enough to buy some time though and he was able to drop down in front of the throng just before they broke through. The loss of his friend filled him with a burst of anger that a saner Death would have found problematic. As it was, he was too busy savagely attacking those ghouls in front of him to truly comprehend its consequence.

His muscles were starting to ache and shiver from all the exertion. He was fuelled on by the sounds of Anna's frightened whimpering and Tess's desperate barking. Death punched and tore at the horde, shattering bones and spreading gore all over the alleyway. He was being grabbed and pulled in all directions, but it did nothing to deter him. He simply kept on sinking blows into the mass of rotting flesh until the undulations and moaning started to diminish.

In the melee his robe was ripped and torn until only a few scraps remained on his chiselled body. He was getting scratches and teeth marks from multiple sources. Death barely felt them. He just kept striking out, absorbed by an outrage towards this collective absence of life.

Despite his flurry, the damage he gave out was starting to

be overwhelmed by what he received. The wall of appetite was starting to resemble a thick brown soup at this point. Still, there were more on the other side of the disgusting mass trying to eat their way through.

Death had a moment of desperation when he realized his efforts were not going to be enough to stop the baying hunger of the dead. He glanced around for some source of aid and to the two he swore to protect. Then to the remains of the former man who started him on his journey. He could not comprehend the idea of failing them all, but what could he do?

His physical and mental presence was not sufficient any more. He was out of power and will. He felt himself give up. He thought he might be fading from existence. At that moment, an unearthly screech and bang yanked him back to reality.

It was not the sound of a super mutant come to feast on them at his weakest moment. It was the heavy wooden block at the end of the alleyway being lifted. He wished he had thought of that through all this punching.

Jenny and Steve were there, signalling for them to come through, panting from the effort of lifting the heavy blockade. Death wasted no time in scooping up Anna as Tess ran in by his side. They cleared the doorway and their two saviours let go of the rope, slamming the slab down over the entrance before any shambles could get close.

***

Steve ended up blocking the doorway using a couple of metal filing cabinets from ex-Michael's office. He piled them with the heaviest jars he could find, all put against the board that used to function as a door. It would take a tremendous force to get through and cause a hell of a noise in the process.

He felt a sense of guilt while doing so. Death was Death, but he looked drained when heading out. Even if he could pass through the barricade like he had in Steve's kitchen, there was the problem of the 'friends' he mentioned. Hopefully, he could take them with him.

There were a lot of unknowns with the reaper. Least of all was his choice of footwear. Steve had noticed the addition of the wooden sandals during the scramble, but did not have the time or nerve to ask.

He was dealing with a force of nature. Still, he needed to kick the door in last time. Surely if he was able to phase along with others, then he would have done so. Or else he broke in out of spite. Although if this was the case it would have been completely out of order.

Another concern was what type of friends these were to begin with. He was not sure Death would be the best judge of character. What could Steve do if they were a gang of merciless bikers, revelling in apocalyptic glory? The answer was not much frankly.

He would have to worry about it later. Now the shop was relatively safe downstairs he needed to check on those above. He climbed the stairs and was relieved not to hear screams or struggle on the way.

Then again, this could mean that everybody was dead up there. However, if this were the case, you'd think you'd at least be able to hear a moaning from the now turned. Or gnawing of undead teeth on the flesh of his former friends.

People sometimes remarked that Steve had a morbid way of thinking. He would argue it was practical. He could see their point though.

Upstairs he saw Lucy crouched in the corner, cradling her sister. Someone had already gagged Joyce's mouth and tied her hands. That was smart, Lucy was probably too traumatized to protest. Dave was laid up on the armchair, pale and perspiring. Likewise bound and gagged, although with a damp flannel on his forehead.

That was thoughtful.

Jenny came out of the bathroom, looking refreshed and drying her hands. Apparently, she had gotten over the sight and smell of Michael that was still present. She smiled at him when she saw him. Methodical calmness, it was an attractive trait.

He smiled back.

"I'm guessing things are all settled downstairs?"

"No! They are coming for us right now!" Steve replied in faux frantic fashion, hoping his sarcasm would make him seem cooler and ease any remaining tension.

"I'm not sure that is appropriate." She narrowed her eyes at him. Inside he melted but managed to stay together.

He shrugged. Pedantic humour was no match for her and her ability to cope with even the most messed up situation.

"I'll chalk it up to trauma." She said with a wry smile. "But seriously, is it alright down there? And where is Death for that matter?"

"He's…"

"If you say he is dead I will slap you." She cut him off.

Steve hesitated.

"…Well, technically…"

Jenny gave him a reasonably hard punch to the arm.

"Hey! You said slap!" Steve winced and pulled back.

"Oh, I'm sorry. How duplicitous of me!" She gasped.

Then she slapped him.

He rubbed his face before throwing caution to the wind. Maybe it was the adrenaline, or the feel of physical contact. He went to kiss her.

She caught his mouth in her hand.

"I'm not really sure this is the right time for that."

Steve sighed, as much as he could with his face still in the palm of her hand.

"I dever doe da right dime." He said through pursed lips.

She shrugged, then gave him a soft peck on the lips as she let him go.

Steve was, as ever, confused.

Then she grabbed him and kissed him firmly while he was standing there dumbfounded.

He was cocky after the second kiss. Confusion cleared up.

"Too romantic. Two out of ten." He crowed.

She gave him a brutal kick to the shin.

"My shin!" He cried.

This ended any romantic exchange as he hopped up and down for a few seconds. He now needed to be off his feet. He hobbled about before seeing that there was nowhere available.

"We really need to relocate." He said, as much to himself as anyone else.

He wondered how Jenny had coped being left here on her own. What if he hadn't come back? Could she have dealt with a zombified Dave and Joyce popping up and attacking her? The gag and ties suggested yes, in a practical sense, but perhaps not emotionally.

Again, maybe he was underestimating her, and she really was able to be that logical about the situation. If that was the case it only made him even more attracted to her. The ability to detach from a stressful situation was something he always liked about himself, and clearly in others. Even if that did sound far more egotistical than he thought it should.

It was the frustration of having a high self-confidence and low social skills. People presumed you didn't have one because you didn't show the other. You were encouraged to big yourself up, and when you did, they would tell you to calm down. It was a terrible trap.

This is why he was not a fan of most people. They were all full of generic advice and sentiment. Then when you responded with any thought or depth, they thought you were the weirdest person they have ever met. It was almost as if they didn't really expect you to be listening or to take what they say seriously. A strange mind-set in Steve's estimation.

He was not sitting down still. A frosty part of his mind said they should lock Dave and Joyce in the bathroom with Michael and be done with it. That would be admitting they were already goners. The more human side of him couldn't do it.

People talked about how stupid characters were in horror films. They make bad decisions and get themselves killed. Steve himself had been a big believer in this.

The problem was when you were actually in that situation it is much harder to follow through with logically sound actions. Can you really blast a loved one in the face just seconds after they turned? Could you really pass judgment over the worth of someone's life in a split second? And worse, if these choices did lead to your survival, can you really live with yourself?

Steve had already made this choice once and it nagged at him. Especially since he was confronted with what he had done and how someone else managed to do what he could not. Sure, this person was the grim reaper, but he still felt bad about it.

Being decisive was one thing, being downright negligent of the human condition was another. It was much easier not to make a choice. So, when presented with people already bound and gagged, he found it easier just to leave them like that.

Dave and Joyce were walking around fine about an hour ago. He couldn't help thinking they might still be alright. He did not even know completely what had happened earlier either.

It looked like both could be on the turn, but what if Joyce was only in severe shock? What if Dave was sick from ingesting rotting bodily fluids when Steve beheaded his attacker? Not to mention that in some ways you could say it was Steve's fault it happened in the first place.

He was the one who charged in with a shovel. Then again if he hadn't Dave would definitely have been bitten now. On his face. If he would even still have a face.

Going back on all this was making it impossible for him to decide. He wondered how Jenny felt about it. Maybe she would think Steve was being soft. But also, if she thought they should be taken care of in a permanent manner she would have done so herself while she had the chance.

Maybe she wanted them to be taken care of but did not want to do it herself. In turn Steve did not want to be the one to make the decision if so. He had great reservations over being forced to make choices for others, especially when those others were reluctant to do the same.

His brain tried to access some logic to excuse himself. He

managed to pull out a nugget that could at least rescue him for now. This was the reasoning that one could turn and the other could fall prey to them if they were put together.

That was good enough. The general uncertainty over who could be infected was a decent excuse. Frankly, it was a dodgy situation no matter how you sliced it.

He hoped Jenny wasn't holding anything back. There was always the possibility that she had gone postal and turned into an unstable psychopath. That might explain the kiss before, it would be just his luck.

Steve decided to dodge the issue, while trying to look for signs of mania behind her eyes.

"I think we should get everyone to another location. The smell in here alone is enough to finish us off." He said.

"Well, you aren't wrong. I think it might be a little difficult though. Death might be the only option."

Steve was taken aback. Both by the reply and the slight dip in grammar. That was not like her.

"Honesty Jenny, I can see what you mean. Maybe killing them outright is the best way to go. But I don't know if I can do it while they're still alive." He sighed. "There is a line between living and dead. I'm not sure I can bring myself to be the one to force someone across it. Even if they are on the way out."

She fixed him with a hard stare. It felt like an eternity. He began to get a little panicked. She moved towards him.

Steve wanted to evade her. He was frozen. Too overcome with fear and confusion. Jenny put a hand on his shoulder and exhaled in exasperation.

"No Steve. I meant that we would probably have to wait for Death to come back, since we probably can't move them on our own. I wasn't suggesting that we kill Dave or Joyce, you big weirdo."

This was a relief, also an embarrassment.

The sense of intimacy they had so quickly developed, had completely evaporated. If going by her tone was any indication anyway. Still, she was staying in his physical proximity. Without questioning her directly he couldn't know exactly what she was planning. Somehow, he felt like asking was not the right thing to do.

They had kissed, and now she was calling him a weirdo. Did that mean that he shouldn't kiss her again. Or should he try to kiss her to make up for being a weirdo?

Steve was always afraid of making an unwanted advance to anyone, but now that they kissed it could be just as offensive not to. How could something you wanted open such a chasm of confusion and worry after you obtained it? It was like becoming famous. You could dream about it for years, but then when it happens it's all questions and outstretched hands!

When was it appropriate to kiss someone you had already kissed? It felt like some sort of barrier had been broken down, but had it really? Maybe if he just stayed still the awkwardness would go away. Like a Tyrannosaurus of romantic anxiety.

She was moving closer. Oh no, what if it was not a T-Rex, but a raptor instead! Clever girl.

This was almost worse than the contemplation of killing of Dave and Joyce. It was certainly just as stressful. She brushed past and opened the window behind him.

"We might not be able to move them right now, but we can at least air the place out a little." She said casually.

Steve thought he felt relief. It could have been the breeze from the window. Had he failed some sort of test? Or was this fine, had he passed?!

A dog was barking.

This was eerie. Steve had heard of feeling butterflies, but never hearing a dog barking. His feet were hurting from having stood in the same spot for so long.

Jenny gave him yet another questioning look. He started to panic even more. What could she want now?!

"Can you hear that?"

That was good. The sound was not just in his head.

Before Steve speak, he heard the distinct sound of a little girl crying out. He checked himself, it wasn't his inner child. He didn't stop to ask why his inner child would be a girl.

Jenny was much quicker to react. She stuck her head out of the window and sharply looked around to locate the source of the noise. She ducked back in and said that it sounded like it was coming from the end of the street.

He was still puzzled by the whole situation. She grasped him by the shoulders. More physical interaction.

"Steve! Is there any way to get the barriers up at the ends of the street?!" She was shaking him a little.

He thought. It was a slow process right now.

"Umm...Yeah, I mean I designed them to be raised if need be. It just made sense." He paused, sensing this was not a good enough answer. "If someone was waiting there to be let in then they would be pretty silly though. After all they would be stuck in a tight alleyway with the undead all around and no way of knowing if anyone was coming to help. It would pretty much be a hopeless situation if someone didn't go to lift the barriers."

He nodded to himself, thinking this explanation was good enough to cover it.

"Okay!" Jenny went to run off.

"What?" He said dumbly.

She didn't wait for him to catch up.

"...Oh yeah, sure." He added, realising what was going on.

He ran after her, hoping the others would be alright until they got back. As they rushed down the stairs, he shot a glance to the barrier he hastily constructed at the back. He was pretty sure it would hold.

Still, it made him worried about what they were heading towards. They hadn't fully discovered the source of the sounds, only that they were likely coming from the alleyway. In the end it didn't really matter as they were on their way now.

Jenny had at this point taken him by the hand to lead him on and he was not about to let go. As they reached the street, they could clearly hear the constant barking coming from down the road. At least they were heading in the right direction.

They reached the barrier. It was clear a dog was behind it,

there were also the moans of the undead and a severe amount of scuffling. It sounded like a full-on brawl on the other side. He was not sure raising the block was really the best thing to do.

Steve looked at Jenny. They had a split-second wordless conversation about the pros and cons. Then a girl's whimpering changed the look on her face and the conversation was over.

He took hold of one of the ropes hanging down from the metal fencing positioned above the block. He tossed the other to Jenny. She grasped the rope and nodded. They pulled at the same time and with some effort the block started to raise.

There was something nice about the symbiotic effort. He usually found this uncomfortable. Again, the sofa memories.

He didn't want to let Jenny down. But also, he needed to rapidly ascertain what the situation was on the other side. That way he could let go quick and have it slam shut if what he saw was not something with a desirable outcome. His male brain wanted to impress the girl he liked, but didn't want to get them killed in the process either.

Unspoken demands to be a protector were stressful, not to mention nonsensical. For a guy like Steve it was problematic. He mostly wanted to be left alone. But there was also a need for companionship buried in his psyche that was not satisfied.

Along with this came expectations.

Unwanted but apparently necessary.

She gritted her teeth under the strain. Seeing her struggle beside him drove him on. She clearly cared, even if some of her choices seemed to be a bit cold. He had never met anyone who could remain so practical while also so passionate.

Hand over hand in swift succession, the block was raised. Steve found a panting and nearly naked Death standing guard over a girl and her canine protector. Beyond them was a wailing pack of mushy shambles.

He readied himself to do something heroic when Jenny called out for them to get behind the barrier. The more sensible option. Steve realised there was enough space between them and the undead to make it without any conflict and erased any thoughts of rushing into unnecessary danger.

Instead, he dedicated himself to making sure the block went back down as soon as they were clear. No one had to be asked twice. The unusual trio crossed through the opening and the dead did not get a chance to close the gap. They were not exactly quick on the mark at the best of times. Their speed and threat level didn't increase simply due to dramatic tension.

Steve let go of the rope at the same time as Jenny and they were clear. He knew a group of regular humans had little hope of budging the wood without engaging the pulley system. The mass of rotting flesh on the other side stood little chance. He smiled and patted the barrier. Job well done.

CHAPTER TWELVE

With Death and his strange crew now saved, Steve wanted to take them to the shop to regroup. Jenny instead suggested they go into his place since it was right there and the three did not look to be in the greatest of shape. None of them were.

He was a bit perturbed by the thought of letting strangers into his house, even in this situation. They were all high risk for staining and accidents; children, animals and even…old people? Death was looking haggard, technically ancient, no matter what face he chose for himself. If he managed to get his scythe back it might now resemble more a walking stick than an implement of destruction.

Still there was little he could say that would justify making them all walk up the road. Let alone through the store and up the stairs to Michael's apartment, where there was nowhere to sit. Not to mention the possibility of the others having turned, another problem that should be dealt with. So, whether Steve liked it or not, they all headed into his house.

There might be tea at least.

It was scary to see how Death's physical demeanour had changed since he first made his appearance in Steve's kitchen. The air of invulnerability he exuded had completely fallen away, much like most of his robes. Rather than standing proud like a chipper inhuman tea-making machine, he was collapsed on the sofa, barely able to keep his eyes open.

The small girl was sitting to Death's left looking up at him, and the dog was at his feet. There was something very human about the scene. He had clearly bonded with this rag-tag pair. It appeared like he had taken on a protector role in a way Steve never could.

Practicality was his strength. When it came to someone in distress, he could think of a dozen solutions to potentially solve their problems or remove them altogether. But he would never think to just hold them and tell them it was alright.

Surely it was not alright though, why else would they be upset? It was hard to process.

At the same time, he cast his mind back to when his SNES used to break on him. Sometimes all the banging and blowing in the world would do nothing. If you unplugged it and left it to cool down for a bit on the other hand, it would be right as rain. Maybe humans were similar, some of them at least anyway.

He was not sure if he ever felt that way though. If Steve had a problem, it nagged at him until he thought of something to do about it. Being told it would be okay never helped.

Admittedly he never tried forgetting about such issues. Or really go to anyone else for help either, so there was that. Steve found it hard to get past his relentless logic. Problems needed to be addressed and worked through until solved damn it!

The idea of leaving something undone was nearly hellish. Then again the persistent need to put things right occasionally caused more harm than good in the long run. Conceivably it could be less to do with finding a solution and more a person recognising you were putting your full support behind them.

In practice this never felt good enough for people either. Looking for someone's keys was not really any good unless you found them. Intention and devotion were trumped by results.

The world was always a confusing place for Steve. Values spoken were often not fitting of actual reality. It could be quite depressing.

He often felt like he missed out on some basic training as a human, or at least was given the wrong manual. Things that came across as obvious to others were at best questionable to him. Other times they were downright alien.

His whole life was spent trying to fit in and failing. When he was himself there was a sense given off from others that he was wrong. Or else they outright told him so.

This was why he constantly kept people at arm's length. Relationships took a lot of time and effort to forge, and could be broken at a moment's notice. It was a code he struggled to crack even after all this time.

While Death appeared to know next to nothing about the human experience a few short days ago, he had already come so far. It almost made Steve jealous. Was he that broken?

Then again, the reaper had been observing humans for so long. At least some of the key fundamentals must have been taken in somehow. It was possibly like someone is brought up around an industry or skill. As soon as they tried it themselves they were quick to master it.

Who knows, he could even ask him for some advice when the moment was right. Steve himself had been studying these dynamics for a good amount of time, and like Death was unable to connect beforehand. For him to be able to forge a genuine connection with others gave Steve hope it wasn't impossible.

He glanced to Jenny, watching the former reaper interact with these newcomers. She looked in his direction and smiled. Maybe you just had to be open and eventually you would find people who will accept you on your terms.

It was possible he already found what he was looking for.

***

Lucy cradled her younger sister in her arms.

She didn't understand how they ended up in this position.

One minute they gathered around their father's grave.

Then a noise...No that's not right.

They had been in the flat, hadn't they?

She remembered running, there had been running.

They were digging their dad's grave...No, they were going to get their father. They had to check if he was alright.

He was dead. They knew he was dead.

He could be undead.

That was it. They were waiting to check if their father was a shambles. He had already died. That had happened. He had always been a shambles.

Lucy was sad. Joyce had seemed fine, together even. Not now. Lucy remembered having thoughts of hope, but that was stupid.

Noises from the bushes.

Lucy saw her sister's fists clench. She ran away. Towards the sounds. Angry. Stupid.

She should have been faster, have been there to hold her back. Help stop her little sister from making any mistakes. She had been to university, she knew better. You could not let your anger get the better of you.

Too late.

Sobbing turned into sprinting.

Her sister cleared the garden wall. They both cried out at the same time. It wasn't good enough.

Then Jenny was there, calling for someone to help. Lucy couldn't wait. She needed to get there. Needed to be there for her sister. Her heart was beating so fast, so, so fast.

Everything else faded. Only glimpses of struggling.

She sat with Joyce. Noises all around her. Muffled voices and indistinct movements.

In a world of ghosts, all Lucy could do was stare down at her sister's pale face. Her eyes had been closed for so long and she was trembling.

There was blood. It was starting to dry on her fingertips. She looked at her nails, they were caked in the stuff. A crimson tip and polish.

Then suddenly Joyce opened her eyes. Her stare spoke of a deep and burning need. Lucy's heart bled for her sister. She could see her lips move under the cloth over her mouth.

There was a vague memory of Jenny telling her why she had done this. She couldn't place exactly why anyone would do something like that. Why would Jenny silence her sister in her time of need?

They had all let her down.

Joyce needed to speak. Lucy had to let her. To hear what she wanted to say. You should always give someone a voice.

Her eyes were locked on her sister as she loosened her grip. Still trying to support her as she reached for the cloth. She pulled back the material, hoping this miniscule gesture would make up for some of her failure.

She should have protected her little sister. The least she could do was let her speak. She leant in close to hear what her sister wanted, her heart filling with hope and love.

***

Joyce was hungry.

***

Dave flickered in and out of consciousness. He heard people talking, a couple of shouts. He was aware of a general sobbing in the near distance. He wasn't sure where he was exactly. All he knew was he had a terrible taste in his mouth.

It was hard to think.

He felt hot and cold all over. When he was younger, he caught the mumps from a girl and things journeyed down to his lower regions. This affliction not only caused one of his testicles to significantly shrink, but also a fever. His skin turned blue and red alternately until he was eventually purple. He imagined the same must be going on with him now.

He tried to look down to see what colour his skin was. His vision was too blurred. Things were starting to clear up slowly though. He was in the flat above that job-end Michael's shop.

He had been here recently, he remembered. Then things had gone to pot. Jenny had called for help and he tried to do his best by them. He didn't want to be left alone.

These feelings mostly came from not wanting to confront

211

any more of the undead. The help in question involved doing just that. He hesitated. Before he could decide it was too late. One of those things was on him and trying to rip his face off.

He'd been helpless. He was surprised he wasn't trying to munch on some tasty brains right now. Good old Steve rescued him he supposed, just like last time.

Imagine though, if you woke up a shambles in the middle of a disgusting feast. Like coming too after being blackout in a kebab shop. You'd probably pretend to still be gonzo to avoid the embarrassment.

Munch down on some sloppy mess that you desperately needed. Fingers covered in sauce, mouth sticky with slobber. Despite the look you were actually completely compos mentis, you were just trying to save face. There was no taxi home.

His mouth was blocked by something and his hands were tied. He tried getting himself free. It wasn't working.

Another compromising position.

He could still hear sobbing. It was coming from the corner of the room. He looked over, not sure what he expected. There were the girls. Lucy was rocking Joyce back and forth.

They were too close. The movement was frantic, it was all wrong. It wasn't Lucy swaying her for comfort. She was being pulled about, like a dog with a treat too big for them. The wet sound Dave mistook for tears was actually the noise of Joyce tucking into her flesh.

He gave out a quiet "Oh bugger" under his gag.

He tried to get his limp and exhausted body to move. His leg flopped to the side of the chair. Mostly useless but a start. It was enough to knock over a glass of water placed on the floor beside him.

Well, that was thoughtful of someone.

As kind as it was to bind his hands and gag his mouth.

Not only did it spread liquid everywhere, but it also made a great deal of cling and clatter.

Clear water mixed with viscous red as it reached the gore siblings. If the Joyce-thing was too busy eating to notice the initial knock, the repetitive clinking of glass against the sodding ratty armchair he was stuck in did the trick.

That Michael was a bastard. Dave was glad he was dead. Maybe that was a little harsh, but he was in a pretty stressful situation right now. He'd probably feel bad about it later.

The ghoulish girl turned on him. Letting go of her sister's neck suddenly caused the body to slump forward, chinning the hungry shambles on the back of its head. The thing turned and growled at the corpse of her sister.

This gave Dave some time to pull himself together. Sibling rivalry could have its uses. His fever was subsiding and he could almost stand now, adrenaline was also good.

In a weakened state it was the only thing letting him get up. At least he might avoid being mauled by a teenage girl. For some older men that could be their greatest fantasy, but Dave had never been that elaborate. He liked his women to have a full figure, a few miles on them, and a pulse.

His feet were not with him enough and he collapsed back down. It was no good. He couldn't walk away. Instead, he tried rocking back and forth to tip the chair over. He hoped he could crawl faster than the artist formerly known as Joyce if it came to that.

He went sprawling over, hands still bound. Unfortunately, it was in the direction of the grizzly pair and he nearly got his eyes clawed out by a vicious swipe before rolling to the side. Joyce wriggled and squirmed to get out from under the dead weight of her sister. She wasn't having much luck.

She pulled and pawed in undead incoordination. Lucy was still holding her back. She reached for him and nearly caught his ankle. This was getting desperate.

If Dave had been in fighting shape, he could have avoided her easily. But still woozy it was all he could do to simply back away and keep out of reach. He kicked at the grasping hands for dear life.

This effort only served to help her to get a grip on his left trainer. He shook it frantically. The movement helped to pull the ghoulish girl away from her sister, who was now starting to stir herself.

Dave managed to use his other leg to slip off the shoe, sending her back. The flailing arm of the shambles clocked her sister, but did little to distract her this time. He was running out of options.

With his legs a little better he tried to get to his feet. It was a struggle but there was some movement and he might actually be able to get away. Then he slipped on a sodding half eaten Mars Bar. The sticky chocolate sent him sprawling back down onto his face. Did no one pick up after themselves in this hellhole?!

***

Jenny's focus was split.. The figure of Death was sitting across from her with the little girl and dog they rescued from a horde of the undead. It was all a little bit surreal. She wondered what Joyce and Lucy would think of him now. Maybe that's why she couldn't shake the nagging feeling she had.

She was not sure when she took on this protector role in the group. If anything, she had expected Steve to step up. And he did, at least to some extent. But a lot of what was happening seemed to require her attention and effort.

It was her idea to make the move to go down the street. As well as being the one to follow the girls when they ran off. Plus, she made sure to tie up Dave and Joyce when suspecting they might turn.

This was a lot of responsibility and it was bothering her. Yes, they now had Death's help to move everyone out of that accursed apartment. Still, she worried it would be too late. She started to doubt her decision to come to Steve's place and not head straight for the Newsagents.

They managed to stay safe for so long and now it felt like the shambles were encroaching on all sides. Maybe she should have left when she had the chance. Jenny wished she could feel content here, it was difficult knowing what was waiting beyond the confines of the street.

Also, the way that dog was looking at her was unnerving.

She made some mental calculations.

"Steve, can you show Anna here to her room?" She tried to imply as much with her tone as possible.

This did not work, he looked completely perplexed.

Steve did have the sense to politely nod before blatantly leaning in closer and asking her what she was on about.

"*We need to check the flat.*" She hissed.

He gave her a look to say "Then why did you said to come here? What are you on about?" She hoped no one else could read his face as well as she could.

"*I know, but I am worried. I was worried about these two before.*" She gestured towards the dog and the girl on Death's lap. "*But now they are fine, and I am worried about the others. Situations change and plans have to be amended.*"

These were words Steve could understand. He clearly had one more question though and she knew what it was.

"*I think you have been through enough without having to potentially kill anyone you might be close to. Also I think Death would fare better. I want to be there in case they are okay. Then we can bring them back here.*" She paused, then added. "*And quite frankly that dog is freaking me out. I'd rather have it with me than where I can't see it.*"

Again, the logic was impeccable, even taking into account the personal opinion about the canine. She knew she delivered her thoughts in a way he could relate to. He would not question it, despite it being an unpleasant pill to swallow. All he could do was utter a passive "I mean..." and shrug, which was his way of giving non-committal consent.

Jenny knew it was the best way not to cause an argument but underline a general problem with her assertions. That way if things went awry it would not be like he did not raise at least some objection. Still, she knew he would not be able to actually say no.

Someone needed to stay and look after the girl. It was his

place, and he knew it the best. Death would be enough on the other end. So that was that.

There was a slight look of ingrained masculine desire to 'protect his woman' buzzing in the back of his eyes. This was quickly dismissed by self-preservation, being excused from this antiquated societal conditioning by Jenny having been the one to suggest the idea. In these post-modern times it was better to trust that she could take care of herself.

Or else at least he would acknowledge that she was safer as part of a group along with a giant supernatural force and an unnaturally unnerving canine by her side. Even if she did need support, it did not have to be him. He could be helpful enough by holding down the fort he built, a rationale that would keep his ego intact.

Stepping up as a man could come in many forms, as long as they helped rather than hindered. Even if this was just in her head, it made sense. You could rely on Steve to see the reason. Reason and faith, this is what any true stable relationship was built on.

If you could call what they had a relationship this soon. If nothing else, it was a connection and shared cause. If physical intimacy got involved once there weren't zombies scratching at the walls, well then that was another thing.

She had to consider one conundrum at a time. There was always going to be a worry in going to investigate something you left unattended. Sometimes you had to expose yourself to threat so things didn't get truly out of control. This again gelled with her logic, steeling her to move on with her plan.

Now it was time to go, Death in tow. As he sat on the sofa his developed physique rippled as he held the little girl. He had been given a spare pair of shorts and t-shirt by Steve. There was an ill-fitting mash up of Star Wars and Christmas, with the classic characters all singing carols on the front. The garish tee barely contained his massive form. His body resembled a statue still, but the colour was slightly off from the last time she saw the reaper.

Although their initial encounter was brief, it was certainly enough to make an impression. Yet, there was also something softer about him now. Dark veins were permeating his skin in a pattern reminiscent of tree roots. She was not sure this design had been there before. The first time they met his robes had been fully intact, despite Dave having told a different story.

That reminded her of the urgency of their situation. They needed to check he had not turned. Let alone what was going on with Joyce and Lucy.

Jenny was filled with a frightful image of a Dave shambles bearing down on the two defenseless girls. Joyce had not even been able to experience life outside of this little grey city. The slobbering hulk could be towering over her right now, hunger in his eyes. Ready to snuff out her life before it began.

She turned to Death and asked him to come with her, to leave Anna behind and take the dog. She didn't stop to see how this was arranged. She was already on her way out the door, assured they would be following close behind.

This was her technique in class for controlling any unruly group of children. Press on and believe that they will catch up. You did not stop to make sure they were ready. If you did so it would cost far too much time and energy.

Jenny wished she could give them more individual care and attention. It only led to more disarray. You needed to think about the group. Otherwise, everything would be lost.

***

Death felt contentment having Anna beside him. She was still quivering a little, but for what they had been through she was relatively alright. He noticed he was shaking somewhat himself. Although he could just be a little chilly, the clothes he had been given were not exactly well fitting.

He tried reforming his robes to no success. The void was growing between him and his mental abilities. Once again, he needed to reassess his place in the world.

This was the rub of existing as a lone agent. You felt more important, but there was no structure, no one to ask about the current state of workflow. On the other hand, if he were Death #652 for instance, a meaningless drone, he would still not know his place in the bigger picture. At least he might have gotten a redundancy package.

He considered that this pocket of time itself could indeed be seen a retirement of sorts. It was a small period to get his affairs in order or else potter around until he truly expired. Not exactly a great bonus as the former embodiment of mortality.

Was he even the grim reaper anymore? No powers could be taken to mean no purpose. Potential tools of the trade that he was required to hand in.

Actually, he did have a purpose. He looked down again at Anna. On the positive side of things he was now free to become a protector of life.

It was a difficult job and arguably he had mixed reviews so far. All he could do was try. There was less certainty, more at stake. Yet he was committed to the role. The ability to conjure a change of clothes and a decent weapon would not have gone amiss. Then again, these were symbols of the old job. Maybe it was time he found some new ones.

He was distracted by movement.

Jenny asked him to follow her in a curt manner. Death did not mind. If someone did not think there was any recourse for politeness it was because the importance of the thing was self-evident, at least to them anyway.

She had also asked Steve to look after Anna. Before there would be a question over if the man was fit to do this. With his abandoning of the girls there had been some friction. However, he had since come to his rescue in Death's time of need, so it was more likely that there was a good explanation.

He believed Jenny and Steve knew what they were doing. They were logical enough as people went. If he was throwing his lot in with them, he had to trust in their decision making. They had already saved him once today.

He was told to bring Tess along as well. This caused him slight pause since he was not sure how the two would handle being separated. However, wherever they were heading might not be the best place to bring a little girl. Also, Tess had to learn to become part of the group.

There was no more time to think, Jenny had already left. He picked up Anna and gently handed her to a reluctant Steve before dashing to catch up. He pointed a stony finger at Tess, who was already semi-growling at the man hesitantly holding the child. She bit it in obstinacy.

This began a game of tug of war that helped him lead her away from Anna and out of the apartment. Then various words of encouragement and distraction kept the canine with him on the way up the street. She was a dog after all, albeit an intense and menacing one.

It became apparent they were heading for that accursed apartment. Death neared Jenny and he felt the trepidation she held amid an outward projection of resolve. He could relate.

She hesitated at the door. He rested his un-chewed hand on her shoulder to convey he was here for her. He wanted to say as much too. Yet it felt rude to intrude on her inner thought process with sentiment he guessed she would not appreciate.

Jenny took a breath and headed through, hopefully more confident with Death beside her. Nothing jumped out, so the reaper decided to relax his body so as to look less like a threat. He could quickly become more intimidating if needs be.

Death saw that Steve blocked off the outside door, which was smart. Potentially life-threatening if he had come back that way, but smart. Also, he had come to rescue them instead, so it all worked out.

This reminded him of the girls and how they were when he found them. Death hoped they were okay. He had dropped them off here, leaving them with Jenny...that is what they must be doing here. They were coming round to get everyone else. But why was Jenny so hesitant? What was she expecting to find upstairs?

They crossed through the shop and peeked round at the surrounding rooms to make sure everything was clear. Jenny started to make her way upstairs. Death followed. He wanted to ask how everyone was, but it would be a moot point since they were about to see anyway.

Despite this there was a little voice in his head wanting to ask anyway. The funny intricacies of social interaction. Being so concerned over people's well-being, it was all so strange.

What they found upstairs was a mess, to put it mildly.

With his concern over the mental state of everyone else, Death had put the potential physical harm to those at the flat to the back of his mind. He had lacked needed urgency. He had not really thought about what dropping Lucy and Joyce off here could lead to.

The full weight of his responsibility, culpability and cost of forgetfulness hit home. He saw the blood smeared across the floor of the upstairs apartment. Dave was ripped open entirely and both sisters were feasting on his insides.

This was so much worse than the Newsagent dying. There he only held some blame. Here his attention and intentions had been split and his carelessness resulted in the current tableau. There was something viscerally unnatural about seeing a man be consumed like a buffet.

His reaction even now felt a little removed.

To be fair, as Death he had seen all kinds of grizzly scenes. In the last month alone he saw multiple people being ripped apart before he had chosen to enter the world again. But he did not know those involved.

The familiarity made a difference. You could picture them talking and moving around. Remember the expressions on their face now rendered lifeless. Did Dave even have time for a last cigarette?

After being initially frozen Jenny gasped, turning away.

As pragmatic as she was, she was not prepared.

This denial of the scene drew the attention of the gorging girls. They looked up from their horrific meal. Faces stained in gore. They let out a set of low moans on key.

Staring into the dead eyes of both sisters, Death was hit with an overwhelming sense of sadness and loss. It was as if the air had been sucked out of the room and he could not breathe. His emotional state was impacting his physical form as much as the stimulus of the external world.

This was instinctive. He had not willed it as with his nose. The sight impacted him, the effect took hold. It was admittedly lessened now by this internal analysis.

A sense of hopelessness nagged at him. He just wanted to turn his back and shut the door. Take Jenny and Tess with him and leave this cursed flat once and for all.

He was stopped by the thought of his found friends being trapped in this state. It was too late to save any of them from their fate. But he could stop them from suffering an eternity of rattling around this tomb as shades of their former selves.

Sadness turned to determination as he once again took on a purpose. Death was still finding his feet in his new role as a guardian. However, here he could embrace his former calling of a helper of the deceased. Even though now it was towards only the nothingness of oblivion.

Anything must be better than being trapped in a husk of your former self. Being unable to think or feel anything except a gnawing hunger. It was unfathomable that this state could be preferable.

He stepped towards the girls as they stumbled over the now dead Dave. He came to meet them in a sweeping embrace. They struggled and scratched as he held them close, overcome with emotion over what he was about to do.

Death tried to draw his right arm up for a killing blow, but it was caught on something. He turned to look, thinking that somehow Tess was still clinging onto his digit. Instead, he saw that the now undead body of Dave was hanging onto his arm, as if in supplication.

A reminiscence of Barry pained him even more. He could not shake him loose. The force it would take to remove the former man would be too indelicate for close quarters and the company around him. So, he persisted in the tug of war.

At the same time the girls continued to claw at him. It was getting difficult to hold them at bay. His grip loosened just a little too much and it allowed them a better angle at biting into his grey flesh. Their teeth sank into his skin and he could feel his muscles tear just like his robes before. He let out a yell of pain and began to lose focus.

He was slightly unsure as to what happened next.

He recalled a blur of fur and teeth, his hand coming free.

There were screams amidst a sea of grunts and growls.

By the time he was able to focus again the apartment was covered in pieces of human and blood beyond anything he had seen as the grim reaper. This many miscellaneous body parts in a small space were rare. Although it was possible his personal stakes in the events were colouring his perception.

Jenny was standing in the middle of the pile, clutching an axe and out of breath. She looked to be alright apart from the gore caked all over. He hoped she was okay. Death could not stand the thought of another one of his friends succumbing to the human condition in such a short time.

With that thought he glanced around for where Tess was. He could not see her. Then he spotted a pile of fur amongst the debris, unmoving.

He rushed to where the dog lay. Shaking and letting out a low growl, Tess had a gash down her side. Her fur was matted with blood and one of the girl's severed arms was still clutched between her jaws.

Death was speechless. Leaking from his own wounds, and they were not healing. He was utterly exhausted physically and emotionally, but this finally broke him. He looked helplessly to Jenny, then back to Tess. He fell to his knees, gathered her up in his arms and began to weep.

EPILOGUE

While it had only been a few days, Steve was getting used to interacting with Anna. He'd never really been around children to any degree before. Although, to be fair she was not exactly a normal child all things considered.

At first, she would not even speak to him. But gradually she started to open up of her own accord. A word here and there would let him know if she needed food or comfort.

He was surprised how quickly he was taking to having a dependent. He had thought safeguarding the street was a big step in terms of caring for the wellbeing of others. This was an entirely different level.

Steve was thriving actually. Having to worry about Anna's needs meant he took care of his own more too. Never before was he able to have a real bedtime, or a balanced diet.

Caring about what to feed a child gave him the excuse to take a full inventory of their supplies. They certainly had plenty of sweets and goodies left from the Newsagents. The stock of which he removed from that accursed place at the first chance he got.

In terms of nutritional food, they were running pretty low though. They would have to go foraging in the surrounding area at some point soon. There were still enough tinned vegetables to keep a growing girl happy, if that was even a thing.

Luckily there was an ample supply of children's clothing in the surrounding houses. The morbid reasoning for this slightly obscured by just how happy Anna was with all the new fashion choices she found. This had surprised Steve given her reserved nature.

He supposed some inherent value systems are ingrained no matter what. Each day had turned into a little fashion show. She had developed a habit of combining outfits that made little sense to him. Still, she enjoyed letting him know all about them anyway.

She came running in to the kitchen while he was washing up, prancing around in just such an outfit. It was a combination of a light blue dress, cargo shorts, knee socks and baseball cap. Plus a couple of those floaty arm bands kids wear in swimming pools. He was surprised she had not found a pair of flippers.

Steve had to appreciate this from a pure logic standpoint. It was pretty much everything you would need for a summer's day. Just maybe not crammed all together like this. Realistically each thing kind of countered the other when combined.

There was probably no way to explain this to her without coming off as a bit condescending. Besides it wasn't like he was about to attempt to deflate the joyous smile plastered on the little girl's face. She was far too pleased with herself.

It was funny how malleable human nature was. Despite what someone went through, in the moment to moment you can always find some joy. Whatever the greater context of the world, there were still reasons to smile.

Steve threw up in his mouth a little.

He knew she wasn't happy simply because of the clothes themselves. It was also who else she wanted to show them off to. He grew tired of the pretense.

"Anna, is there someone you would like to pay a visit?"

"Yes!" She beamed.

"Alright then, let's go up."

The girl didn't hesitate. She rushed up the stairs as fast as her little legs could carry her. Steve followed at an even pace. His house had become a staging ground.

All the supplies were there now. Anna was staying there. He was there obviously. And then there was Death. He was laid up in his spare room like something from the English Patient.

Anna flung herself on his prone body. He groaned in pain but greeted her with genuine warmth, rather than the cordial politeness that was his trademark before now. He lifted her up and began discussing with her all aspects of her new summer style.

"He's getting better."

Steve jumped at the familiar voice. Jenny had snuck up on him and was holding him by the waste. He was powerless to stop the kiss she planted on his cheek.

Jenny brought back Death from the apartment. He had looked like his namesake and yet not. The complete opposite some might say, close to death but more human than ever.

They were caked in carnage and could barely speak. They had both collapsed on the sofas. Steve's sofas were white, or at least they were. It was a whole thing.

At the time he had only cared about what happened in the apartment. He felt bad about badgering them, but finally learned that Dave and the girls were gone. While this made him sad, he was at least relieved that they made it out alive.

When he said alive, he meant it. Death seemed entirely human now. Although thankfully one who was entirely immune to zombie bites. You could tell by the sheer amount covering his body, which now was healing at a normal rate.

He remembered their first encounter, where Death had literally pulled an axe out of his head to no ill effect. That axe was now resting by the bed he was laid up in. Jenny had come back with it, dragging it behind her as she supported the former grim reaper.

It had been quite a sight. He was as scared of her as he was in awe. Somehow, she had stepped into a house of horrors and come out relatively unscathed.

Steve was sure the whole thing must have been traumatic in some way. After all he was the one who had to clean it all up. It had been an agreement.

Despite this, Jenny didn't seem to be showing any signs of

distress despite the ordeal of having to hack up several undead acquaintances. This worried him a little. He was trying to focus on the positives.

A fury of fur bounded past the pair and ran up to Anna and Death's bedside.

It was Tess.

The circumstances of her being alive were more than a little confusing. As Jenny described it, Tess was torn to shreds. Death was holding her and then his tears had revived her.

Then again, she also said that before being taken down she had seen the dog rip a zombie Lucy limb from limb. Then use one of those limbs to beat said zombie into a fine pulp. So, he wondered about her credibility in this case.

Whatever had really happened, it was miraculous. All in all, the past couple of months were a bit overwhelming. There had been great loss, but overall, he was perhaps better off now than he had ever been. He needed to learn to take the good that came with the bad.

Plus, Death had told him about a shop with a whole load of guns and ammunition sitting on the edge of town. They all needed to rest up for now, however he felt like defending this place may take a lot more firepower in the future. It could be a long and perilous journey, but it was something to shoot for.

Printed in Great Britain
by Amazon

22809005R00129